The Curious Spell *of* Madam Genova

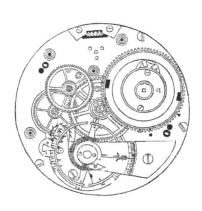

J.G. Schwartz

TABLE OF CONTENTS

ACKNOWLEDGEMENTS

Cover design: Go On Write
Book interior and e-book design: Amit Dey
Editors: Josiah Davis, The Book Butchers
Gary Smailes, Bubblecow
Linda Schwartz-Wright
Alan R. Schwartz
Louise S. Sagor and Bryan T. Sagor

DISCLAIMER

The Curious Spell of Madam Genova is a work of fiction. Many of the names, dates, and actual events that appear in the book are accurate; however, the author has invented the entire story.

LIST OF MAJOR CHARACTERS

*Nicolas Avril—Owner of Avril's General Store. Monique's friend and landlord.

James Addison Baker, III—(James Baker) Served as White House Chief of Staff and United States Secretary of the Treasury under President Ronald Reagan, and as U.S. Secretary of State and White House Chief of Staff under President George H. W. Bush.

David Berkowitz—(AKA Son of Sam) An American serial killer who pleaded guilty to eight separate shooting attacks that began in New York City during the summer of 1976.

Betsy Bloomingdale—American socialite and friend of Nancy Reagan.

Alfred S. Bloomingdale—Heir to the *Bloomingdale's* department store fortune, "father of the credit card," and the lover of murdered Hollywood sex worker and dominatrix Vicki Morgan.

*Bobby—Joshua McMillan's blood brother at Boy Scout Camp.

*Brian—Senior Patrol Leader, Boy Scout Troup 231.

Barbara Bush—Former First Lady of the United States, wife of George H.W. Bush.

George H. W. Bush—41st President of the United States, 1989-1993.

Joe DiMaggio—Played baseball for the New York Yankees. Widely considered one of the greatest baseball players of all time. Married for a brief period to Marilyn Monroe.

Alexander Esau—One of David Berkowitz's (Son of Sam) victims.

Detective John Falotico—Police detective. Helped capture David Berkowitz (Son of Sam).

Detective Sgt. William Gardella—Police detective. Helped capture David Berkowitz (Son of Sam).

*Jenny Genova—(AKA Madam Genova) Jack's mother, clairvoyant, and fortune teller extraordinaire. Best friend of Monique LeClaire.

Irene Rothschild Guggenheim—Child welfare advocate and art collector. Wife of Solomon R. Guggenheim.

Solomon R. Guggenheim—An American businessman and art collector best known for establishing the *Solomon R. Guggenheim* Foundation and the *Solomon R. Guggenheim* Museum in New York City.

Betty James—Richard T. James' wife. Famous for naming the Slinky toy.

*Dolores James—Richard James' mother; neighbor and client of Madam Genova.

*Howard T. James—Richard James' father and famous watchmaker.

Richard T. James—Son of Howard and Dolores James. Engineer and inventor of the Slinky toy.

Jacqueline Kennedy—Former First Lady of the United States. Wife of John F. Kennedy.

John F. Kennedy—35ᵗʰ President of the United States, 1961-1963.

John F. Kennedy, Jr.—(AKA John-John) John F. Kennedy's son.

Robert Kennedy—Brother of John F. Kennedy. Served as the 64ᵗʰ United States Attorney General from January 1961 to September 1964.

Peter Lawford—English-born actor. A member of the "Rat Pack" and brother-in-law of President John F. Kennedy.

*Monique LeClaire—Fortune teller extraordinaire and clairvoyant. Best friend of Jenny Genova.

Anne Spencer Lindbergh—An American author and aviator, wife of decorated pioneer aviator Charles Lindbergh.

Charles Lindbergh—American aviator, military officer, author, inventor, and activist. Won the Orteig Prize for making a nonstop flight from New York City to Paris in his plane, the *Spirit of St. Louis*.

James Arthur Lovell, Jr.—American retired astronaut, naval aviator, and mechanical engineer. Pilot, Gemini 7; Commander, Gemini 12; Command Module Pilot, Apollo 8; Mission Commander, Apollo 13.

Marilyn Lovell—James Lovell's wife.

Charles "Lucky" Luciano—Italian-born gangster who operated mainly in the United States. Instrumental in the development of the National Crime Syndicate.

Nelson Mandela—President of South Africa from May 10, 1994-June 14, 1997.

Thomas Kenneth Mattingly, II—American retired aviator and astronaut on Apollo 16.

*****Fred McMahon**—Furniture store owner, New Iberia, LA.

*****Jeremy McMahon**—Son of Fred McMahon.

*****Eric McMillan**—Joshua McMillan's father.

*****Joshua McMillan**—Childhood friend of Jack Genova and 'adopted' son of Jenny Genova and Monique LeClaire.

Marilyn Monroe—An American actress, model, and singer. Famous for playing comedic "blonde bombshell" characters. The most recognized sex symbol of the 1950s and early 1960s.

Vicki Morgan—Alfred S. Bloomingdale's mistress.

Barack Obama—44th President of the United States, 2009-2017.

Edward Joseph Perkins—American Ambassador to South Africa, 1986 -1989.

Joan Quigley—An astrologer best known for giving astrological advice to the Reagan White House in the 1980s.

Nancy Reagan—Former First Lady of the United States, American film actress, second wife of Ronald Reagan.

Ronald Reagan—40th President of the United States, 1981-1989.

Frank Sinatra—American singer, actor, and producer. One of the most popular and influential musical artists of the 20th century.

Valentina Suriani—One of David Berkowitz's (Son of Sam) victims.

John Todaro, Sr.—A prominent Buffalo, New York, businessman and the Mafia boss of the Buffalo crime family.

*Mr. Alvin Warwick—Scoutmaster, Troop 231.

*Fictitious character

CHAPTER 1

JOSHUA OBSERVES

February 26, 1927

"Well, how do I look?" Madam Genova asks as she stands up, looks in the long mirror, and adjusts the red scarf draped over her head.

As he stares at her image, Joshua can't help but focus on the gold coins dangling from the chain in the middle of her forehead. He takes just one step toward her. It is a small room, and standing right next to her, he can feel her long sleeve gently brushing his bare arm. She smells just like a bunch of freshly picked flowers.

"I—I—Well, I think you look fantastic," Joshua stutters.

Although he has known the fortune teller for a few months, and has listened in on her sessions with her clients, he still thinks she is the most beautiful woman he's ever seen. Madam Genova tucks a few strands of hair back under her scarf before they escape onto her cheeks. Blue and red stripes circle each arm of her white, billowing blouse, and her long red skirt sweeps the floor. The jangly bracelets on her wrists, partially hidden underneath her long sleeves, make music when she moves.

They are in her 'parlor'—well, that's what Madam Genova calls it, anyway. It is actually the back bedroom of her apartment, and it's where she sees clients. Jack, her son, is seated at the small round table which takes up most of the space. A crystal ball sits in the center, and a dark wooden chest with many drawers is against the wall. Although the room is well lit, once the session begins, Madam Genova will only allow light from a small brass lamp mounted on the wall behind her chair.

The fortune teller adjusts her large gold earrings, breathes a heavy sigh, and turns to look at them. "Okay, you handsome young men, we need to get this show on the road."

Jack moves next to Joshua, and Madam Genova leads them into an even smaller room, basically a closet. The walls, floor, and inside surface of the door are lined with thick carpet, making the small room soundproof. A grate covers a small cutaway in the wall, allowing them to peer into her parlor.

"Now, you boys get in there and sit down," she whispers. "Remember, I don't want to hear a peep out of you."

They sit down and get settled, their backs to the wall. Just before Madam Genova closes the door, Joshua realizes he is staring at her with his mouth open. She looks at Joshua, winks, then gently pulls the door closed behind her. He can still see her when she sits at the table and begins slowly shuffling her tarot cards.

There is a knock on the front door of the apartment. Madam Genova greets her client, and escorts her back to the table in the parlor. The client takes off her fur coat and drapes it over a chair. She is thin, with gray curly hair, and is wearing a dark blue suit. After she sits, Joshua observes the woman placing her purse on the floor and grasping the edge of the table with her hands.

"Let us begin," says Madam Genova. "Please shuffle these cards." When the client finishes, Madam Genova turns over the top card. "I see your future very clearly now, Miss McConnell. Within the next two years, you will travel to a land where everyone speaks a foreign language. There, you will find a marketplace exactly two blocks south of your hotel. Fine cloth and magnificent rugs, figs and pomegranates are displayed in the market. Miss McConnell, you must buy a large blue and gold silk scarf from a vendor wearing a brown hat. He will wink as you approach."

"A marketplace? But how am I to tell him apart from some other man in a brown hat?" the client asks, shaking her head.

"You will recognize him, Miss McConnell," Madam Genova sternly insists. "Believe me, you will recognize him. Remember, he will wink at you as you approach."

"Oh, oh I see, that's right," replies Miss McConnell.

"You must listen to me carefully, Miss McConnell. There is a spell upon the scarf you will purchase. You see, it was used to kill this man's wife."

"It was used for what?" Miss McConnell asks, horrified.

"Just listen to me. Because the man strangled his wife with the scarf, her soul still lingers in it. Purchase the scarf and place it in your purse. You will only be able to feel her spirit for three months, but in that time it will guide you in making the most important decisions of your life. After that, the spell will be gone. Do you understand?" Madam Genova asks.

Jack and Joshua look at each other, then cover their mouths, trying not to laugh. It's Saturday, so the boys have been playing together. They live in the same apartment building and have been friends now for nearly four months. Jack has short black hair, wears round, black-rimmed glasses, and can easily fall victim to the giggles. People often mistake the boys for brothers. Both are thin, but Joshua is two inches taller with blue eyes and longer hair. He has a small vertical scar in front of his left ear. Both boys are in the same eighth-grade class at Longfellow Junior High School.

One of Joshua's favorite activities, when not in school, is to listen to Jack's mother, Madam Genova, predict the future for her clients. Madam Genova is not really her name, but it's what she calls herself, so Joshua does the same. He spends a lot of time in Jack's apartment because his mother works as a secretary and is gone until about four o'clock most afternoons. The women who come to seek Madam Genova's advice always wear fancy clothes and jewelry and, it seems to Joshua, have traveled all over the world. Unfortunately, it usually takes some heavy arm-twisting to convince Jack to let him listen to one of his mother's sessions. Jack always tells Joshua he's bored with them because he's listened to them for so long. He would rather be playing cards or board games, but Joshua thinks her sessions are amazing.

They watch as Miss McConnell leaves. Madam Genova escorts her out, then returns and opens her small closet. Jack and Joshua run straight toward the kitchen. They pull out the heavy wooden chairs and sit down at the table while Madam Genova sets about preparing a snack for them.

"So Joshua, how are you doing these days? Are you still enjoying school?" she asks as she serves a large plate of molasses cookies.

"Yes, ma'am. It's great," he says, his mouth full of cookie crumbs. "I especially love reading. Oh, and my mother just signed me up for the Boy Scouts, and I like that, too. I've already been to two meetings."

"I asked your friend over here if he wanted to join the Boy Scouts," Madam Genova says as she nods her head in Jack's direction, "but he didn't want any part of it."

"That's right," Jack says, shaking his head, "I don't want any part of it. Hiking and camping with all those creepy bugs crawling all over you...Who would want that?"

"Huh. Well did you know you can actually get a badge for studying insects?" Joshua says. "In fact, one of the guys in my troop already has his. It's got a big green grasshopper on the front."

"That's disgusting," Jack says while reaching for another cookie.

"Anyway, my troop is supposed to go on an overnight camping trip in May—May seventh, I think. And, yes, I'll be sleeping with all the bugs, but other than that, it should be a lot of fun," Joshua says.

"Well, that does sound like fun now, doesn't it Jack?" she asks.

Jack rolls his eyes.

"Oh, and by the way, Madam Genova, I love hearing you tell the future. Thanks for letting me listen in on some of your sessions." Joshua takes a sip of milk and notices Madam Genova looking at his arms. She looks concerned.

"Joshua, what are those marks on your arms? Those small, round purple marks?"

"Oh, nothing. It's really nothing, Madam Genova," Joshua says while looking at the cookie in his hand.

She moves closer to him and takes his forearm in her hand. "They look like bruises. Like bruises from someone's fingers. I've seen these on your arms before. Yes, it looks like you have marks from someone's fingertips on your arms."

"Oh, those. I...I got up to go to the bathroom last night and ran into a wall. It's nothing, really," Joshua explains.

Madam Genova nods her head, still staring at his arms.

CHAPTER 2

THE WATCHMAKER'S IDEA

March 1, 1927

Mr. Howard T. James is not only one of the finest watch-makers in New York, he is also one of the greatest artists in the city. Howard has worked for Pierre Cartier for the past ten years at the famous Cartier store on Fifth Avenue. He is paid well and takes pride in providing only the finest pieces of jewelry to his customers and the best, most comfortable life for his family. And he has achieved just that: the James family recently moved into an apartment in Tudor City, a fifteen-building waterfront complex on Manhattan's East Side.

Years of working on fine and intricate watch mechanisms have taken a physical toll on Mr. James. His posture is stooped and his shoulders rounded, making his head appear to lean forward. When the New York wind whips around the buildings, he often has trouble securing his flat cap to his balding head.

Mr. James first caught Mr. Cartier's attention after he helped design the 1926 Baguette Watch, now always displayed in its classic red box. The watch even appeared on the Broadway stage in Anita Loos' play, *Gentlemen Prefer Blondes*—now everyone has to have one. In the wake of his design's success, he has been given free rein in creating designs for Cartier.

Although Mr. James is proud of his work at Cartier, he believes his greatest accomplishment, by far, is his handsome, kind, and thoughtful blue-eyed, blond-haired son, Richard. He frequently annoys his coworkers by saying things like, "Is it only me, or does everyone think their child is the smartest and most amazing and most wonderful person in the entire world?"

Richard, almost fifteen years old, joined the Boy Scouts of America a year ago, and Boy Scouting seems to be all the boy can talk about during dinner. He talks incessantly about the newest badges he has earned, where his troop is going to camp, the art of building a fire without matches, and on and on and on. These subjects dominate the conversation.

Richard's mother Dolores—a tall handsome woman with long blonde hair—is pleased her son is making so many new friends and is so enthusiastic about the Boy Scouts. She stays busy with household chores and takes turns with the other mothers baking cookies and cakes to ensure their sons have ample food at their numerous events.

Dolores is deeply religious. She always wears a small gold cross around her neck and attends every Sunday service. However, she also enjoys the occasional séance or tarot card reading from her neighbor, who happens to be a fortune teller.

Richard's fifteenth birthday is rapidly approaching, and after months of trying to decide what to give his beloved son, Howard has decided he will create a pocket watch designed specifically for a Boy Scout.

One night after dinner, after Richard has gone to bed, Howard describes his idea for the watch to Dolores. "The face of the watch must depict trees, streams, and tents," he tells her. "And the twelve disciplines of a Boy Scout, like being obedient and kind, will be written around the perimeter of the dial. The hands of the watch will be in the shape of wooden directional signs, and the words 'BE PREPARED' will be printed on the hour hand and 'A SCOUT IS' on the minute hand. Can you envision it, Dolores? When the minute hand sweeps around the watch, it will point to the various traits of the ideal Boy Scout."

"Oh Howard," Dolores gushes, "I know he will love it."

"Yes," Howard says. "In fact I will create two pocket watches and keep one for myself." *The watches will create an even closer bond between Richard and me*, he thinks. *One watch will be encased in silver, the other in brass. The brass watch will go to Richard. Brass will be a more durable and a more appropriate material for a young scout.*

Howard selects only the finest materials from all over the world for his watches. From Italy, the most expensive and brightest paints made from linseed oil; from England, the finest silver and brass for the watch casings; and from Switzerland, of course, the finest watch mechanisms. But Howard's collection of paintbrushes is his most prized possession. The fine, handmade brushes with bristles of sable are made by English craftsmen, and are the perfect tool for the necessary intricate hand painting.

Creating the watch takes almost two months. After discarding the first ten prototypes—the initial trees were too tall, the river too blue, the letters too big for the dials—Howard installs the elaborate mechanisms and painstakingly paints the fine finishing details on the two watches, which he believes are perfect. He gently seals the crystal in each face, then pauses to admire the watches, satisfied they are identical in every aspect, except for the material of their protective cases.

Howard etches his initials on the inside case of each watch: "HTJ" in letters so small one would need a magnifying glass to see them. He decides to show the silver pocket watch to his boss, Pierre Cartier.

At 5:00 p.m. on Friday afternoon, Howard enters Mr. Pierre Cartier's office holding the silver watch. His shoes sink into the thick, royal-blue carpet. Mr. Cartier is sitting behind his ornate 19th century French Louis XIV walnut desk, signing papers.

"Mr. Cartier, I am sorry to bother you, but I just wanted to show you this watch that I've designed." Howard places the watch on his desk. "You see my son is a Boy Scout, and I thought he would enjoy having a watch like this. I made two of them. This one I made for myself, and the one for my son, I encased in brass. Do you think you might like to begin selling this type of watch in your store?"

Mr. Cartier opens the silver watch with his fingernail and examines the painting. He then looks at Howard. "Although it is a handsome pocket watch, it would not be suitable for the Cartier image," he says.

"So you have no interest in the watch?" Howard asks, surprised.

"No, not really."

"Then, Mr. Cartier, do I have your permission to apply for a patent for this design?"

Pierre looks at Howard and smiles. "Yes, certainly. If you think you can patent and sell them, you have my permission."

By the end of the week, Howard has in his hand a legal document signed by Pierre Cartier relinquishing all rights the company has to the Boy Scout pocket watch and its design.

Howard sells the patent to the Ingersoll Company, which successfully makes and sells the unique Boy Scout watch for decades.

CHAPTER 3

THE WATCHES ARE REVEALED

May 5, 1927

Thursday night, May 5, just one week before Richard's fifteenth birthday, Howard and Dolores are relaxing in their living room; Howard smokes a pipe and reads the newspaper, and Dolores knits a green vest. They look up periodically to admire their newly purchased oil painting, *The Artist and His Mother*, by Arshile Gorky. Howard purchased it recently as Dolores' forty-second birthday present. They are alone this evening, as Richard is spending the night at a friend's home.

"Howard, I think Gorky's mother, the one in our painting, looks a little bit like my mother, don't you think so?"

"Sure, sure, she looks just like your mother," Howard says, not raising his eyes from his newspaper.

Suddenly Howard stands up from his chair. "Oh my heavens, I need to show you something." He walks into their bedroom and returns with two small white boxes. "I made two of these," he explains, handing a box to Dolores. "I thought I would keep one for myself."

Dolores opens the box. "Why, Howard, I don't think I've ever seen anything so fine." She picks up the brass watch. The metal casing is cold, and the watch is heavier than she expects. Dolores looks at Howard, smiles, then opens the watch. "Oh my goodness, look at these beautiful colors. It's just perfect. I know Richard will treasure this gift and keep it with him all his life."

"I was going to give the brass watch to Richard and keep this one for myself," Howard explains as he hands her the second box which contains the silver watch.

After closely examining it, she says, "Howard, darling, I know you're not very religious or spiritual, and I'm sure you'll think this is silly, but I would like to take both watches to my fortune teller, Madam Genova, so she can bless them, or say a chant over them, or do whatever she does to make them special so they will guide and protect you and our son."

"You want to do what?" he asks.

"Oh, I know you don't believe in all that fortune teller stuff, but what could it hurt, really?"

"That's ridiculous, Dolores, just ridiculous. I won't hear of it."

Dolores places the silver watch back in its box, secures the top, and then places both boxes on the small table next to her. She continues with her knitting, but tears begin to form. Her chin trembles, and she dabs at her eyes with the corner of her blouse.

The couple sits in silence for a few moments.

"Oh, Jesus, Dolores. If it's that important to you, then get both of the damn watches blessed. Just go ahead and do it." Howard pauses. "Hey, but don't let those watches out of your sight. I mean it, Dolores. They are precious items, and I don't want some crazy old lady taking them into one of her back rooms and doing I-don't-know-what with them. Do you understand?"

Dolores smiles and nods her head. "Thank you, Howard."

After finishing the row of knitting, Dolores calls her neighbor, the fortune teller, and she makes an appointment to see her the very next day.

CHAPTER 4

CASTING THE SPELL

May 6, 1927

"I will trade you three games of checkers and two games of marbles if we can listen to your mother's session today," Joshua says.

"Three checkers and two marbles, for Monday afternoon? Shoot, yeah," Jack replies.

At 3:55 p.m. the boys walk into the small, padded closet, and Madam Genova closes the door behind them.

*　　*　　*

Dolores' blonde hair is piled high on her head as she leaves her apartment to visit Madam Genova. She cradles the two white boxes in her hands as she makes her way down the four flights of steep stairs. Dolores' purse is heavy, and the handle begins to dig into her wrist.

"I should have put the boxes in my purse before I started down these stairs," she says to herself.

Arriving at her destination, and still juggling the boxes, Dolores uses her fingertip to tap on the door. Madam Genova greets Dolores and escorts her into the back room of her apartment.

Dolores looks at the tarot cards that have been stacked neatly next to the crystal ball on the table. "Oh, Madam Genova, I'm not here for a reading, I'm here to show you something." Dolores sets the two white boxes on the table, removes the watches, and places them in front of the fortune teller.

"My," the fortune teller says, "Mrs. James, these are very fine watches."

"Yes," Dolores replies, fingering the handkerchief in her lap. "It took months for my husband to make them. We are going to give one of them to our son for his fifteenth birthday, and my husband is going to keep the other one." Madam Genova nods her head. "I have always trusted you, Madam Genova, and followed your guidance. I thought, perhaps, you could see what would be in store for their future owners, or, better yet, say a blessing or prayer over them so these watches will protect their owners and bring them good luck."

The fortune teller continues to examine the watches, opening each case to admire the artwork on the faces of the watches. "Well, it so happens that a dear friend of mine specializes in casting spells. I am pretty sure I could make an appointment for you. Yes, I know if I asked her, she would see you."

"I really don't want to involve a stranger with these precious watches. Aren't you capable of casting a spell? You are so talented, are you certain you don't know any spells?"

"Well, Mrs. James, as you probably know, the casting of spells is a completely different art—a different talent, so to speak—from what I am able to do."

They sit for a few moments.

"You know, Mrs. James, I just might have a solution. My dear friend did teach me *one* casting spell about seven years ago…yes, it's been about seven years. It's a good luck spell, and it might work just fine for these two watches. Yes, come to think of it, I believe it would be the perfect spell."

"Well, for Heaven's sake, then please cast it on both of these," Dolores says.

"I am especially intrigued with this watch," Madam Genova says as she looks at the brass watch in her left hand. "This watch, Mrs. James, this is the one that should go to your son. It is important that you give him this one."

Dolores nods. "Yes, that's the one my husband wants to give him."

"Well, that's good," Madam Genova says.

Dolores pauses. "If you think it's possible to cast your good luck spell, how much would it cost to place it on both of these watches?"

Madam Genova looks at Dolores with a serious expression on her face. "It will be one hundred dollars for each watch."

"One…one hundred dollars *each*? Oh my goodness, that's a lot of money. So, two hundred dollars for both of them? Gee, I had no idea it would be so expensive."

"You want the spell to last the lifetime of the watches, correct? You want it to be strong enough to influence the future decisions and actions of the owners, right? If so, it will have to be a very strong spell—which may result in the loss of all of my powers, and that will surely endanger my health," the fortune teller explains.

"Oh, I see. Well then, of course. Of course. I can certainly see why the spell would be so expensive." After a few moments of deliberation, Dolores continues, "Well, I'd have to bring you the rest of the money on Monday. I only have one hundred dollars in my purse."

"That will be fine," Madam Genova replies.

Dolores picks up her purse from the floor, takes out her wallet, and hands all of her paper money to Madam Genova. The fortune teller puts the money in her skirt pocket, then glances at the wooden chest of drawers against the wall.

"First, Mrs. James," Madam Genova says, "I must check one thing."

The fortune teller walks over to the wooden chest, opens the top drawer, and shuffles a few pieces of paper. Madam Genova remembers placing a notebook containing the words to the good luck spell in the top drawer, but it has been years since she has seen it, and she is not certain of the exact words or the exact order in which they appear. She is relieved to find the notebook. In the dim light, Madam Genova examines each line of the spell. When she finishes, she closes the drawer, and returns to her table.

"Okay, I'm ready. Let's begin."

She moves the boxes to the side of the table and places both watches directly in front of her, side by side and just inches apart. The fortune teller stares at the watches, then covers her eyes with the palms of her hands and begins chanting the three sentences of the good luck spell, the spell Monique first showed her many years ago in Louisiana. She chants so softly Dolores cannot make out exactly what she is saying.

After a few moments Madam Genova stops, looks at Dolores, and shakes her head. "It's not working," she says.

"What's not working?" Dolores asks.

"The spell. The spell, of course," Madam Genova states in an irritated tone.

"Well, why not? Why isn't it working? What's wrong?" Dolores asks. "I paid you for the spell."

"Don't you think I know that? I have no idea why the spell isn't working," Madam Genova says waving her hands in the air. "Give me a moment to think."

After a few minutes of uncomfortable silence, Madam Genova says, "Mrs. James, I know why the spirits will not allow me to cast this spell in front of you."

"For goodness sake, just tell me," Dolores exclaims.

"It's because…" Madam Genova hesitates. "It's because you are too religious. Your belief in Jesus is too strong."

"What? What in the world are you talking about?"

"That's it. I'm certain that's why this is happening. The Spirit World and the Religious World often conflict with one another," Madam Genova explains as she stares at the gold cross dangling from Dolores' necklace.

They sit in silence at the table. "Well, we could try one other thing. Why don't you step out of the room for a few minutes and let me try once more to cast the spell? Maybe the spirits will be more forgiving if you are out of the room."

Dolores lowers her head and then looks back. "Okay. Let's give that a try." She stands up, but then stops. "Oh, no. I can't do that. I made a promise to my husband that I would not let these watches out of my sight. Honestly, he made me promise."

"Oh, for goodness sake," Madam Genova says, "you will be right outside the door. What possible harm could come to these watches in the few minutes they will be under my care? Don't you trust me? You have known me longer than your husband."

Dolores hesitates. "Oh, you're right. Of course you're right. I've placed my trust in you all these years, and you've never steered me wrong. You even told me Howard was the man I should marry." Dolores pauses. "I remember you told me the specific day when the stars would all be perfectly aligned so I could set the date for my wedding. I do trust you, Madam Genova. I'm just being silly, I know. So, let's continue."

"Okay, then, I want you to leave the room," instructs Madam Genova. "I'll come and get you when I'm ready for you to return. Don't enter this room again until I tell you to do so, understand?"

Dolores nods and exits the room. She closes the door behind her and waits just on the other side with her hand still holding the doorknob.

Madam Genova then takes out the notebook containing the spell from the chest. She reads the spell once again, then closes the drawer. Madam Genova glances at the watches on the table, breathes a heavy sigh, then sits down and stares at the watches for a moment.

Placing her palms over the watches, and with her eyes closed, she begins to chant:

Great stars in the heavens, shine your brightest tonight.

Good fortune we seek, let it be in our sight.

Hope and wonder, please do come our way,

For this is our wish, for luck to stay.

She keeps her palms pressed against the watches, which begin to vibrate as she chants. Thin strands of white smoke and a bright light emanate from each. The light is so bright, Madam Genova has to turn her head.

"Oh Jesus," Madam Genova says to herself. "I don't remember any smoke or flashing lights when I watched Monique perform this good luck spell. Maybe I wrote it down wrong.

Maybe the sentences are out of order...or I left something out...Something has gone terribly wrong."

After about five minutes, Dolores hears Madam Genova walking toward the door. The door opens, and she invites Dolores back into the room. Her red scarf is lopsided, and she appears out of breath. Dolores notices the two pocket watches appear to be in the exact same position as when she left the room.

"It's done," Madam Genova explains to Dolores. "The spell has been cast."

"Oh my, that's wonderful," Dolores says.

"Yes, yes, the spell is complete," Madam Genova says. "Extraordinary good fortune will come to pass for the owner of each watch. Success beyond their wildest dreams will be theirs for the taking."

"Why, that's unbelievable," Dolores exclaims. "I am just delighted."

"Yes, the spell is definitely complete, but let's sit down here for a moment, Mrs. James." Dolores complies.

"I should tell you," Madam Genova explains, "along with the gift of luck, I sense each watch now seeks its own destiny."

"Its own what? The watches seek what?" Dolores asks.

"Its own destiny, each watch now seeks its own destiny," Madam Genova says. She holds the brass watch in the palm of her hand, closes her eyes, and wraps her fingers around it. "This watch longs for the brightest stars."

Dolores looks at her. "Huh, well, I really don't know what to say. That's a good thing, right?"

"Yes, that's a good thing," Madam Genova says, opening her eyes and returning the brass watch to the table. She picks up the silver watch, clasps it with both hands, then brings the watch up close to her chest. With her eyes closed, she says, "This watch seeks the man with the greatest hope." She opens her eyes and returns the silver watch to the table.

There are a few moments of silence.

"The greatest hope?" Dolores says. "The greatest *hope*? Well, that's very interesting and all—strange, but interesting, nonetheless. Actually, I have no idea what you're talking about, Madam Genova, I just want to make sure my husband and son will have luck with these watches. That's all I care about."

"I understand, Mrs. James, and I want to assure you, the owner of these watches will undoubtedly have good luck. However, there is one final thing I must tell you," Madam Genova says. She swallows. "If the true owner of either watch should lose it, or abandon it, bad luck will follow. For as you must know, Mrs. James, bad luck often follows good luck."

"'Bad luck'? What do you mean 'bad luck'? I didn't ask for that. And what do you mean 'bad luck often follows good luck'? What kind of nonsense is that? All I wanted was a good luck charm placed on the watches, for God's sake."

"I'm sorry," Madam Genova says. "I actually didn't realize it would be part of the spell. It's a very powerful one, and there was really nothing I could do once the spell was cast. And remember, the bad luck will only occur if the watch is lost or abandoned."

Dolores stares at Madam Genova for a moment, shaking her head and pursing her lips. She returns the two pocket watches to their respective boxes. "I'll stop by on Monday with the rest of the money," she says.

As Dolores begins to reach for the boxes on the table, Madam Genova picks up the box closest to her and places it in her lap. "You know I trust you, Mrs. James, so I know you won't mind if I keep one of these watches until Monday, when you return."

Dolores stares at her. "What? You are actually going to keep one of the watches? You must be kidding."

"Just until you return on Monday."

Dolores breathes a heavy sigh. "Well, okay. I guess that will be alright."

Madam Genova stays seated as Dolores takes the one remaining box from the table and walks out of the room.

"Okay, boys. You can come out now," Madam Genova says, and she returns the white box to the table.

Joshua opens the padded door, and both boys step out of the closet. Jack immediately heads for the kitchen.

"Come here, Joshua," Madam Genova says after she turns up the lights and sits back down at her table.

She reaches out, takes Joshua's right arm in her hand, and begins to examine it. "I see you have more bruises on your arms. Have you run into more walls?" she asks.

He hesitates, then looks down at the floor. "Yes, ma'am," he says. "That's what happened." Joshua feels hot tears beginning to roll down his cheeks, so he closes his eyes.

She is silent for a moment but doesn't release his arm. "Oh, hon," she whispers, "I can help you. Would you like me to help you?"

Joshua shakes his head. "No. No one can help us. No one can know."

"Here, take this tissue," she says, reaching into her skirt pocket. "Listen, Joshua, I know you don't want to talk about this, but I am going to do something for you." Madam Genova opens up the white box and takes out the shiny silver pocket watch. She opens up the case and hands it to him.

Joshua sees the Boy Scout tents, the dark green trees, and the blue river painted on the face. "I've never seen anything so nice," he says.

"Joshua, what you just saw in this room today, you must never tell anyone. I placed a spell on these watches…a very powerful spell that I learned years ago from a Vodou Queen in Louisiana. She had great powers, and she made her living by selling amulets, lucky charms, and magical powders. She cast spells that were guaranteed to grant one's desires or to destroy one's enemies. I helped her one day, and, in return, she taught me a very powerful spell."

"M-magical powders?" he asks.

"Yes, magical powders."

"And you say you helped her?"

"Yes, a man was tormenting her and killed one of her pets, so I helped her with her problem," Madam Genova explains.

"How did you help the Vodou Queen?" he asks.

"Well, never mind about that now. Joshua, this watch… this watch will protect you and keep you safe. I know you are going on a camping trip tomorrow, and you should keep this watch with you. It is very important that you bring this back to me in pristine condition on Sunday night. Do you understand? Pristine condition. No scratches. Okay?"

He nods, still staring at the watch. "Yes, Sunday night. I promise I will bring it back to you on Sunday night." He places the watch in his pocket.

"Oh, and Joshua, don't tell your parents anything about this."

"I won't," he calls, already running out of the apartment.

CHAPTER 5

ERIC MCMILLAN

May 6, 1927

Madam Genova is washing dishes when she hears loud banging on her front door. She opens it to find Joshua's father, Eric McMillan, standing in front of her. Eric's long, oily black hair has a terrible odor. Ashes drop from the cigarette dangling from the side of his mouth, and the stubble on his face appears to be about three days old. She notices his sleeveless T-shirt has yellow stains on the front, and the zipper on his pants is only halfway up. He wobbles on his feet, then reaches for the doorframe to steady himself. They are both the same height, and now Eric is standing just inches in front of Madam Genova. He drops his cigarette to the ground and crushes it into the hallway carpet with his shoe.

"So here we meet again, huh?" Eric asks with his acrid breath. "Listen to me, you bitch, or is it *witch*? I told you I don't want you to have nothin' to do with my kid. Do you remember that? Can you hear me? Are you listening? Are you DEAF? I was down here just last week. Listen, I know my kid has been here to visit you. You tell him he CANNOT visit with you, that you don't want to see him anymore. UNDERSTAND?

DO YOU UNDERSTAND NOW?" He wobbles again and grabs hold of the other side of the door frame. Madam Genova stares at him. "If I catch him down here, there will be a big price to pay. I will beat the shit out of both of you. Do you understand me?"

He reaches into his shirt pocket, takes out a cigarette, fumbles for the lighter in his pants pocket, and lights it. He blows the smoke of his first inhale into Madam Genova's face. She continues to stare at him.

"Well, bitch, are we clear?"

"Yes, Mr. McMillan, I understand you perfectly."

As Eric turns around to leave, he wobbles and almost falls. Madam Genova reaches out to steady him.

"Hey, bitch, don't help me. I don't need your fucking help. And don't touch me. NEVER TOUCH ME AGAIN," he yells as he heads toward the stairs. He takes a few steps, then grabs hold of the banister and uses it to help pull himself up the steep stairway.

Madam Genova watches him climb the stairs, and after he disappears, she walks back into her apartment and examines the cigarette lighter she just picked from Eric's pocket. She notices the initials 'EM' engraved on its side. Madam Genova sits down on her couch, but after a few moments she gets up and goes into Jack's bedroom. He is already in bed.

"Who was that, Mom?" he asks.

"Oh, no one, dear. Listen, I need to go out for a couple of hours. Will you be okay?"

"Sure, Mom, I'm a big boy."

"Of course you are, my love." She kisses Jack on the forehead, grabs her purse, and leaves her apartment.

CHAPTER 6

MADAM GENOVA ASKS A FAVOR

May 6, 1927

Madam Genova knocks on Monique's apartment door, and as she opens it, she sees Monique is still wearing her work clothes—a long blue skirt, white blouse and her favorite gold-hooped earrings. The walls of Monique's apartment are covered in dark paneling, and the living room is filled with expensive antique furniture.

The women have been best friends since they were in elementary school, when each discovered the other had a unique gift of clairvoyance. Monique, born into a Louisiana Creole family, is tall and slender with dark skin and emerald-green eyes. Even at a young age, her appearance was striking, and men noticed when Monique walked by wearing her flowing skirts.

"Hi Jenny. Is something wrong?" Monique asks.

"Monique, I'm so sorry to bother you this late in the evening. I'm sure you just got home."

"Oh for goodness sake, please come in and sit down," Monique says. "I'm always glad to see you. What's going on?"

"I have a big problem," Jenny says as she enters the apartment and sits on the long, plum-colored, Edwardian couch.

"There is a little boy in my building, a very sweet, innocent little boy, and his father beats him and his mother. It's a horrible situation. The boy's father came to my apartment this evening, drunk, and threatening me. What an asshole! Anyway, as he was leaving, I picked his pocket and got his cigarette lighter."

Jenny takes the cigarette lighter out of her purse and hands it to Monique.

"Is there something you can do with this?" Jenny asks. "You really are so talented when it comes to placing curses on objects."

"Yes. I'm certain I can find just the right spell."

"Monique," Jenny says, "the spell needs to work quickly. I never want this man to come to my door again."

"What's his name?" Monique asks.

"Eric, Eric McMillan," Jenny replies.

"It shouldn't be a problem," Monique says as she walks over to a cabinet in her living room. She takes out a bottle of brown powder and sprinkles a bit on the lighter. "Eric McMillan," she says to the lighter, then takes a deep breath and blows it forcefully onto the lighter, "will breathe no more." She hands the lighter back to Jenny.

"That's it?" asks Jenny.

"That's it, my dear. You must simply make certain this man has the lighter in his hands within seventy-two hours. It will not harm anyone but him."

Jenny takes the lighter, places it in her purse, and stands up. "I love you, Monique."

"I love you, too, Jenny."

The women hug, and Jenny departs.

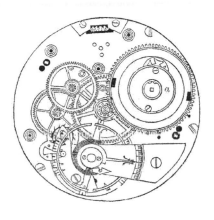

The Journey of the
Silver Boy Scout

Pocket Watch

CHAPTER 7

CAMP BARTON

May 7, 1927

"Oh my God, how long have we been on this bus?" Joshua whispers in Bobby's ear.

He shakes his head.

Joshua reaches into his pocket for the Boy Scout watch and feels the cold metal case. He takes it out and attempts to pry it open with his fingernail. After a few tries, it opens. Joshua already knows the watch well. He stared at it in his room for a long time after Madam Genova gave it to him. 'BE PREPARED' is printed on the short hand, and 'A SCOUT IS' on the big hand. Individual words describing the ideal traits of a Boy Scout form a printed circle around the edge of the watch: '*REVERENT, TRUSTWORTHY, LOYAL, HELPFUL, FRIENDLY, COURTEOUS, KIND, OBEDIENT, CHEER-FUL, THRIFTY, BRAVE,* and *CLEAN.*' As the big hand sweeps around the hour, it points to each of these words. Currently, at twenty-three minutes past the hour, the watch says, 'A SCOUT IS *COURTEOUS.*'

The loud motor and constant rocking of the bus have lulled almost everyone to sleep. At each turn of the bus, Joshua feels

31

Bobby's arm push against his. Bobby is focused on shredding a rather large wad of tissue in his lap.

"Hey Bobby," Joshua whispers. "Did you remember to bring some toilet paper?"

"Yeah, my mom packed two rolls," Bobby replies.

"Two rolls for two days?"

Bobby nods his head. "I guess she figured there'd be a lot of pooping."

They both giggle.

"My mom forgot to set her alarm and I almost didn't make it. It's a good thing I packed everything last night before I went to bed," Joshua explains to Bobby.

The old bus is winding along the bumpy road to Camp Barton, on Frontenac Point on the west shore of Cayuga Lake one of New York State's Finger Lakes.

Bobby, a thin, frail boy with thick glasses pauses. "We got to the bus an hour early this morning. My mom wanted to make sure I didn't miss it."

Joshua catches sight of another wad of tissue stuffed into the side pocket of Bobby's vest. "What's with all the tissue?" he asks.

"Oh, sometimes I get a bloody nose," he replies. "I hope it won't happen on this trip, but I need to be prepared, just in case."

"I hope you don't get one either," Joshua says, nodding his head.

It's beginning to get light outside, and a few of the Boy Scouts are starting to wake up. Joshua and Bobby listen to their conversations along with their periodic shrieks of laughter, but they spend most of their time staring out the window.

Bobby and Joshua have only recently joined Boy Scout Troop 231. Their Senior Patrol Leader and their Scoutmaster are on the bus as well and will be guiding them on this trip.

Brian, the Senior Patrol Leader, just turned eighteen years old. They're not sure how old Mr. Alvin Warwick, their Scoutmaster is, but he looks ancient. The rest of the boys in their troop range in age from fourteen to seventeen years. Bobby and Joshua are the youngest; both of them are fourteen years old.

This is their first sleep-away adventure. Their troop is heading for a two-day, one-night campout. The boys hope to meet the requirements for earning merit badges in things such as backpacking, bird study, hiking, and insect study. Joshua hopes they won't run into difficulties and end up earning badges for things like lifesaving or first aid. Most important of all, Joshua hopes he doesn't start crying because he's homesick and make a fool of himself.

They were instructed to pack very sparingly; a sleeping bag, a change of underwear, a canteen for water, toilet paper, and a few utensils are all they've brought.

After nearly a three-hour bus ride, an impressive wooden structure made from logs greets them at the entrance to the camp. The words 'Camp Barton' appear on a massive horizontal log perched at the top of the entrance. The bus continues under the tall wooden structure, and they bump along for another two miles until they reach their campsite.

Mr. Warwick, balding and with a beard of short, grey stubble, is about forty pounds overweight. But he seems confident and speaks with an air of authority. Today he has on his tan regulation cap, which seems a bit small for his head. He is wearing a short-sleeve brown shirt that matches the rest of their uniforms. Even though his red neckerchief usually covers the front of his shirt, whenever he moves, Joshua can see the buttons are pulling on the front, eager to pop open. The hem of Mr. Warwick's shorts falls just below his knees. Mr. Warwick, among other things, reminds their troop his son was an Eagle Scout. Joshua is certain he has forgotten he told them about his son just last week.

The bus stops, parking on a piece of dry, flat land. They all stand up, put on their backpacks, and start walking slowly toward the front of the bus.

Brian is the first to step off the bus, and he begins shouting, "Let's go, let's go, let's go," while motioning with his hand as they step off the bus and onto the parking lot.

A few feet away from the bus, Joshua feels the cool air on his face. He looks up at the blue sky. It smells like pine, and he sees the tall trees dotting the steep hiking trails that wind among the distant hills. The air is much colder than he thought it would be, not hot and sticky like back home.

Brian is around six feet tall, with dark red hair cut close to his head in a crew cut. The scarf around his neck is almost the same color as his hair, and the freckles on the bridge of his nose spread across to his cheeks.

"Now partner up," Brian says. "Make sure you've taken everything off the bus that you brought with you, and then find a partner. You must know where your partner is at all times. Your partner will also be your tent mate. As you get off the bus, each pair of boys will get a set of stakes to help steady your tents. If your partner already has a set, you do not need to get another set from me. Look around and find a spot to set up camp and put your gear down. Mr. Warwick and I will begin unloading the canvas tents and we'll distribute them to you."

Bobby looks at Joshua as they walk away from the bus. "Say, Joshua, will you be my partner?"

"Of course," Joshua says. He turns and takes a set of stakes from Brian.

"John," Brian yells at one of the scouts. "Don't set your gear down so far away. Bring it in closer to the rest of us. Now all of you, listen up. Start setting up your tents. When you're through, put on your backpacks and find your partners. We're about to go on a short hike. Be sure you have water. After we get back from our hike, Mr. Warwick and I will inspect your tents."

After a few missteps, Bobby and Joshua finish setting up their tent. It looks pretty good. Joshua unzips his backpack and is surprised to find a banana his Mother placed inside. She has carved on the yellow peel: "I love you, Joshua. Mom." After he stares at the banana for a few seconds, tears begin to form.

"Hey, anything wrong?" Bobby asks.

"No, no," Joshua replies. "I just have some allergies."

"You have allergies, too?" he asks.

"Yeah, sometimes," Joshua nods, wiping the tears away and walking out of the tent. Joshua sees everyone is gathering for their hike. He takes out his watch and notices the tent pictured on the face of the watch looks just like theirs. It's 10:03 a.m.—'A SCOUT IS *TRUSTWORTHY*.'

All fifteen boys from Troop 231 walk in single file up the closest trail. Joshua checks his pocket to make certain the watch is safe. Brian leads the way, and Joshua walks directly behind him.

The trees are gigantic, and Joshua knows he wouldn't be able to touch his fingers if he were to wrap his arms around the trunk. Pinecones, gravel, a few scattered large rocks, and tree roots cover the trail. Squirrels dart across the path in front of them, then scamper up the trees. Joshua hears someone running up the path. When he turns, he sees Rodney—a short, stocky boy with round brown glasses—approaching. Unsteady in his oversized hiking boots, Rodney slips on the gravel, then regains his balance. When Brian notices him, he motions the line of scouts to stop. Rodney, out of breath, stands on his tip-toes and whispers in Brian's ear.

"Just go in the bushes over there," Joshua hears Brian instruct Rodney. "We'll wait for you right here."

Rodney remains standing in front of Brian, looking up at him. He is not heading for the bushes. Joshua is close enough to Rodney to see tears forming and his lower jaw trembling. Mr. Warwick walks over to Brian and Rodney.

"What seems to be the problem, Rodney?" he asks.

Rodney looks down at his shoes, then looks up at Mr. Warwick. "Sir," he says, "I have to go number two."

Delbert, a large, lumbering boy standing behind Joshua, turns around and shouts to the rest of their troop, "Hey, guys, Rodney has to take a poop."

There are some giggles among the boys.

Mr. Warwick turns around and faces Delbert. "Son," he says, leaning very close to Delbert's face, "I think you need to start minding your own business, don't you?"

"Yes sir," Delbert replies, his face turning red.

"And Rodney, that's absolutely no problem." Mr. Warwick takes off his backpack, reaches into it, and hands Rodney a small shovel. "Well, okay then," he says. "Do you have toilet paper in your backpack?"

"Yes sir."

"Okay. Good. You'll need to remember to dig a deep hole. Oh, and when you are done, be sure to cover it with enough dirt. We want to leave these beautiful woods just as we found them, don't we?"

"Yes sir," Rodney says while holding the collar of the small shovel.

Rodney scurries into the woods until they can no longer see him.

"Everyone take your packs off and sit down," shouts Brian. They do so in the middle of the trail.

Soon Rodney reappears, and Mr. Warwick looks relieved. Rodney hands the shovel to Mr. Warwick, and Joshua is surprised he doesn't examine the shovel to see if any poop is on it. He guesses Mr. Warwick isn't bothered by such things. Mr. Warwick puts the shovel back in his pack and they continue their hike.

After an hour, Brian turns the troop around and marches them back toward their campsite. As they start back, there is a loud shriek from one of the scouts.

"Get it off. Get it off. Oh Jesus...get it off."

Joshua turns and sees Cameron, one of the older scouts, has a gigantic furry spider with green eyes on his forehead. Cameron's partner, Jeff, is frozen, and all he can do is stare at the spider. But he quickly recovers, and steps forward. He swats Cameron's head, knocking the large spider to the ground.

Mr. Warwick rushes over and looks at the spider, now scampering away. "That's a wolf spider," he announces. "Are you okay, Cameron?" he asks.

Cameron smiles sheepishly. "Yes sir."

"Their bite is not deadly," Mr. Warwick continues, "so let's just move on."

Still, there is nervous laughter.

"Good work, Jeff," Brian shouts.

"Oh my God," Cameron says, "can you believe the size of that spider?"

Yikes, Joshua thinks, *that was probably the biggest spider I've ever seen.*

Once they arrive at the campsite, a few of the scouts dig a hole for the fire pit while others make sure their tents are ready for the upcoming inspection. The rest head out to collect sizable logs for the campfire.

Mr. Warwick checks that all the food is in good shape, then he hangs their large, wooden, bear-resistant trash barrels by a rope about eight feet off the ground, dangling them between two trees.

Mr. Warwick blows a whistle to get the scouts' attention and asks them to gather around the pile of logs. He hands out peanut butter and jelly sandwiches and, with Brian's help, places a large metal container of water on the ground. "Fill up your canteens with water if they're starting to get low," Mr. Warwick instructs them.

They sit in a circle eating, and Joshua notices a small pile of rocks near the logs.

After lunch, the scouts carefully put away any leftovers from around their campsite, lest the smell attract wild animals. Since Joshua's and Bobby's tent is located closest to the trash barrels, they gather the trash and help Mr. Warwick lower the barrels to place the trash inside. The barrels are heavy, and it takes all their strength and weight to raise them and secure them in place.

Mr. Warwick and Brian walk around inspecting the tents, making certain they are stable.

Bobby and Joshua crouch down on the ground in front of their tent while they wait their turn. They clear a small area of rocks before sitting down. Joshua notices Bobby has suddenly stopped. Bobby stands up slowly, his eyes widening as he looks over Joshua's shoulder. He shakes his head and repeats the word "no" so softly he can barely hear him.

As Joshua turns around, he hears a loud *thwack* like something hitting wood.

"Okay boys," Mr. Warwick, tells them in a soft but firm voice. "Stay calm and remember what you've been taught. Let's all line up right here."

All fifteen boys form a straight line. Joshua reaches into his pocket and squeezes the cold metal of the watch. For a moment, it seems as if it's vibrating.

Kevin, the boy to Joshua's right, looks at him, and they reach for each other's hands. Joshua reaches out to his left, for Bobby's hand, and clasps it with a firm grip. They all raise their hands above their heads. The line stands straight and tall. Joshua focuses on the astonishing sight in front of him and tries to ignore the few whimpers from the other boys. The deep guttural sound shakes the air. A massive brown bear is standing erect, battering the wooden barrel with his huge paws. *Thwack.* The barrel swings against the tree and lands with a loud crash as branches fall to the ground. When the trash barrel swings back toward the bear, his paw pounds it once again, making a thunderous sound.

The bear, still standing on his hind legs, stops and looks at them. He is now thirty feet in front of them. The scouts freeze. No one breathes. And then their entire line wobbles back—one small, unsteady step. Glancing to his left, Joshua sees everyone still holding each other's hands, high in the air.

The wind picks up, and for the first time he smells the musky odor wafting from the bear. Joshua glances to his right and sees Mr. Warwick has positioned himself in the middle of the line. He has a firm grip on Tommy and Kevin's hands, the smallest boys in the troop.

After a moment of silence, Mr. Warwick, while never taking his eyes off the bear, states in a steady but soft voice.

"Remember what I taught you, boys, hands high in the air, and sing like you mean it."

With timid and trembling voices, they sing. "Old MacDonald had a farm." They get louder. "EE-I-EE-I-O. And on his farm he had a cow. EE-I-EE-I-O. With a moo-moo here and a…"

The bear snaps its jaws together, making a *whoofing* sound. He puts his head down, lays his ears back, and then moves one step toward their line, his front paws swinging in the air. They stop singing.

Joshua hears Mr. Warwick say, "It's okay, boys, it's okay. I want all of you to slowly take two steps backward."

They do.

"Now," he says, "I want you all to keep your hands in the air, wave them around a little, and keep singing."

Joshua begins singing, quite loudly, "With a moo-moo here and a…"

The rest of the boys join in. "…moo-moo there, here a moo, there a moo, everywhere a moo-moo, old MacDonald had a farm, EE-I-EE-I-O."

Another *whoof* from the bear, and, with a loud thud, his front two paws land on the ground. The bear looks again at the trash barrels, then at the boy scouts, and finally turns around and disappears into the woods.

The boys look at each other, slowly bring their arms down to their sides, and release each other's hands.

"I'm very proud of you," Mr. Warwick says firmly. "You were all very brave, and you remembered to do just what you were taught."

Brian is crying, his hands over his face. Mr. Warwick walks over and puts his arm around his shoulder.

"We're okay. We're all okay," Mr. Warwick consoles Brian.

Brian is the only boy crying. The rest of the boys are still in shock.

"Let's all go to our tents for about an hour," Mr. Warwick announces. "We'll rest up, and then we'll cook dinner."

They walk back to their tents.

Bobby and Joshua lie down on their sleeping bags. "Can you believe how close we were to that bear?" Bobby asks.

"No," Joshua replies. "I thought we were going to die for sure."

"Me too."

There are a few moments of silence. "I hear Delbert pooped in his pants," Bobby says.

"Hey, I heard that too," Joshua says. They both giggle.

Their hearts are still racing as they gaze at the tent's ceiling and watch the canvas gently move in the wind for the next hour. When they hear a whistle blow, Brian, apparently now recovered, is barking out dinner assignments for everyone.

"Kevin and Rodney, get the plates and the hot dog buns. Tommy and Nelson, unwrap the hot dogs. Rusty and Larry, gather some long sticks so we can roast our hot dogs and marshmallows, and then give the sticks to Steve and Noe. Steve and Noe, when you get the sticks, take your pocket knives and start sharpening them to skewer the hotdogs. Be careful and don't cut yourselves. Bobby and Joshua, go collect some kindling for the fire."

Bobby and Joshua head for the woods. "Wait," Bobby says. "It's too hot. I'm going to leave my vest in our tent."

"Okay," Joshua says. "Yeah, it's pretty warm. I'll wait for you here."

Bobby returns, a little out of breath. His brown regulation Boy Scout shirt, previously hidden under his dark vest, is heavily starched and well ironed. It looks brand new. Joshua glances down at the few holes and loose threads in his own shirt.

They walk into the woods and find an area dense with small sticks. Soon, their arms are filled with kindling. They look at each other for a moment and decide to inspect each other's arms, heads, and clothing to make certain there are no spiders hanging around. Finding none, they walk back to camp.

Close to camp, Bobby says, "Oh no, I have to sneeze."

"Wait, what? You have to what?" Joshua looks at Bobby as he lifts his head slightly and squeezes his eyes shut. He holds the bundle of small sticks against his chest.

"I have to…I have to…AHHH…AHHH…ACHOOOO. ACHOOO. ACHOOO. ACHOOO."

The kindling falls and scatters around Bobby's feet. The front of his brown shirt is now splattered with bright red blood.

"Oh my goodness," Joshua says, looking concerned.

"What?" Bobby asks. "What's wrong? A bear? Another bear?"

"No, no. It's the front of your shirt," Joshua points while still holding onto the kindling. "It has blood all over it." He notices blood dripping out of Bobby's nose. "And Bobby, it looks like you might have a little nosebleed going on there." He points to his nose.

"What? My nose is bleeding?" he asks.

Bobby pulls out the bottom of his shirt, which had been tucked into his shorts, and wipes his nose. The blood is bright red, and there is a lot of it. The stain spreads quickly across the bottom of his shirt, adding an additional pattern to the already splattered blood.

"Is there anything I can do?" Joshua asks.

"Well," he says, "I'm just going to lie here on the ground for a few minutes and put my head back while I pinch my nose. That's worked before."

After Bobby lies down, Joshua places his kindling on the ground and sits down next to him. After a while, Bobby sits up and looks down at his shirt, but he has difficulty finding an area free of blood. Once he finds one, he touches it to the end of his nose. The bleeding has stopped, so they gather the kindling and head back to camp.

By the time they return, the sun is starting to set. They bring their kindling to the fire pit, and a few of the boys help them arrange it strategically underneath the larger logs.

"Hey, Nelson," Brian yells. "Come on over here and start this fire with these rocks."

Joshua sees Brian lean toward Mr. Warwick and nudge him. "Watch this, Mr. Warwick, it will be funny. He'll never be able to light the fire with those rocks."

Nelson, though very quiet, is certainly one of the most coordinated boys in their troop. He is tall, with dark, straight hair that keeps falling into his eyes, and he lives on the poor side of town. Everyone knows that his father is a carpenter.

During only the second meeting of Joshua's Boy Scout troop, the boys went to an archery range. Mr. Warwick positioned each of them about 100 miles from the archery target, or at least that's how it seemed to Joshua. When it was Nelson's turn, Joshua saw him stare at the colorful circles on the target, turn sideways, and stand up straight. He took one of his arrows out of his quiver and placed it on the string, then pulled it back, taut, while squinting with one eye. Nelson held steady— maybe five seconds or so—still staring at the target, and then he let her go. It hit smack dab in the middle of the center circle.

Bull's-eye. Nelson continued to make bull's-eyes all afternoon, to the entire troops' astonishment, and scored well over the required sixty points. He earned his Archery Merit Badge that day, and he was the only one to do so.

Nelson goes to the small pile of rocks and crouches on his knees. After examining a few of them, he chooses one of the larger rocks, which has quite a bit of quartz in it. Next to him is a matted pile of kindling, which looks like a bird's nest. He sets it on the ground in front of him. Joshua notices his rock has multiple sharp edges. Nelson pulls out what appears to be a broken-off steel file from his pocket. He holds the quartz rock while he strikes the file against its sharp edges, maybe five or six times in rapid succession, and sure enough, sparks begin to fall onto the ground, and some into the bird's nest. Nelson blows, ever so gently, into the nest. Within a few seconds, it is in flames. He quickly sets the flaming nest next to the kindling. The kindling catches fire, and soon the smaller and then the larger wooden logs are bursting into flames.

Although the boys' eyes are mostly glued to Nelson's fire-making production, their gaze often shifts to the front of Bobby's shirt, eyes widening at the sight of the now darkened, splattered blood.

"Well, I'll be," Brian says to Mr. Warwick. "If I hadn't seen it for myself, I never would have believed it."

"Well done, Nelson," Mr. Warwick shouts. All the boys clap and rush to congratulate him.

Nelson grins and lowers his head.

"Amazing, Nelson. I don't know if I could have done that well," exclaims Mr. Warwick. "Good job, son. Very good job."

As it gets dark, the scouts gather around the campfire and have fun roasting their hot dogs and marshmallows. They accidentally sacrifice two hot dogs and marshmallows, too numerous to count, to the fire gods.

Brian tells a ghost story about a man who drives his girlfriend to Lovers' Lane to make out. Listening to the radio, the couple learn a murderer with a hook for a hand has just escaped from the insane asylum, which is only two blocks away. The woman hears strange noises outside their car and insists they head home. When they arrive at her house, her boyfriend walks around to open the car door and finds a large steel hook in the handle.

The boys nervously laugh, then go totally mute.

"Alright, boys, everyone get to bed. It's late and we've had enough excitement for the day," Mr. Warwick says.

The fire is low as they head for their tents. Bobby and Joshua crawl into their sleeping bags. Joshua is almost asleep when he sees Bobby get up and walk toward Mr. Warwick's tent. He follows him to see if something is wrong. Joshua sees Bobby is crying, and he seems to be trying to explain something to Mr. Warwick. Although Mr. Warwick is in his sleeping bag, he listens intently.

Bobby sees Joshua is behind him, then turns back to face Mr. Warwick. His bloodied brown shirt is unbuttoned, revealing a white T-shirt underneath, which is also heavily stained with blood.

"Mr. Warwick," he says, "with this blood all over my clothes, I'm afraid the bear will come back and kill me. I don't have an extra T-shirt and I've asked around and nobody has one." Tears flow down Bobby's face.

"Oh my, Bobby. The bear won't come back to get you," Mr. Warwick explains.

Mr. Warwick sits up. "Hey, Bobby," he says, "did you know bears like peanut butter much more than blood?"

Bobby shakes his head.

"Well," Mr. Warwick says, "let's go get some peanut butter."

He grabs his lantern as Bobby and Joshua follow him to the large wooden barrels hanging from the trees. They help him lower one.

"Hey, Joshua, shine that light over here into this container," Mr. Warwick tells him.

Looking into the container, and after digging around a bit, Mr. Warwick brings out a large yellow and red tin bucket of Shedd's peanut butter.

"Ahh. Here it is," he says.

He opens the lid, sticks his hand deep into the bucket, and smears a large glob of peanut butter down the front of his own T-shirt. Mr. Warwick still takes some time to clean the remaining peanut butter from between his fingers with the bottom of his T-shirt.

"Now," he says, "you have nothing to worry about. If any bears are nearby, they will come after me, okay? And, hey, don't tell any of the other boys I stuck my hand in the peanut butter tin."

Bobby and Joshua look at each other and grin, then look at Mr. Warwick. "Okay," Bobby says. "Thank you, Mr. Warwick."

CHAPTER 8

ADVENTURES AT CAMP BARTON

May 8, 1927

It's the second day of camp, and the sun is just coming up. Mr. Warwick is standing at the opening of their tent.

"Bobby," he whispers. "Brian packed an extra Boy Scout shirt and a T-shirt. Why don't you put these on?" He offers Bobby the shirts.

"Thanks, Mr. Warwick," Bobby says, taking the items. He crawls out of his sleeping bag, removes his bloodied T-shirt, and replaces it with the slightly big T-shirt. He examines the fresh brown Boy Scout shirt. 'Troop 231' is sewn just above the pocket in bright blue thread.

Joshua notices Mr. Warwick has on a clean T-shirt this morning, no peanut butter anywhere.

Soon after breakfast, Delbert twists his ankle on a rock and spends the day in his tent. The rest of the troop attempts to earn their merit badges by finding and cataloging different species of trees, plants, insects, and birds.

At the end of their final day, and just before the bus is scheduled to arrive, Bobby and Joshua walk to their tent to disassemble it. Once inside, Bobby says, "Hey, Joshua, would you like to become blood brothers?"

"Blood brothers?" he says. "Heck yeah."

Bobby removes a Swiss army knife from his backpack and makes the tiniest prick on the palm of his right hand. Joshua takes Bobby's knife and does the same. They both press their palms with their thumbs to make certain enough blood is coming out, and then they shake hands.

"Blood brothers for life," Bobby says, looking at Joshua.

"Yes," Joshua says. "Blood brothers for life."

At 4:00, they load up on the bus to head for home. Mr. Warwick and Brian are across the aisle from Bobby and Joshua. The bus engine starts with a roar and they slowly head down the steeply graded hill.

Mr. Warwick leans over to Joshua and says, "Hey, Joshua, did I tell you my son was an Eagle Scout?"

"Why, yes. Yes sir. I believe you did," he says.

Later, Joshua looks at his watch. It's almost 7:00. 'A SCOUT IS *REVERENT*.'

It's beginning to get dark outside, and Joshua is the only one still awake. He looks at Bobby, fast asleep, and then at his right palm and smiles.

"Blood brothers," he whispers.

CHAPTER 9

JOSHUA RETURNS HOME FROM CAMP BARTON

May 8, 1927

A rriving back at the parking lot, Joshua sees his mother's car waiting for him, and quickly runs toward it. She greets him happily, and while they drive home, she tells him to be quiet when he arrives home, as his father is asleep in their bedroom—though it's only 8:30 p.m.

Their apartment looks just like Madam Genova's; well, it has the same number of bedrooms, at least. Joshua's room, and, in fact, all their rooms, smell like cigarette smoke, and a few empty beer bottles and whiskey bottles are always on the kitchen counter. He and his mother try to keep everything organized and straight, because his father gets very angry if there's a mess, or if dinner isn't ready on time, or if they're out of beer. Actually, almost anything can upset him.

Joshua throws all his camping gear on his bed and rushes toward his front door, as he promised to return the watch to Madam Genova immediately.

"Where are you off to, dear?" his mother asks.

He makes an excuse, telling her he has to see Jack about something.

"It's late, dear, and he's probably already gone to bed. I'm sure you're tired from your camping trip. Why don't you just wash up and go to bed? After all, you've got school tomorrow and you have to wake up early."

"I promised, Mother. I promised I'd go see Jack as soon as I got home tonight," Joshua says. "He knew I'd be coming home late and is waiting up for me. I'll only take a few minutes... then I'll be right back. I promise," he says, walking to the door. He makes certain the watch is in his pocket.

His mother purses her lips. "Joshua, I don't think your father wants you going down there."

"Mother, I swear, I'll just be gone a minute."

There is a moment of silence. She looks at her watch.

"Well, go on then," she says. "Just hurry back."

He races down the two flights of stairs to Madam Genova's apartment.

Before he has even knocked on her door, she opens it and smiles. Joshua stares at her for a second, then retrieves the watch and hands it to her.

"The watch saved me and my entire troop from getting eaten by a bear."

"Well of course, I know that," she says, nodding her head and closely examining the watch. "Thank you for bringing it back, Joshua. It looks perfect. Oh, and Joshua, please do me a favor. I found this cigarette lighter on the hallway carpet the other day, and I believe it belongs to your father. See, it has the initials 'EM' on it. Would you please return it to him for me?"

"Sure. Yeah, it looks like my dad's lighter. He'll probably be glad to get it back. Thanks."

"I'm sure he will be. Please tell him I found it."

"Okay, I will," he shouts as he runs up the stairs.

Joshua's mother is in the kitchen, and after he shows her the lighter, she places it on the kitchen table. Together, Joshua drinks milk while she drinks coffee, and he tells her about his camp-out adventures. She is very interested, asking a lot of questions. When he looks at her closely, he sees the skin around her left eye is bruised. Joshua doesn't tell her about the bear, thinking it might frighten her.

"Was Father drinking again tonight?" he asks. His mother nods her head. "Did he hit you?"

Again, she nods her head and reaches out to gently stroke his cheek. "Yes, my darling boy," she says, "but tomorrow's another day, and I'm sure he'll apologize."

In the middle of the night, Joshua is awakened by his father yelling at his mother. "He went to that damn fortune teller's apartment tonight? Goddamn it, woman. Why did you let him go? We've talked about this. I'm going down there. This is NOT okay. Goddamn it, how many times do I have to explain this to her? She's had fair warning. I don't want her to have anything to do with Joshua. Do you understand? Do you? Do you really understand? Because I don't think you do."

"Eric, calm down. You're drunk. Please calm down. He just went to see Jack to tell him about his camping trip."

"'Calm down'? What the hell do you mean, 'calm down'? Are you now telling me what to do? Are you the boss of this house, lady?"

Joshua hears a loud thud against his bedroom wall and hears his mother moan. "Eric, please don't."

Joshua hears him storm into the kitchen. He opens his bedroom door slightly and sees his father standing near the kitchen table, smoking a cigarette. Joshua's father notices his son's door is open and walks into his bedroom. They look at each other, then Joshua takes a step backward. He knows his father is too angry and too drunk, and nothing he can say will make any difference. Joshua watches as his father raises his hand above his head, then it comes down hard and fast against Joshua's left cheek and almost knocks him off his feet. He grabs his bedpost to regain his balance. Joshua is determined not to cry, but he is too tired from the camping trip, making it impossible to fight back the tears.

Joshua's father looks at him and starts to say something but, instead, turns around and walks back into the kitchen. Joshua closes his door and sits on his bed, holding his throbbing cheek and wiping his tears with the corner of his sleeve. *I hope a bruise won't be there tomorrow when I go to school,* he thinks.

"I'm going to go back down to that goddamn fortune teller's apartment again, that witch downstairs, and give her a piece of my mind," Joshua's father shouts. "She'll never want to set eyes on Joshua again when I get through with her." He stomps out the front door. It slams behind him.

Joshua stays on his bed, frozen, until he collapses from sheer exhaustion. He is startled when his alarm rings at 6:30 a.m. Though he is still exhausted, he gets up and dresses for school. When he opens his bedroom door, he's surprised to see a uniformed policeman talking to his mother.

She looks surprised to see him standing in the doorway, and says, "Come here, darling. Come over here, son."

He walks over to the table and the policeman stands up, turns around, puts his hand on Joshua's shoulder and says, "I'm so sorry, son, but your father appears to have tripped when going down the stairs last night. Unfortunately, he is no longer alive."

"What did you say?" Joshua asks.

"I'm sorry, son, but we believe your father fell down the stairs and broke his neck. He died last night. One of your neighbors found him at the bottom of the stairs this morning."

"Well, where is he now?"

"We've taken his body to the city morgue. Your mother has already identified him."

"She identified him? This morning?" Joshua turns and looks at his mother.

"Yes, and again I am very sorry for your loss," the policeman says staring at the red and blue welt on Joshua's cheek. "What happened to your face, son?"

Joshua puts his hand up to his cheek. "Oh, nothing, nothing at all," Joshua says as he shakes his head. "Well, I better be getting off to school."

Joshua's mother covers her face with her palms and begins to sob.

"Now, now, there," the policeman says as he places his hand on her back. "Everything will be okay, Mrs. McMillan. And Joshua, I don't think you'll be going to school today."

Joshua stares at his mother. He feels nothing but relief.

*　　*　　*

Early Monday morning, Dolores James goes to Madam Genova's apartment and hands her the one hundred dollars, as promised. In return, she receives the box containing the second watch—which is in pristine condition.

*　　*　　*

Madam Genova contacts one of her wealthy clients and ensures Joshua's mother gets an excellent, well-paying job, which allows her to earn enough money to send Joshua to one of the finest private schools in New York City, with plenty left over for their livelihood.

CHAPTER 10

THE DINNER

May 11, 1927

Three days following the death of his father, Joshua stands in front of Jenny's apartment, holding a hot tin pie plate. Joshua is certain he has serious burns to the tips of three of his fingers from carrying the pie down the stairs. His mother baked it, then left to visit her sister in Poughkeepsie.

Joshua is wearing a well-pressed, slightly large, long-sleeve white shirt with tan trousers and a leather belt. His hair is clean and slicked back. He taps on the door with the tip of his shoe, and Jenny opens it. A long white apron is tied around her neck, partially covering her blue flowered dress.

"My, Joshua, don't you look handsome this evening?"

"Why thank you, Madam Genova."

"Joshua, you may call me Jenny."

"Oh...okay. Thank you, Jenny."

"What a nice shirt you're wearing," Jenny says.

"Oh, thanks. It was my father's. We cleaned out his closet, and most of his things look brand new because he didn't get out of the house that much."

"Well, it looks very nice on you. Why don't you come on in?"

"Oh, and here's an apple pie my mom baked," Joshua says. "Would you like me to put it in the kitchen? The plate is pretty hot."

"Yes, Joshua. That would be great. I'm sorry she wasn't able to join us this evening."

"Boy, it smells wonderful in here," Joshua says as he places the pie on the kitchen counter.

"Well, I hope you'll enjoy the meal. Why don't you go in and join Jack? He's already at the table waiting for you. Oh, and I've invited my dear friend, Monique, to join us tonight, too."

Joshua sits down at the dining room table and introduces himself to Monique. She is strikingly beautiful—with dark skin and bright green eyes. Her hair is long and she wears it entwined with a colorful scarf and tied into a fancy knot on top of her head.

Jenny finishes bringing the dishes to the table, and they begin passing the plates, which are piled high with food.

"So, Joshua, I am very happy that you're finally able to meet Monique. We have known each other since growing up in a small town in Louisiana. We both moved to New York around the same time. She, like me, is a fortune teller—a very talented one—and she knows how to cast spells, too."

Joshua looks at Monique and she nods her head. "Wow. That's amazing," he says. "Did you go to school together?"

"No, says Jenny. "We went to different schools, but our houses were close together, so we got to see each other a lot."

"We went to different schools, Joshua, because of the color of our skin," Monique explains.

"Oh, I understand," he says nodding his head. "So how did you and Monique learn to tell the future?"

"Well, I don't think either of us actually *learned* to tell the future," Jenny explains. "It just seemed to come naturally. By the time I was ten or so, for example, I would walk to the front window of my house, and my father would always show up at our front door about five minutes later. And it's not like he had a regular job or anything like that. He worked on a shrimp boat off Louisiana's coast, so his comings and goings were quite unpredictable."

"You could predict just when he was coming home?" Joshua asks.

"Yes, I could. At first I thought everyone could see what was going to happen next, but soon I realized it must be something special. On occasion, I would tell my mother what was going to happen; then, when what I predicted actually occurred, my mother would be horrified, so I learned not to tell her anything about the future.

"When I was young, I seemed to know silly things that would soon occur, like I would know my father was going to cut himself when he shaved, or what the school would be serving for lunch the next day, or which piece would be played next in a game of checkers—simple things like that. But as I got older, I learned how to predict even more accurately and further into the future."

"That's incredible," Joshua says, looking at Jack. "So are you able to see into the future?"

"No, I've tried," Jack says. "I can't predict anything."

"And what about you, Monique? Is that how you discovered you could see into the future?"

"Well, Joshua, I come from a long line of Creole fortune tellers who practiced Louisiana Vodou. I learned all my spells and incantations from my mother, grandmother, and great

grandmother, and from the books they used. My great grandmother, in fact, taught me her most secret, most complex, and
most powerful magic spells."

"Her most powerful spells?"

"Yes, that's correct," Monique says. "My parents and
grandparents died when I was quite young, and I still use the
books I inherited from them to look up specific charms, love
potions, or plant poisons."

"So all the women in your family could tell the future and
cast spells?" Joshua asks.

"Yes, that right," Monique replies.

"Well, were there other people in your town who could tell
the future?" Joshua asks.

Jenny looks at Monique, and they both shake their heads.
"No, I don't think so."

"And, Jenny, when did you learn to cast spells?" Joshua
asks.

"Oh no. Only Monique is able to cast spells; however,
she did teach me a good luck spell many years ago," Jenny
explains as she looks at Monique and smiles. "And sometimes
you use very special ingredients to cast spells. Isn't that right,
Monique?"

"Yes, it's important to have the right ingredients."

"I remember the first time I went over to Monique's
house," Jenny says. "The shelves that lined the back room of
her home were filled with bottles made of clear, brown or green
glass, all filled with a variety of seeds, stems, crushed powders,
feathers, rat poisons, ants, bees, cat and dog fur, rooster combs,
teeth—from every creature imaginable—small tree roots, rat
tails, fly wings, green beetles, snake tongues, and a million
other things."

Joshua and Jack look at each other and smile. Their eyes widen. "Wow," Joshua says with delight.

Jenny continues. "Some of the bottles' contents, as I recall, appeared red, and others, yellow. Some smelled sweet and others rancid. And although Monique's collection of bottles looked disorganized, she knew exactly where everything was located. Isn't that right, Monique?"

"Yes, although things might have looked a bit messy, I had my own system of cataloging my ingredients."

"We both dropped out of high school and got jobs working at local businesses," Jenny says. "I worked at the Ford Dealership, helping with paperwork and filing in the office, and Monique worked at McMahon's Furniture Store, where she helped clean, swept the floors, and dusted the pieces stored in the building."

"Is that how you supported yourself in Louisiana?" Joshua asks.

"Well, you have to remember I had a young child to raise—Jack here. So Monique helped me financially."

"I just helped her a little bit," Monique says.

"Oh, don't let her fool you. She is the reason Jack and I survived. Monique's knowledge of herbs and poisons, and her ability to cast powerful spells and create amulets to ward off evil spirits, brought her great fame in Louisiana. So, although she worked at the McMahon Furniture Store during the day to maintain the appearance of a normal life, the main source of her income was from her Vodou skills. People from all over Louisiana paid her handsomely to make someone love them or to harm their perceived enemy."

"Is that true?" Joshua asks Monique.

"Yes it is," Monique says and smiles.

They sit in silence, then Joshua says, "I feel very lucky to know both of you."

"Well, we're lucky to know you," Jenny says as she pats his arm.

"Hey, somebody pass the mashed potatoes, please," Jack says.

After the meal, thick slices of warm apple pie topped with vanilla ice cream are served for dessert, then everyone gets up from the table to leave. Jenny escorts Joshua to her front door. "Just let me know if you need anything while your mother's away."

CHAPTER 11

A BOND OF TRUST

May 14, 1927

Late Saturday morning, Jack and Joshua walk to Lincoln Park Field, only one mile from their apartment building. The Wildcats, their school's baseball team, are playing for the city championship. When they arrive at the baseball field, a large crowd is assembled, but they find two empty seats high up in the bleachers. Four hours and three extra innings later, the Mustangs, the opposing team, are ahead by one run. The Wildcats are up to bat, struggling with two outs and one man left on base.

"Jesus, it's hot today, right?" Joshua asks.

"I know, my shirt is soaked through."

"And, to make it worse," Joshua says, "I've gotten a few splinters in my butt from these bleachers."

"My butt is so numb I can't even feel the splinters," Jack says. Both boys laugh.

"Three extra innings. Who would have thought we'd be here so long?" Joshua asks, wiping his forehead with his handkerchief.

"Oh dang—and there it is, the third out," Jack says as he watches the foul ball fall into the glove of the Mustang's catcher. "Well, there's always next year, right?"

Joshua nods his head.

After the game, the boys console their school's players, then head over to the local A&W Root Beer stand. Joshua and Jack find a table in the back and order root beer floats—a thick, creamy, white mixture of root beer and homemade vanilla ice cream—Heaven in an ice-cold frosted glass mug.

"It was nice meeting Monique last night," Joshua says.

"Yes, she's been my mother's friend for as long as I can remember—a very close friend."

"Well, I guess they have that fortune teller thing in common."

"No, Joshua, they have a lot more in common."

"What do you mean?" Joshua asks.

"Well, it's a long story—a long, strange story."

"What happened?"

"You know we all lived in a small town in Louisiana, right?" Jack asks.

"Yes, you've told me that."

"I was pretty young when we lived there. Mother and I moved to New York when I was seven, and Monique moved to the city just a few weeks after us. Anyway, mother would always tell me a story when she put me to bed each night. That was just our routine, you know? So one night, she told me this story about something that happened in Louisiana that involved her and Monique. It was about a young man named Jeremy who had this big crush on Monique back in Louisiana."

"I can understand that," Joshua says. "She's very pretty."

"Yes, she is pretty, and I can understand about the crush and all, too. But according to mother, Monique didn't feel the same way about him."

"So what happened?" Joshua asks.

"Well, when mother first told me the story, it really frightened me, but then, for the next couple of weeks, I made her tell it to me again—the same story about Jeremy, the man who had a crush on Monique—every night for two weeks straight. Each night she would ask me if I wanted to hear a different story, but I didn't."

"The same story?" Joshua asks.

"Yes, the same story every night, although sometimes she would add an extra detail or two. And I asked her a bunch of questions."

"Why did you want to hear the same story?" Joshua asks.

"I have no idea. Maybe I didn't believe it happened—or maybe I was so terrified when I first heard it I had to hear it again and again, hoping it might become a little less scary. You know, kind of like watching a scary movie. If you watch it over and over, after a while, it's not so scary."

"Well, what in the world happened?" Joshua asks.

Jack glances around at the crowded tables, then begins. "You see, back then, Monique worked at McMahon's Furniture Store. The owner, Mr. McMahon, had a son named Jeremy, and he was kind of wild. Mother told me he had gotten into some trouble with the sheriff—stealing things, setting small fires to property and all—but anyway, he had a huge crush on Monique. Mother told me she made an effort to be nice to him at first, because, after all, he was the owner's son. But Jeremy wanted there to be something between him and Monique.

"Even though she was colored, and he was white, Jeremy wanted a romantic relationship with her. But because that kind of relationship was totally frowned upon in Louisiana, he wanted to hide it from his friends. Eventually Jeremy's advances became aggressive, and Monique refused to have anything to do with him. In fact, she told his father to keep Jeremy away from her. After that, he got very angry and killed one of her pets."

"He what? Killed one of her pets? Oh my God, that's terrible. But, hey, you know what? I do remember your mother telling me a long time ago she helped a woman with a problem after one of her pets was killed."

"Yes. It was Monique's dog, and the way mother described it, she loved that dog more than anything. Monique was afraid Jeremy would kill her two cats, or maybe even harm her, next."

"So what did she do?" Joshua asks.

"Monique thought up a plan—a plan to get rid of Jeremy. But she needed mother's help. Monique's house was located beside a deep freshwater lake which was home to a large number of alligators—and since it was alligator mating season when this all happened, it didn't take long for her to hatch a plan for what to do about Jeremy.

"Monique contacted Jeremy and invited him over for an early dinner. She told Jeremy she was actually flattered by all of his attention, and that she wanted to go out with him.

"Mother arranged for me to spend a few hours with a neighbor, then went to Monique's at about 5:00. By the time mother arrived, Monique had sprinkled sleeping powder in Jeremy's coffee," Jack explains.

"Sleeping powder? *Sleeping powder?*" Joshua asks.

"Well, it was either some heavy-duty sleeping powder, or some poison I guess," Jack says. "Anyway, by the time mother arrived at Monique's, Jeremy's head was already slumped down on his dinner plate. Mother said it took both of them to pull his chair away from the table. They eventually slid him onto the floor, dragged him across the kitchen, and got him out the front door and onto the porch. After they caught their breath, she said, they tugged and pulled him a short distance down to the river and laid him out just about ten feet from the river-bank, with his feet facing the water."

"Jesus, I can't believe I'm hearing this," Joshua says as the bottom of his glass mug lands hard on the table.

"Well, do you want to hear the rest of it?" Jack asks. "It's pretty disgusting."

"Yes, yes. Go on."

"Then Monique and mother, each with small, sharp knives, made cuts in Jeremy's body."

"They cut him all up?" Joshua asks, with his eyes opened wide.

"No, not too much. Just enough to let him bleed a lit-tle—enough to entice the alligators. Within a few minutes, a huge alligator stuck his eyeballs up, just above the top of the water. Mother said it was dark green and must have weighed about a thousand pounds. The alligator slowly turned his head from side to side, checking them out, then turned and faced forward, frozen for a few minutes, starring at Jeremy's bloody body. Then, suddenly, quick as lightning, she said, the alliga-tor scurried up on shore and chomped down hard on Jeremy's left foot."

"Holy cow, this is incredible," Joshua says, shaking his head.

"I know, right? And it's all true. Both women were stand-ing very close to the alligator, but they didn't move, and after a minute, the alligator slowly released his bite and then opened his mouth as wide as possible. It remained in that position for a few seconds, then moved a few steps closer to Jeremy. In the blink of an eye, Mother said, the alligator chomped down with incredible force directly into Jeremy's upper left thigh."

"Jesus, Mary, and Joseph. Unbelievable. Wait, don't tell me any more," Joshua says holding up his hand. He shakes his head and then takes a big gulp of his root beer float. "Okay. I've changed my mind. Tell me the rest of the story."

"Yeah. Believe me, I know. It's pretty gruesome. Mother said when the alligator snapped his jaws shut, Jeremy's whole left leg, almost up to his hip, was in the alligator's mouth—and Monique was covered in blood from the spray, from when the alligator shut his jaws so quickly. Can you imagine?"

Joshua shakes his head.

"After a few minutes, and never taking their eyes off the alligator, they both slowly stepped backward toward Monique's house. They watched the alligator drag Jeremy, still unconscious, down the grassy slope and into the river, pulling and tugging in a herky-jerky fashion. Mother described that scene to me quite a few times. After an initial splash and some gurgling sounds, she said, the alligator pulled the body under the water. The air was silent except for the crickets and the bullfrogs."

"Jesus, and you kept asking your mother to tell you this story? You must have been scared out of your mind."

"Yes, I really don't know why it seemed to help hearing the story over and over. It was terrifying," Jack says, "but after a while, I became really proud of mother for being so brave and for helping Monique. I'm certain no one else would have helped her. Anyway, after Jeremy's body disappeared under the water, they cleaned up, and then mother walked back to our neighbor's house to pick me up, and then we headed for home."

"I am speechless, just speechless," Joshua says. "No wonder the women have such a strong bond."

"Yes, they would do anything to help each other."

"Well, apparently so," Joshua says.

"So, the next day, about five in the morning," Jack continues, "a strong storm blew in and lasted most of the morning. It knocked down a few large trees and even blew the roofs off of some of our neighbors' houses. It must have dumped at least five inches of rain in our area, and it wiped out any evidence of their crime. After that, Monique cast a good luck spell on both of them, to protect them, I guess, and she taught mother the same spell."

"The same good luck spell we saw your mother place on the pocket watches?"

"Yes, that's the one."

"And no one investigated Jeremy's disappearance?" Joshua asks.

"Oh, sure, it was investigated," Jack explains, "and the local sheriff probably had an idea that the women were somehow involved, but Monique had given the sheriff a medicinal powder a few weeks earlier that saved his son's life. You can imagine he was indebted to her, so, to put an end to the investigation, the sheriff made up a story and told Jeremy's father his son had purchased a bus ticket to Atlanta."

"And all this is really true?" Joshua asks.

"Swear to God."

They sit quietly for a few moments.

"Why do you think your mother told you this story?"

"We have no secrets from each other," Jack says, "and she thought I was old enough to hear it."

Joshua looks down at the ground and then back at Jack. "Did your mother know you were going to tell me about this?"

"Yes, she knows."

"Huh," Joshua says, shaking his head. "Well, thanks for trusting me enough to tell me about it, and of course I promise I will tell no one."

"Thanks, Joshua."

They leave the root beer stand and head for home.

"You know, Jack, I have to tell you, I admire your mother even more now—both your mother and Monique. They are pretty amazing women. It sounds as if that asshole got just what he deserved."

CHAPTER 12

THE HONOR OF SEEING THE
SPIRIT OF ST. LOUIS TAKE FLIGHT

May 14, 1927

Richard James, the handsome young son of Howard James, arrives home late Saturday morning, exhausted but still excited from attending the week-long Boy Scout Jamboree at Camp Glen Gray in Bergen County, New Jersey. As the family sits down to lunch, Howard prepares to hear all about his son's adventures. Richard leans forward in his chair as he speaks, and Howard and Dolores nod and smile, trying to follow Richard's erratic recap of events.

"Oh, it was so much fun. And so cold. And, oh my gosh, we cut down old dead trees, we canoed up and down the river all week...and there were rapids, big rapids, Our Scout Master lost his ring in the rapids. We tried to find it, but no luck. Oh, and we almost got sprayed by a skunk...a big skunk. You could smell it a mile away. And I saw this huge spider. Jerry found a snake in his cabin. An actual snake. Can you believe that? We never found out what kind of snake it was, but it didn't bite anybody anyway. And we had a contest to see who could catch the biggest frog, and guess what? I won. Oh, and I saved Tommy from going over the falls."

"What? You did what?" Howard asks.

"Yes, Father. Tommy lost control of his canoe, so I grabbed it by the bow and pulled it to shore so he wouldn't go over the steep falls," Richard explains.

"Well that sounds dangerous," Dolores says with concern. "Where was your Scout Master?"

"Oh, he was about five canoes back."

Howard and Dolores look at each other and shake their heads.

"Oh, and I forgot to tell you the exciting news. The five Boy Scouts who acquired the most badges won a trip to see a man by the name of Charles Lindbergh take off on his flight. When they're done building his plane, he's supposed to take off from Roosevelt Field on Long Island. They don't know exactly when he'll leave, but our troop will be notified as soon as the date is set. I was the top badge earner; can you believe that? So I get to go on the bus trip to Long Island."

"Who is Charles Lindbergh?" Dolores asks.

"I've read about him recently," Howard says. "He apparently received backing from several people in St. Louis to compete for the Orteig Prize—a $25,000 reward, put up by a man named Raymond Orteig, for the first person to fly an airplane non-stop from New York to Paris, or vice versa, from Paris to New York. I read that Mr. Lindbergh is now looking for the ideal plane to make the trip."

"I imagine a trip like that would be awfully risky," Dolores says. "No wonder there's such a large amount of prize money."

"Yes," Howard says. "Unfortunately, a few pilots have already tried to make the flight and failed. It's a long shot that anyone could make it. The engines they put in planes these days are too heavy for that long of a flight."

Howard turns to Richard. "But enough of that. Let's get back to the birthday boy! Tomorrow's the big day! And son, congratulations. I am very proud of you for winning all those badges, although I would expect no less. Now you'd better slow down and eat some lunch before it gets cold."

*   *   *

While Richard goes to his room to unpack, Dolores and Howard relax in their living room.

"I'm excited about giving Richard his birthday present tomorrow," Howard says.

"I've invited his Boy Scout Troop over for cake and ice cream tomorrow afternoon. When the kids leave, you can give him his watch," Dolores says.

"He'll really be surprised," Howard says and smiles.

CHAPTER 13

THE BIRTHDAY GIFT

May 15, 1927

At 6 p.m., Dolores removes a small vase of yellow flowers sitting on top of the round kitchen table, and places it on the countertop. Howard asks Richard to join them at the kitchen table.

"Richard," Howard begins, "I want to let you know I spoke with my boss, Mr. Cartier, and guess what? He knows quite a bit about Mr. Lindbergh's flight, since he's good friends with Harold Bixby, the head of the St. Louis Chamber of Commerce and one of the financial backers of Mr. Lindbergh's flight. Well, anyway, before I go on, here is a gift I want to give my wonderful son on his fifteenth birthday. I hope you know I am the luckiest man alive to have been blessed with such an amazing son. Your mother and I love you very much, so here you go."

Howard places the white box with the gold bow on the table directly in front of Richard. Howard's heart is racing. He hopes Richard will love the watch as much as he does.

Richard looks at both his parents, then begins to untie the bow. When he opens the lid, he sees the shiny brass pocket watch and slowly removes it from the box. "Why it's beautiful," he says.

"Open it," Howard says. "You have to open the watch."

Richard takes his fingernail and begins to pry open the watch. He stares at the face. "Oh my gosh. This is the most beautiful thing I've ever seen. Look! Trees and tents, and a river, and the Boy Scout traits are printed all around the rim...And look at the big and little hands. This is so great. Where did you find this watch?"

"I made it for you, son," Howard says. "I know how much you love the Boy Scouts."

"It took your father two months to make your watch," Dolores says.

"It is the best present in the world. I love it. Thanks so much," Richard says.

"Son, I made two of these watches so we could each have one, but Mr. Cartier said since you and a few other scouts were going to see Mr. Lindbergh take off, he could arrange a special ceremony where you could meet Mr. Lindbergh and give him the other watch just before he departs. And, although I would have liked to keep the watch, I would also like to do Mr. Cartier a favor, so I don't mind giving the watch to Mr. Lindbergh. Would you like to present it to him?"

"That would be fantastic, Father."

"I thought you'd like it. Happy birthday, son," Howard says as he stands up from the table and leaves the kitchen.

Richard starts to get up from the table, but Dolores touches his arm. "Stay here with me for a minute, dear." She pauses. "You know the watch your father made for you is very precious, and you must promise me you will never lose it."

"I won't, Mom. I won't lose it. I'll take good care of it."

"Richard, the watches will bring you and Mr. Lindbergh luck," Dolores says.

"They will what?" Richard asks.

"Oh, never mind. Just be sure to tell Mr. Lindbergh that you're giving him a lucky watch."

"Sure, Mother," Richard says, and he runs out of the kitchen.

Dolores holds her breath, nods, and then closes her eyes.

CHAPTER 14

CHARLES LINDBERGH

May 20, 1927

In the early morning of Friday, May 20, 1927, it is raining at Curtiss Field, where three asphalt runways, in a triangular layout, sit in the middle of a large grass field. Workers are soaking wet while loading fuel aboard the *Spirit of St. Louis*. Once this is done, the plane is towed to Roosevelt Field, where nearly a thousand people have gathered to watch Charles Lindbergh begin his flight to Le Bourget Field in France. Charles' mother stands near him under a large canvas tarp as they wait for the weather to clear.

Among the crowd are five Boy Scouts and their Scout Leader, Gerald Smith. One of the Boy Scouts, Richard James, was able to earn the most badges during the recent Boy Scout Jamboree at Camp Glen Gray. Because of his accomplishments, but mostly because his father designed and made the watch for Mr. Lindbergh, Richard was given the honor of actually handing the watch to the aviator.

Local police attempt to manage the jubilant crowd but have little success. Although the presentation of the watch has been approved by the airport personnel and by Raymond Orteig, the sponsor of the flight, Richard has little hope that it will actually take place after surveying the large crowd.

Wearing his official Boy Scout uniform, which includes his sash decorated with numerous badges, and holding the watch box tightly, Richard steps away from his troop and pushes his way through the crowd toward Mr. Lindbergh.

After getting pushed, shoved, and even elbowed quite severely in the eye, Richard manages to make his way to the front of the crowd and now stands about twenty feet in front of Mr. Lindbergh.

"Mr. Lindbergh," he shouts. "Mr. Lindbergh. Over here. I have something for you here. Look at me."

Jumping up and down, Richard waves the white box over his head, though he stops periodically to cover his now greatly swollen left eye. Just as he is about to give up, Richard sees—out of his right eye—he has caught the attention of Lindbergh's mother. She tugs at Charles' sleeve and points at Richard. Charles sees Richard, motions for him to come closer, and instructs the policemen to let him approach.

"Oh my God," Richard shouts over the crowd, "I can't believe I actually got through to give this to you. I am Richard James, sir, and I am with Boy Scout Troop 832," he says, still panting.

Charles bends down, closer to Richard's face. "Welcome to Roosevelt Field, son."

"Oh God, now I've forgotten my speech, but I want to give you this gift from the Boy Scouts of America. We wish you the very best of luck, Mr. Lindbergh, and I want you to know, this is a lucky watch, so you should always keep it near. It is a great honor to meet you, sir," Richard says as he hands the box to Mr. Lindbergh.

As he opens it, a small break in the clouds allows the sun to shine on the silver pocket watch, and it glimmers.

"Why it's beautiful, Richard," he says, opening it with his fingernail. Charles stares at the intricate details of the design, smiles, then closes the watch.

He looks at Richard and raises his voice so the boy can hear him. "It could be the finest watch I've ever seen." He slips the watch into his left pants pocket and says, "It will serve as my lucky watch and accompany me to Paris, son. Thank you for this marvelous gift, and please thank all the members of your Boy Scout troop for me."

Charles looks up and luckily finds the sky is clearing. He kisses his mother on the cheek, and then walks to the *Spirit of St. Louis* to begin his long, hopeful journey to Paris.

CHAPTER 15

CHARLES LINDBERGH'S FLIGHT

May 20, 1927

The fully loaded aircraft weighs over five thousand pounds, and the muddy, rain-soaked runway hampers the takeoff. Charles' plane clears the telephone lines at the far end of the field by only twenty feet.

"LINDBERGH GETS AWAY AT 7:52 A.M. WITH FULL LOAD AT FIRST ATTEMPT"
– St. Louis Post - Dispatch

Over the next thirty-three and one half hours, sitting in the cramped cockpit of his plane, Lindbergh encounters numerous hazards. Twenty hours into the flight, his windshield begins to ice over. He becomes frightened, and his heart starts to race. Suddenly he feels a strong vibration on his thigh. He reaches into his pocket, and holds the cold metal of the pocket watch. It slowly stops vibrating. Lindbergh proceeds to decrease his altitude slightly and the ice begins to vanish.

Thirty hours into the flight, Lindbergh encounters a thick fog, and he feels he can no longer keep his eyes open. He turns the light on in the cockpit, takes out the pocket watch, opens it up, and stares at the tents and the river. He begins to sing campfire songs he learned as a boy. After singing loudly for a while, he then drinks some water and eventually feels more awake.

Lindbergh initially mistakes the Le Bourget Aerodrome Airfield in France for a large industrial complex because of the many bright lights. But the lights are actually due to the tens of thousands of spectators' cars caught in 'the largest traffic jam in Paris history'; all them are attempting to be present for Lindbergh's historic landing.

Charles Lindbergh lands at 10:22 p.m. on Saturday, May 21, completing the first solo, nonstop transatlantic flight from Long Island, New York to Paris, France. The moment his plane touches down, he reaches into his pants pocket and grasps the silver pocket watch in his hand. Then he brings his plane to a stop.

"LINDBERGH LANDS SAFELY AT PARIS"

– *St. Louis Post – Dispatch*

For this amazing accomplishment, he wins the $25,000 Orteig Prize.

Lindbergh is not a superstitious man, but just because there might be a slim chance that the watch has brought him such astounding luck, he keeps it with him at all times.

Lindbergh makes a series of brief flights to Belgium and Great Britain in the *Spirit* before returning to the United States. On his arrival back aboard the U.S. Navy cruiser USS *Memphis* on June 11, 1927, a fleet of warships and multiple flights of military aircraft escort him up the Potomac River to the Washington Navy Yard, where President Calvin Coolidge awards him with the Distinguished Flying Cross. This is the first time the physical medal has been presented as part of the award. The U.S. Post Office Department issues a ten-cent air mail stamp depicting the *Spirit* and a map of the flight.

On June 13, Lindbergh flies from Washington, D.C. to New York City, arriving in lower Manhattan where a ticker-tape parade has been planned. Hundreds of thousands of New Yorkers line the streets to celebrate the return of "Lucky Lindy." Paper and confetti, thrown from the windows of the tall skyscrapers lining the route, slowly float down on top of the parade participants. Policemen on horseback and on motorcycles attempt, as best they can, to control the excited and happy crowd.

While Lindbergh is in the United States attending various celebratory events, the Boy Scouts often serve as his escorts and help local officials manage the throngs of well-wishers. He always takes pride in showing them his unique silver pocket watch.

On December 14, 1927, a Special Act of Congress awards Lindbergh the Medal of Honor. *Time* magazine names him "Man of the Year" and, on January 2, 1928, at age twenty-five, he appears on the magazine's cover. Between December 13, 1927, and February 8, 1928, Lindbergh tours sixteen Latin American countries. Although he is exhausted from his extensive travel, he remains delighted to be hailed as a hero by so many adoring fans.

In 1928, one year and two days after its first flight, Lindbergh gives the *Spirt of St. Louis* to the Smithsonian Institution, flying it from St. Louis to the old Bolling Field in Southeast

Washington. Escorted by motorcycle police, it is towed, partly disassembled, to the Smithsonian's Arts and Industries Building on May 11.

As he walks away from his plane, out of habit, he touches the outside of his left pants pocket and realizes the Boy Scout watch is missing. He stops and searches his other pockets. No watch. His heart begins to race. He doesn't remember when he last saw it…Was it yesterday? Last week? He runs back to the Arts and Industries Building and frantically looks everywhere, inside and around the plane. Over the next few days, Lindbergh continues his search, asking everyone if they have seen it, but he realizes he has visited too many places and has traveled across too many miles. There is no hope of finding it.

CHAPTER 16

MONIQUE LECLAIRE
AND THE MAFIA

September 4, 1929

Monique LeClaire tells fortunes and casts her spells from a room she rents above Avril's General Store, located just off Bleecker Street in Manhattan. Mr. Nicholas Avril, the proprietor, is a tall, thin man with bushy eyebrows and bushy hair, who dresses formally in a three-piece suit every day.

One wall of Monique's room is lined with dark wooden shelves which store hundreds of glass bottles, many brought from Louisiana. Since moving, she has added a few items to her collection, including a few new elixirs, clear and pink quartz crystals, and a collection of special coins. Massive cabinets, built specially for the room, take up most of the space on two of the walls. Each cabinet contains one hundred miniature drawers, each of which has a small card on its front, describing its contents. A colorful, hand-knotted Persian rug, woven with patterns of floral design, covers most of the floor, and a round wooden table surrounded by three chairs sits in the center of the dimly lit room. Small candles flicker in antique silver candle holders.

Mr. Hyram Javits, a heavyset man, black-hatted and black-clothed, sits at her table stroking his long, white beard. He checks periodically to make sure his hat is secure on his balding head.

"Now, Mr. Javits," Monique says, "tell me again about your wife and what you want to do."

"As I just told you, when I come home from work, actually the minute I step into the house, Rachel, my wife, begins to yell, 'Ravi hasn't done his homework,' or 'Leah won't help with the dishes,' or 'Levi hit someone in school,' or 'They don't have enough kosher meat at the deli,' or 'Our neighbor Daniel is now charging to sweep our sidewalk.' It's always something. I get no peace at home. You have to help me. I get a headache and just dread going home from work," he says, shaking his head.

"I see, I see. And just how would you like to be greeted when you arrive home? What would be the ideal situation?" Monique asks.

"Well, I guess I would like to have Rachel greet me at the door and say nothing, nothing at all, or perhaps, 'Good evening, dear. I'm so happy you're home. Dinner is prepared for you in the dining room whenever you're ready,' or something like that."

"Hmm...I think I have just the spell—a mild mummifying charm that should work perfectly." Monique walks over to her large cabinet.

"Ahh...it's in here, Mr. Javits," she says, opening a drawer. "This is where I placed the perfect antidote for your problem. I am certain this will work."

"Now this won't hurt her too—" he begins to ask. He is interrupted by the sound of a loud crash coming from downstairs. "What was that?"

"Oh, probably nothing," Monique says. "Maybe someone just dropped something. Let's continue. Now, Mr. Javits, I'll give you a charm that looks just like the mezuzah you wear around your neck, your mezuzah necklace."

He fingers his mezuzah, which contains a tiny scroll of parchment. Monique takes a small, gold cylinder-shaped charm out of the drawer. It is the same size as his mezuzah. She looks carefully at it and carries it back to the table.

"You can keep this charm in your pocket, but you must be careful not to lose it, and you have to be the only one who touches it. Each day, just a few seconds before you step into your home, I want you to hold on to this charm with one hand and say to yourself three times, 'Gay kocken offen yom.' You must repeat this chant to yourself and not actually say it out loud. Do you understand?"

"'Gay kocken offen yom'? You want me to say, 'Gay kocken offen yom' when I hold this?"

"Yes. That is exactly what I want you to say, and you must repeat it three times just before entering your home," says Monique.

"Okay, Miss LeClaire. I understand. How long will it take to work?"

"It will begin working the first day you use it, and—"

They hear screaming from downstairs: "Oh my God! Help me! Someone, help me please! You're going to kill me. I'll pay, I'll pay. I promise I'll have it for you. You're killing me! Stop!"

Monique heads for the stairs. Mr. Javits grabs her arm.

"Wait, wait. Maybe we shouldn't go down there," he says.

"What? Didn't you hear that?" Monique asks.

"Help me! Someone, I need help. Can anyone hear me? I'll pay! I'll pay! I'll get the money by next week. Stop for God's sake!"

Monique runs down the stairs, and Mr. Javits follows. They stop when they see Mr. Avril on his back, sprawled out on the floor, being kicked by a short young man wearing a dark suit and a flat cap. Broken plates, shattered glasses, bags of candy and boxes of cigars are scattered across the wooden floor.

"Hey. What are you doing to him?" Monique screams.

"Get out of here, Miss LeClaire," Mr. Avril moans as the blood trickling down his forehead becomes trapped in his eyebrows. "Get out of here quickly."

The young man stops kicking Mr. Avril and looks at Monique and Mr. Javits. "Who the fuck are you two?"

"Please leave them alone. They have nothing to do with this," Mr. Avril pleads, holding the side of his ribcage.

"Mr. Javits," Monique instructs, "get out of here. Get out of here now."

"Are you going to be okay?" he whispers to Monique from where he stands behind her.

"Yes, I'll be fine. Just go," she says, never taking her eyes off the young man, who has a severely pock-marked face, a scar on his left cheek, and one droopy eye. His starched white shirt rides up high and tight on his neck.

As Mr. Javits walks backward toward the front doors of the shop, the young man watches Monique. When he reaches the front door, Monique turns to him. "Don't forget, Gay kocken offen yom. Gay kocken offen yom. You must say it three times for the charm to work."

"Okay, I've got it," Mr. Javits shouts back and then runs down the street.

"Mr. Avril," Monique asks, "who is this man? What's happening?"

"He's here for protection money."

"Protection money? From whom? It sure doesn't look like you're being protected," she says.

The young man walks toward Monique. "I protect Mr. Avril here from violence, looting, from someone raiding his property, and other bad stuff," he says. "But he didn't pay me this month, so he might not be protected. Unless, of course, he pays me. *Capisce?*"

"Yes, I understand," says Monique.

"Ya kind of a pretty young thing," he says, looking her over, then touching her gold earring and her cheek with the back of his hand. "What was ya doing upstairs?"

"That's where I conduct my business," she says.

"A business? Mr. Avril never told me there was a business upstairs. He said it was just a storeroom. I shoulda checked the place myself." He turns and looks at Mr. Avril, who is groaning in pain. "So there are two businesses here? From now on ya gonna pay me twice as much? No?"

Mr. Avril nods his head and sits up.

The young man turns his attention again to Monique. "So tell me, pretty lady, just what kind of business ya runnin' upstairs? Something I might be interested in? Ya service men, perhaps?"

Monique glares at him. "Are you alright, Mr. Avril?" she asks and walks toward him.

"Hey, *bambina*," the young man barks, and he grabs her wrist. "Ya need to look at me when I'm talking to ya. Let's go see exactly what's upstairs. *Andiamo.*" He pushes her toward the stairs.

Monique starts up the stairs with the assailant following closely behind.

As they both ascend the stairs, he shouts, "Hey, Avril, I'll be back on Tuesday. Ya like your legs? On Tuesday, no money, no legs. *Capisce?* No money, no legs." He pushes Monique's back, and she picks up her pace as she climbs up the stairs.

Once in her room, the young man approaches the shelf containing hundreds of bottles. "Oh Jesus, lady, what the hell are all these bottles? Are ya some type of *strega?* A fortune teller? What the hell do ya do up here?" he asks, picking up a bottle. "Hey, what's in this? It looks like teeth, human teeth."

"Yes, those are teeth, and yes, I am a powerful witch. I can be of great service to you."

He laughs and lifts up his jacket. "Ya see this gun? Ya see this knife, lady? I don't need any of ya service. These are all I need." He opens the door of a large cabinet, revealing all the labeled drawers. "Is this where ya stash your money?"

"It's where I store all the ingredients for my medicine... and for my spells."

"For your what? Your spells? Are ya like a witch as ya say, or more like, what was his name...Harry—Harry, like a Harry Houdini or something?" he asks.

"Well, sir, Mr. Houdini was a magician, a genius of escape artistry, and, just before his death, he tried to debunk individuals who supposedly spoke to the dead. I, on the other hand, am gifted and can see into peoples' lives, predict their futures, and cast spells against their enemies. The skills that Harry Houdini had and my skills are quite different."

"Ya can tell people's futures and kill their enemies? Hey, what did ya say your name was?" he asks as he opens the labeled drawers and peeks inside.

"I don't believe I told you. It's Monique, Monique LeClaire."

In one drawer he finds white fur, in another, a small box of silver beads, and in the next, branches from a rose bush with sharp thorns. "Well, Miss LeClaire, if ya such a great fortune teller, what's my name and what's my fortune?"

"Your name, sir, is Salvatore Luciana," she says. "I know that because I read the newspapers and I recognize your face—not because of my fortune telling abilities. The press often misspells your name. They call you Luciano, correct?"

"Yeah, that's right. Now everyone calls me Luciano."

"Well, Mr. Luciano, I would have thought you would have sent one of your lowly henchmen to harass Mr. Avril for a payout today. I am surprised to see you performing such a menial task."

"Paolo was sick today, so I decided to check things out for myself. But why am I telling ya my business?" Luciano smiles as he continues opening drawers in the cabinet. "So, ya think you're pretty good at fortune telling and casting spells?"

"Yes, I do. I've been able to make a good living doing it for many years."

"Lady, let's see just how good ya are. Come sit down here. I've never had my fortune told, and I would like to know what's in store for me. If you're a fake, which ya most likely are, ya will need to immediately begin paying my people for protection."

"And if I'm not a fake?" she asks.

"Well, we'll see."

Monique sits next to Luciano. She glances at the three candle holders, now cold and glued to the table with melted wax. "Of course I can tell by the scars on your face you've had a difficult life," she says.

"That's too general," he says, laughing. "Ya need to be way more specific."

"Let me see your right palm," she says.

He holds his hand out, and she studies it for a moment. "You have recently received a severe beating from three men. Your throat was slashed, and you were strung up by your hands from a beam because you refused to work for another mob boss."

"Huh," Luciano says. "Maybe that was in the newspaper, too. What else?"

"You are lucky when it comes to gambling, you deal in blackmail, bootlegging, and robbery. A man named Arnold Rothstein has taught you many valuable lessons."

"Interesting, but again, too general. Tell me something ya couldn't have picked up from the newspaper."

She looks at his palm more closely. "You are superstitious and cross yourself when you walk under a ladder. Last night, you slapped your girlfriend when you learned she was talking with one of your soldiers. This morning she complained you weren't giving her enough money. You called her 'a cunt,' then put on your coat and walked out of the Waldorf Towers." Monique releases his hand and looks at his face. "You have recently been asked to murder someone you know by the name of Gaetano Reina."

Luciano stands up quickly, his chair tilting back. "Fuck me. How the hell do ya know that, lady? Shit, no one knows that information. What the fuck?" He then draws his gun and points it at Monique. "Tell me exactly who gave ya this information."

"Mr. Luciano, please sit down and think for a moment. Who could have told me anything? And how would I know I would run into you today? I just have the ability to see into peoples' lives. Think about it. Your girlfriend and you were alone this morning. Who could have told me about her, or much less what you said to her?"

Luciano sits down and nods his head. "You're good… pretty good, I have to give ya that."

"Perhaps, if you would like, we could help each other."

"We could what? What are ya talking about?"

"If you give me and Mr. Avril protection from your gang, and from all other gangs," Monique says, "in return, I will guide you through life and warn you against your enemies."

"Hmm…You'll warn me against my enemies? That hardly seems possible. I'll have to think about it. Let me ask ya another question. Will I always work for Masseria?"

"No," Monique answers. "No, you won't."

"Really? Huh. And what do ya mean, 'help guide me through my life'?"

"Keep you out of jail. Keep you alive. I will give you two coins. One will keep you out of jail and the other will return you to Italy and allow you to die there when you are old."

"Coins?"

"Yes. I will place a spell on the coins. The spell will only work, however, if you keep the coins and, of course, if you protect Mr. Avril and me. I will expect you to make periodic visits to me so I may ensure your safety and make you aware of your enemies."

"This seems like a very strange offer…very strange. Ya know I don't believe in all this crap," he says.

"Well, perhaps it's something you should think about."

"Ya know, Monique, I am a very powerful man with powerful friends, and if ya don't follow through with your promises—say, if I go to prison for some reason, or if one of my enemies harms me in any way, if ya cross me in other words—ya will suffer. Youse both will suffer."

Monique nods her head. "I realize that, Mr. Luciano. And, of course, you know if you don't keep *your* word, there will be consequences."

"Are ya threatening me, lady? Because that would be a very dangerous proposition."

"No, Mr. Luciano, I'm not threatening you at all. I'm just clarifying what we are both agreeing to do for one another."

Mr. Luciano thinks for a few moments. "Okay, let's give this a try."

Monique opens a drawer in her cabinet and removes two coins. She holds one coin in each hand and whispers a separate phrase onto each. When she finishes, she hands the coins to Luciano.

"The spell I have placed on the coin that will keep you out of prison is very strong," she says. "So strong, in fact, people will be amazed you are not behind bars. You will be nicknamed 'Lucky.'"

"Well, we'll see about that," he says and smiles.

*   *   *

Luciano leaves that afternoon with two coins — one, a 1920 Saint-Gaudens double eagle gold coin to keep him out of prison, and the other, a 1921 Peace silver dollar to allow him to die in Italy.

Over the next few years, Monique holds true to her word and gives Luciano sound guidance. From her, he learns he will work for Salvatore Maranzano as his lieutenant. Eventually, she informs him, Maranzano will become a threat and will have to be killed. With her advice, Luciano becomes the most dominant crime boss in the United States, and he knows he owes much of his success to her.

*   *   *

On January 8, 1931, Mr. Avril's landlord informs him his rent will double, and the city of New York suddenly threatens to revoke his business license. Monique contacts Luciano, and they are never bothered again by the landlord or by the city.

*   *   *

After a horrific car wreck on Staten Island, Gay Orlova, Luciano's girlfriend, is taken to Richmond Memorial Hospital. A surgical resident, Dr. Joshua McMillan, who recently trained at Johns Hopkins Hospital in Baltimore, operates on Miss Orlova and saves her life.

Three weeks after Miss Orlova's surgery, while she is recovering in the hospital, Luciano meets Dr. McMillan in the hospital's cafeteria. "I want to sincerely express my gratitude to you, young man. I understand ya saved Gay's life, and I want ya to know how grateful I am."

"Thank you, Mr. Luciano. Recently I learned a new technique used to repair the pericardium, the sack surrounding the heart. I was just lucky to be at the right place at the right time and all. Just lucky, you know."

They sit quietly for a few moments. "I know you'll think this is very strange, and actually I've never told anyone this, but every once in a while I visit a woman who works," Luciano says, "or tells fortunes, rather, in a room above a general store. She claims she can tell the future, and I have to tell ya, so far she's been pretty accurate. Anyway, about a month ago she told me there would be an accident and that a young surgeon would save my girlfriend's life."

"A fortune teller with her place of business above a general store, you say?" Joshua says, and he smiles.

"Hey, yeah, I know that sounds crazy, but she's pretty good. In fact, I think she has saved my neck a few times and has managed to keep me out of prison."

Joshua nods his head. "Do you want to know something even crazier, Mr. Luciano? I think I just might know who you're talking about. Is it Monique LeClaire?"

Luciano stares at Joshua for a moment. "Now how in the hell do ya know Monique?"

"Well, sir, it's a long story. Monique's best friend is Jenny Genova, and she has looked after my mother and me for many years now. Such a strange coincidence, I realize, but I've accompanied Jenny many times to visit Monique above Avril's General Store. Oh, and by the way, you're correct. Monique is amazingly accurate at telling fortunes, and the spells she casts are very strong. She learned her art from her Creole parents and grandparents, and her great grandmother taught her some unique spells, too. Over the years, Monique taught a few spells to Jenny, so she, too, is pretty incredible."

"I can't believe we both know Monique," Luciano says, shaking his head.

"It is a bizarre coincidence, for sure," Joshua says.

"And even though Monique has helped me so much over the years," Luciano explains, "it's still hard for me to wrap my head around it all. The car accident, and Gay being taken to this specific hospital, and ya just learning a new surgical technique which would save her life, and being here just at the right time...It's just all too crazy to think about."

"I know, sir. It can be overwhelming." Joshua looks directly at Luciano. "It was hard for me to believe both Jenny and Monique could tell the future. And if I hadn't known both women for as long as I have, and if I wasn't familiar with their knowledge of the future, I, too, would be very skeptical. But I have to tell you, I've lived around both of these women since I was very young and have grown accustomed to the weirdness—to all the amazing coincidences that have occurred during my lifetime." Joshua pauses. "Well, I'm sorry, sir, but I need to get back to work now."

"Thank you for meeting with me today, son," Luciano says as he shakes Joshua's hand.

When Gay Orlova is released from the hospital, Luciano rewards Dr. McMillan with a suitcase filled with one million dollars cash. Joshua at first refuses, but then accepts it after deciding to purchase two rooms, adjacent to one another, at the 80th Street Residence Retirement Home in New York City. Though he doesn't need the rooms now, when he does, the retirement home agrees to allow anyone to occupy one or both rooms at a moment's notice, and for as long as needed. A contract is provided, and his generous gesture guarantees him two of the most luxurious penthouse rooms, with all the amenities, including the highest quality food, and the most experienced, carefully selected twenty-four-hour nursing care and medical staff. Joshua reserves the rooms in the names of Jenny Genova and Monique LeClaire, for when they eventually retire.

Salvatore Lucania, or 'Lucky Luciano,' as he is commonly known, discovers how Dr. McMillan spent the reward money. He visits the retirement home to ensure everything will go smoothly. Aware of who he is, the management assures him it will.

By 1936, 'Lucky Luciano' has been arrested twenty-five times on charges including assault, illegal gambling, blackmail, and robbery, but spends no time in prison.

But in May 1936, Luciano loses the Saint-Gaudens double eagle gold coin Monique had given him. He is tried and successfully convicted for compulsory prostitution as well as running a prostitution racket, after years of investigation by District Attorney Thomas E. Dewey. Found guilty on June 5, 1936, Luciano knows he will not be able to take the Peace silver dollar with him to prison, so he gives it to Dr. Joshua McMillan, the only person who would understand its importance. Luciano is sentenced to thirty to fifty years in prison. On June 19, 1936, he is transferred to Clinton Correctional Facility, a maximum-security prison in Dannemora, New York.

"LUCANIA SENTENCED TO 30 T0 50 YEARS; COURT WARNS RING"

– The *New York Times*

On July 24, 1936, Dr. McMillan visits Luciano in Dannemora prison and, unbeknownst to the prison guards, returns the Peace silver dollar to him. That afternoon, Luciano sits on his cot, staring at the coin and wondering how in the hell the coin will be able to transport him to Italy, his place of death, as the fortune teller had predicted.

At the height of World War II, an agreement is struck with the Department of the Navy through Luciano's associate and childhood friend, Meyer Lansky, for Luciano to provide naval intelligence. His prison sentence is commuted in 1946 for his wartime cooperation on the condition he be deported to Italy. Luciano dies in Italy on January 26, 1962, and his body is transported back to the United States for burial. In his will, he leaves instructions for the 1921 Peace silver dollar to be buried with him.

CHAPTER 17

TELLING THE FORTUNES OF THE RICH IN NEW YORK

August 26, 1929

Irene Rothschild Guggenheim, a child welfare advocate, avid art collector, and wife of Solomon R. Guggenheim, is sitting with Jenny at her round table, gazing at her crystal ball. Mrs. Guggenheim, a pale woman, wears a long white dress with intricate lace on the collar and cuffs and a matching white hat.

During their session, Jenny predicts Mrs. Guggenheim and her husband will build a grand art museum and that a man named 'Wright' will be the architect. Irene tells her husband that evening over dinner what the fortune teller told her. Solomon laughs.

"Well, she must have known that you love art, or you must have told her. What else did she say?" Solomon asks.

"She told me that you should immediately take all your money out of the stock market," Irene replies.

"What's that? What was that you said? Take my money out of the stock market? Why, that's ridiculous," Solomon says. "And how much did you pay her for this sage advice?"

"She didn't want any money. But she said I would return soon, and that I would become a regular client," Irene says.

"And who told you about this woman, Irene? This so-called fortune teller?"

"Oh, just someone I know who works at the Brightside Day Nursery."

"Well, she sounds crazy to me," Solomon says. "You should stay away from her."

Irene looks at him, shocked, and after a moment, she says, "She told me you'd say that. That you'd say those exact words. And you'd tell me this evening at dinner that she sounds crazy and to stay away from her, word for word! But she also said it was extremely important that I convince you to remove all your money from the market."

"Well, that's not going to happen," he says.

Irene cries all night, explaining periodically through the night to Solomon how vital it is that he obey her wishes. She has never been this adamant about anything, yet Solomon refuses to be persuaded.

"What harm could possibly come from taking the money out of the stock market and locking it in our home safe for three months?" she pleads. "If you loved me, you would do this for me."

He refuses to listen.

The next morning, as the couple is seated for breakfast, Irene stares at an untouched plate of eggs and toast. Her eyes are dark and puffy.

"Solomon," she says, "I'm calling my uncle this morning and telling him to stop funding all of your projects. I'm certain your friend, Hilla Rebay, will be disappointed that you will

now not be able to buy those paintings by Bauer and Kandinsky she suggested. In fact, no more artwork period."

Solomon stands up. "You're going to do what? Call your
uncle?"

"Yes. I will call him right after breakfast," Irene says. "I
have no doubt he will honor my request."

"Oh my God, Irene. You've lost your mind. Really lost
your mind," he says, waving his fists in the air.

"Well, Solomon, maybe I have, but will you finally listen
to me? Will you take all of your money out of the stock market for three months? It's only for three months, for Heaven's
sake."

Solomon slumps down in his chair and shakes his head, his
palms covering his face.

That afternoon, Solomon R. Guggenheim places an order
to sell all of his stocks, and within a period of three days, all
have been liquidated. Irene watches as Solomon locks the cash
in their home safe.

Two months later, On October 29, *1929*, Black Tuesday
hits *Wall Street*, and investors trade some sixteen million shares
on the New York *Stock Exchange* in a single day. Billions of
dollars are lost, wiping out thousands of investors.

"BILLIONS LOST IN WILD STOCK MARKET CRASH"

– CHICAGO TRIBUNE

Irene Guggenheim sees Jenny again on October 30 and
becomes a regular client. She refers her friends and acquain-
tances to Jenny and encourages them to seek her advice.

Madam Genova is then able to keep an even smaller clientele, allowing only the richest and most influential individuals to participate in her sessions.

*   *   *

Following Black Tuesday, Irene and Solomon Guggenheim eat dinner in their opulent dining room. Solomon stares at the candles' flickering lights in the silver candelabra then says, "You know, I can't believe it, but your friend saved us millions of dollars."

"Yes, she did," Irene says. "Maybe we should give her a reward."

"You're right," he says. "I'll take care of it."

*   *   *

Many years later, the renowned architect, Frank Lloyd Wright, designs the Solomon R. Guggenheim Museum which opens on October 21, 1959, in New York City. The unusual gallery provides many visitors a first encounter with great works of art by Wassily Kandinsky, as well as by his followers, including Rudolf Bauer, Alice Mason, Otto Nebel, and Rolph Scarlett.

CHAPTER 18

MADAM GENOVA AND ANNE MORROW LINDBERGH

March 23, 1932

"LINDBERGH BABY KIDNAPPED FROM HOME OF PARENTS ON FARM NEAR PRINCETON; TAKEN FROM HIS CRIB; WIDE SEARCH ON"

— The *New York Times*

Charles Augustus Lindbergh, Jr., the twenty-month-old son of Charles and Anne Lindbergh, is kidnapped at 9 p.m. on March 1, 1932, from the nursery on the second floor of the Lindbergh home near Hopewell, New Jersey. The child's nurse, Betty Gow, discovers the child's absence, and reports it to his parents, who are then at home, at approximately 10:00 p.m. A ransom note demanding $50,000 is found on the nursery windowsill. Once the Hopewell police are notified, the report is telephoned to the New Jersey State Police, who assume oversight of the investigation.

On the morning of March 23, 1932 Anne Lindbergh contacts Madam Genova to make an appointment. The fortune teller knows her as a well-recognized author of children's novels, as well as the recent victim of the horrible and tragic kidnapping of her young son.

Madam Genova cancels the rest of her appointments for the day and arranges to meet with Mrs. Lindbergh, who arrives that afternoon. She is very thin and wears a black dress and a small black hat with a veil that partially covers her face.

As they sit at the parlor table, Mrs. Lindbergh begins to speak tearfully in a low, soft whisper. "Of course you know why I am here, Madam Genova. I have heard of your wonderful reputation. Please help me! Do you know where my son is? I desperately need to find him."

Madam Genova hands her a tissue. "Let me see what I can find. Please shuffle the tarot cards and turn over the top one." The fortune teller looks at the card, then into her crystal ball for a few moments before she takes Mrs. Lindbergh's hands gently into hers. "I'm afraid I have terrible news, Mrs. Lindbergh. There's no easy way to tell you, but your son is no longer alive. I'm so sorry."

"Are you certain? Are you absolutely certain?" she asks.

"Yes, there's no doubt. You and your family will be asked repeatedly for a ransom, but no ransom should be paid. The child, sadly, is no longer alive."

Anne Lindbergh puts her hands up to her face and sobs.

"Mrs. Lindbergh," Madam Genova says after a few moments, "I see your son's soul among the brightest stars. He is looking down and watching over you. I'm so sorry, I'm so terribly sorry for your loss." She hands her another tissue.

"No, no, I'm certain you're right. As a mother, I already knew deep down that he was gone. It's just—it's just that I had a bit of hope left. Just a little bit of hope," she says. "Of course Charles will never believe you, and he will never stop looking for our baby."

"I know," Madam Genova replies.

Mrs. Lindbergh regains her composure. "Madam Genova, this must sound like a strange question, but just prior to my husband's flight to Paris, he was given a silver pocket watch… some silly Boy Scout pocket watch. He actually believed the watch brought him luck. Ridiculous, I know. But he lost the watch a while ago, and since then, well, he's been having a lot of difficulties…And now, oh my God, and now our child is gone. I even hate to ask you this, but do you think there could possibly be a connection between the two? Between the loss of his watch and this horrific thing that happened to our little boy? Charles thinks there may be some connection between the two, and I'm afraid he has become somewhat obsessed looking for that watch."

"A lucky silver Boy Scout pocket watch?" Madam Genova asks. "I really don't know, Mrs. Lindbergh. It could be possible." The fortune teller hesitates for a few moments, then continues, "Mrs. Lindbergh, I have a strong feeling your husband will eventually find his watch; however, it might be many years from now. When your husband does find it, please suggest to him, not to keep it, but instead to give it to a very powerful man."

"You want me to do what?" she asks.

"When your husband does find his watch, even if it's years from now, please tell him not to keep it. Instead, he should give it to a very powerful man."

"A powerful man? Which powerful man?" Mrs. Lindbergh asks. "Will he know?"

"Yes," Madam Genova says. "Your husband will know."

"Okay. I hope to remember that…to tell him," Mrs. Lindbergh says as she stands up from the table. "And thank you, Madam Genova, for allowing me to meet with you today. I knew you would tell me the truth."

Over the next two and a half months, a total of thirteen ransom notes are delivered to the Lindberghs, all requesting various amounts of money. After the thirteenth note is received, a man claiming to be the kidnapper picks up a cash ransom of $50,000. Part of the ransom is in gold certificates, all of which are soon to be withdrawn from circulation and will therefore attract attention. The bills' serial numbers are also recorded.

On May 12, 1932, the body of the kidnapped baby is accidentally found, partially buried and badly decomposed, about four and a half miles southeast of the Lindbergh home. The coroner's examination shows that the child had been dead for about two months and that death was caused by a blow to the head.

Bruno Richard Hauptmann, a German immigrant carpenter, was arrested for the crime in September, 1934. He was tried, found guilty, and sentenced to death. He continued to profess his innocence, but all appeals failed and he was executed at the New Jersey State prison on April, 3, 1936.

CHAPTER 19

NANCY DAVIS AND ZASU PITTS

February 8, 1946

Anne Frances Robbins, born on July 6, 1921, was called "Nancy" from birth. Her mother, Edith Prescott Luckett, was an actress, and her godmother was the silent-film-star Alla Nazimova. Nancy knew from the time she was very young that she was destined to become a famous actress.

Edith divorced Nancy's father, Kenneth Seymour Robbins, a farmer turned car salesman, in 1928, and in 1929 she married the prominent conservative neurosurgeon Loyal Edward Davis, after which the family moved to Chicago. Dr. Davis formally adopted Nancy in 1938 when she was seventeen years old. She legally changed her name to Nancy Davis. To help achieve her ultimate goal of becoming an actress, Nancy attended Smith College in Massachusetts, where she majored in English and drama.

In February, 1946, Nancy, alone in her apartment in Beekman Place on 51st Street in Manhattan, calls her mother's friend, ZaSu Pitts.

"What in the world am I going to do, ZaSu? I have absolutely no friends here in New York."

"No friends? Well what am I?" ZaSu asks.

"Well, of course you're my friend, ZaSu."

"I know what you mean, Nancy. You mean no friends your own age, right?"

"Well, yes, that's right."

"You've just recently moved here, dear. You'll have many friends very soon. Just wait and see. Nan and Walter Huston, Lillian Gish, and Spencer Tracy, why they're all your friends."

"Yes, I realize that," says Nancy.

"And we all promised your parents that we would look after you while you're in New York."

"And I greatly appreciate it, ZaSu," Nancy says.

"Hey, I've got an idea. Let's meet at Bergdorf Goodman this afternoon and then have lunch. What do you say?"

"Oh, I have a lunch date with someone this afternoon."

"You do? Why that's wonderful. See, you *do* have friends here in the city. And if you're going out, be sure to wear your long mink. It's very cold outside."

"I definitely will, and thank you for everything, ZaSu. I'll talk to you soon."

ZaSu Pitts, an American actress who starred in many silent dramas and comedies, transitioned successfully to mostly comedic films with the advent of sound motion pictures. Well-connected and friendly with luminaries such as Bing Crosby, Al Jolson, W.C. Fields, and Rudy Vallée, she gets Nancy her first acting job—a minor role as Alice in *Ramshackle Inn*. Nancy has only three lines of dialogue. The play opens on Broadway and then closes quickly.

Through their connections, Nancy then gets a non-speaking part in Broadway's *Lute Song,* starring Mary Martin and Yul Brynner. Mary Martin demands that Nancy be given a larger part—the role of her lady-in-waiting.

But Nancy doesn't believe *Lute Song* will have a long run, and she longs for the role of Dolly Tate in *Annie Get Your Gun*.

As Nancy begins to get ready for a lunch date with Vera Briner, she has a difficult time deciding what to wear. Both women have appointments to see Madam Genova following lunch. What does one wear to hear one's fortune?

CHAPTER 20

NANCY'S ADVENTURE
IN NEW YORK

February 8, 1946

At the Carnegie Deli, Nancy joins Vera Briner, who is already seated at a table. The smell of corned beef and hot matzo-ball soup fills the air. The restaurant is crowded, with customers sitting shoulder to shoulder at the long, thin tables. The women split a corned beef sandwich, after which Vera orders cheesecake for dessert. She offers to share, but Nancy claims she would never fit into her costume if she ate even a bite.

Nancy is acquainted with Vera, since her brother, Yuliy Brynner, is appearing in *Lute Song*. Ever since Yuliy introduced the women, they have become close friends. Vera has been a client of the fortune teller Madam Genova for the past few years, and now wants to introduce Nancy. Vera made an appointment for both of them this afternoon.

"Vera," Nancy says, "I've noticed you and your brother's names are spelled a little differently. He has now started to refer to himself as 'Yul Brynner,' and he spells his name 'B-r-y-n-n-e-r.' Is there any reason for the difference?"

"No, no reason," says Vera. "He just liked the look of the 'y' and the two 'n's' in the name, I guess."

"Huh. That's interesting. So anyway, I'm excited about seeing your fortune teller this afternoon. You've been to her before?" Nancy asks.

"Oh, many times, and I think she's pretty accurate. My brother went to her last week and came home very excited," Vera says.

"Really? What did she tell him?"

"She said he was going to be a very famous actor and that he would star in an amazing play on Broadway. She told him he would be the lead in movies that cost millions of dollars to make, that his movies would be shown around the world, and that he would win many acting awards. But she also told him a strange thing."

"What was that?" Nancy asks.

"Madam Genova told him he would have to shave his head to be truly successful."

"Hmm…that is rather odd," Nancy says. "You know, I work with Yuliy every day, and I love your brother, but he still has a really thick Russian accent. And it still hasn't faded at all. No offense, but that accent would be hard to overcome as an actor. Don't you think this Madam Genova tells everybody wonderful things about their future just to make them happy so they'll come back and see her?" Nancy asks.

"Heavens, no," Vera says. "She's told me some awful stuff about my career, and many of the people I know who long to be famous actors, well, she's advised them not to pursue their careers."

"And they actually followed her advice?" Nancy asks.

"Well, yes. At least most of the people I know did. As I said, I think she pretty much knows what she's talking about."

CHAPTER 21

MADAM GENOVA'S SESSION

February 8, 1946

Madam Genova greets both women, who are prompt in arriving for their appointments. Vera is wearing a flower-print dress with puffy sleeves and a small black hat. Nancy is wearing a green suit with a matching hat and a knee-length mink coat.

Madam Genova asks to speak with each woman separately and begins with Vera. Nancy waits in the adjacent room.

"Vera, it's nice to see you again. Please come and sit down."

"Thank you, Madame Genova. I am anxious to hear what's in store for me."

"Today I would like you to shuffle these tarot cards, then place them in a single stack, and turn over the top card."

Vera attempts to shuffle the cards, but they scatter over the small table. "How clumsy of me. I'm so sorry," she says, gathering up the cards and placing them in a neat stack. She turns over the top card. It is 'The Moon,' the eighteenth card of the major arcana.

"Ah, The Moon," Madam Genova says, placing her fingertips gently on top of the tarot card. "The Moon tells me a situation in your life is not what it appears to be. You need to trust what your instincts tell you in order to see past this illusion. I see a man offering you small parts in a few movies."

"I get to be in some movies?"

"Yes, but you must be wary. This man, this producer, will think you owe him for this favor. Although you will have a few small movie parts, you will have little success in acting. But you will be remembered for your singing, for your high-pitched soprano voice, and for your Russian folk songs."

"Well, at least I have a career singing," Vera says with disappointment.

Madam Genova looks into her crystal ball. "I also see a bit of your brother's future."

"Oh, really? What's he doing?"

"Yuliy, will become world famous in the next few years and will have success beyond his wildest dreams."

Vera looks down at her lap and frowns.

Madam Genova senses jealousy, but nevertheless, she entrusts Vera with the task of telling Yuliy to befriend a woman named 'Mary.'

After Vera leaves, Nancy comes in and takes a seat at Madam Genova's table.

"Hello, Madam Genova. My name is Nancy, Nancy Davis, although you probably already knew that…you being a seer and all," Nancy says.

"Good afternoon, Miss Davis. I am happy to meet you. I understand you are a good friend of Vera's."

Nancy nods her head.

"Would you like to take off your coat and get a little more comfortable?" the fortune teller asks.

"Why, yes, yes I would," Nancy says as she stands up and drapes her coat over another chair. "I am—I am a little nervous because I've never been to a person who can see the future," Nancy says.

"Oh my. Don't be nervous. There is nothing to be nervous about. Let's see what your future holds."

Madam Genova looks into her crystal ball for a minute, then looks at Nancy. "Nancy Davis, Nancy Davis. Why that's not the name you were born with, is it? You weren't born 'Nancy' or 'Davis' were you?" she asks.

"That's true, Madam Genova. I was born 'Anne Frances Robbins' right here in New York City, and everyone just called me Nancy as a child. I don't know why...And my stepfather adopted me in 1938 when I was seventeen, so that's why my last name is now Davis. I find it amazing that you knew that."

The fortune teller smiles and nods her head. "Well, Miss Davis, I am very happy to say that you have an amazing future. You will date famous movie stars."

"Well, Spencer Tracy is trying to fix me up with Clark Gable," Nancy says and laughs.

"I see you are tremendously ambitious and that you long to get specific roles in acting," Madam Genova says.

Nancy nods her head.

"You are thinking of performing in a Broadway play that hasn't opened yet. Is that correct?"

Nancy opens her mouth and stares at the fortune teller. "Yes," Nancy says. "Yes, that is correct."

"This new play, it requires quite a bit of singing and dancing, is that right?"

"Yes, that's also true."

"I see someone, another woman who is quite talented, will also be trying out for the same part," Madam Genova says.

"Well, will she get the part, or will I? What do you see?" Nancy asks.

"That answer depends on what you decide to do next. It depends on whom you will ask to get involved," the fortune teller informs her.

"What do you mean by that? Get involved? Do you see me getting the part?" Nancy asks.

"Again, all I can say is it depends on what decisions you make in the next month or so. I'm sorry I can't tell you any more than that. However, Miss Davis, I would strongly suggest you turn your sights to Hollywood."

"Hollywood? Well, I've actually been thinking seriously of moving to Hollywood," Nancy says.

"I must warn you, however, I see some sort of dark shadow in the future of Hollywood itself—a bad aura. I cannot explain it. Someone in power will create a list of names of people who are not allowed to work in Hollywood. I cannot actually see why your name will be on the list, but you will seek help from a man, and he will be able to help you with this. He will be the love of your life."

"The love of my life? Why that's wonderful news," Nancy says. "In Hollywood, you say?"

"Yes. That's correct."

Madam Genova looks closer into her crystal ball and is very surprised by what she sees. One of the Boy Scout watches has resurfaced after all these years. The fortune teller then looks directly into Nancy's eyes. "Miss Davis, I also see, years from now, a silver pocket watch will come into your possession, given to you by a dear friend. Be certain to keep it close, as it will bring luck to you and your husband."

"A silver pocket watch?" she asks.

"Yes, a silver watch. Take good care of it, and keep it close. It will eventually bring you great power."

"It will bring me what?" Nancy asks.

"The watch will bring you power. That will end our session for today. It was nice to meet you."

"Well, alright then," Nancy says, slightly bewildered. "It was nice meeting you, too."

CHAPTER 22

NANCY CALLS FRANK SINATRA

March 6, 1946

"Hello, Frank, darling. How are you doing these days? It's been a while since I've seen you."

"Hello, doll. Yes, I haven't been to New York in a few months."

"Well, when do you plan to be here next? There's something really important I need to discuss with you," Nancy says.

"My schedule has been crazy, hon, just crazy. Hey, but I plan to be in Hoboken and then in the New York area next week to visit some relatives. I have to spend most of my time going to different radio stations in the area for interviews. My agent has lined them all up with a little help from Lucky and his *consigliere*, Costello. I believe Costello is actually running the show now, but hey, have you heard my newest song, 'Five Minutes More'?"

"Yes, Frank, and it's wonderful, just wonderful," says Nancy.

"In fact, Nancy," Frank says, "there's more good news. I've heard rumors that your governor, Mr. Thomas Dewey, is about to commute Lucky's prison sentence with the understanding that he agrees to be deported to Italy. I think Lucky helped the government out with some inside information during the war or something like that. Anyway, my hunch is that Lucky will eventually end up in Cuba."

"You're talking about Lucky Luciano, right?" asks Nancy.

"Yes, my friend Lucky. I told you about him when I was in New York, when we were having dinner at Peter Lugers, remember? I told you he was being moved around to different prisons in New York and that he built a church at the Clinton Correctional Facility in Dannemora."

"Oh, yes. Of course I remember hearing about him. Dewey put him behind bars when he was the New York D.A., right?" she asks.

"Yes. That's right."

"Well, he must have given the government some pretty important information for them to let him out of prison," Nancy says.

"Yeah. I suppose so."

"Frank, I'm so happy about the success of your new song, but darling, I really need your help with something, and it's much more important than your record."

"More important than my record? Well, that's just not possible. I'm really aiming for the number one spot. Nancy, my friends have guaranteed it, if you know what I mean. They've assured me my record will get to number one if I put in a little effort and follow their suggestions."

"Sure, sure, I get it! And, oh, Frank, I was just kidding. Of course nothing could be more important than your wonderful singing career and your records."

"And my new 78, *The Voice of Frank Sinatra*. How do you like the title of the record?" Frank asks.

"Why it's just perfect, darling. I actually couldn't have picked a better title myself," Nancy says. "But Frank, I desperately need to see you. There really is something I need to discuss with you."

"Wow, desperate, huh?"

"Yes, I have to admit it. I am desperate to see you. I think you're the only one who can help me."

"Well, as I said, I'll be in New York next week. I could squeeze in a lunch with you."

"That would be perfect. How 'bout we meet at Schrafft's on Wednesday at noon?" Nancy asks.

"Okay, I'll see you then, but you'll owe me a big favor if I meet you," Frank whispers into the phone.

"I always repay good deeds, you know that, Frank."

"Yes you do, Nancy. Yes you do. I'll see you next Wednesday."

CHAPTER 23

LUNCH AT SCHRAFFT'S, FIFTH AVENUE & 46TH STREET

March 13, 1946

Frank arrives at Schrafft's wearing dark glasses, a long trench coat, and a trilby hat. The restaurant has dark wood paneling along the walls, and the tables and chairs are of the Colonial style. The restaurant's front hostess, who wears a long black gown, recognizes Mr. Sinatra; however, she has been taught to remain aloof and to never gush over any celebrities who might enter the restaurant.

"Mr. Sinatra, it's nice to see you. How many will there be in your party today?"

"There will be two of us, and I'd like a table in the back of the restaurant. A table where we won't be disturbed."

"Certainly, Mr. Sinatra," the hostess replies.

She holds up two fingers, then walks over to the floor hostess and whispers something in her ear. The floor hostess walks over to Mr. Sinatra. "Please follow me, sir."

He is seated in a semi-private area at the back of the restaurant, and Nancy Davis soon joins him at his table. A small vase containing a single rose sits in the center of the table, but Nancy pushes it to the side.

The waitress, wearing a dainty white apron and a black dress with a starched crisp white collar and cuffs, approaches their table. Speaking in an Irish brogue, she says, "Good afternoon. Would you like to see some menus or do you know what you'd like to order?"

Frank notices the waitress's hair net doesn't completely cover her hair, and a loose strand of red peeks out from under the front of the net.

"I know what I'd like. How about you, Frank?" Nancy asks.

"I know what I want, you go ahead."

"I'll take your egg salad sandwich and hot chocolate with whipped cream. No wait. On second thought, skip the whipped cream," Nancy says.

"And I'll take your chopped chicken sandwich with a martini. Do you serve martinis at lunch?" Frank asks.

"I'm certain we can get you a martini, Mr. Sinatra," the waitress says.

"No, no, never mind. I've changed my mind. I'll take a peach ice-cream soda instead, and some coffee. Bring me the coffee first."

Frank is able to see into the main dining room, and he notices a Black couple just being seated at a table. After ten minutes, he realizes no one will wait on them. Schrafft's policy is that white women do not wait on Black people.

"I hate this goddamned restaurant," Frank says to Nancy as he nods in the direction of the Black couple. "There's no reason they shouldn't be served, too."

The floor hostess brings the coffee and hot chocolate to their table, and soon their waitress appears with her arm extended, carrying a tray with their order. The waitress sets the plates down in front of them. Both sandwiches have their crusts removed. The chopped chicken sandwich is cut into quarters and the egg salad sandwich into thirds.

"I should take our plates and just walk over there and put them on their table. In fact, that's just what I'm going to do," Frank says, and he begins to stand up.

Nancy places her hand on Frank's arm. "Frank, please, I beg you," Nancy whispers. "Don't make a scene. Please just sit back down and let's eat our lunch."

Frank sits back down and begins eating. "We're never coming back here," he says.

"That's fine with me," Nancy replies.

"This is just wrong," Frank continues. "We shouldn't pay good money to eat here."

"I know, Frank. I know. I shouldn't have chosen this restaurant. We won't come back here again."

After a few minutes and a few bites of his sandwich, Frank regains his composure and looks at Nancy. "Well, darling, I am just noticing that you look wonderful. Great looking suit. Is that Chanel?"

"Of course," says Nancy. "And how do you like my earrings?"

"Very nice. Hey, didn't I give those to you last year?"

"You sure did."

"Well, as I remember, you deserved them," Frank says, smiling.

"Oh, Frank," Nancy says. She reaches underneath the table and squeezes his knee.

"So what's this problem you have, doll?"

"Frank, Frank, I really need your help. You know I'm in this play on Broadway called *Lute Song*, and, well, although I like being in the play, it's not really that great. You know what I mean? Not that great. The scenery and costumes are great, but not the play itself. Once you've seen it, you know, you really wouldn't want to see it again. The songs and the script are just not very good. You wouldn't leave the theater humming one of the tunes."

"Well, okay, so what do you want me to do about it?" Frank asks.

"I don't think the play will last much longer, is what I'm saying."

"Nancy, darling, you have a lot of connections. Why don't you just audition for another play?"

"Now that's exactly what I want to speak with you about, Frank. Another play."

"I don't really know much about the current plays on Broadway or the auditions, Nancy. I'm pretty well tied up with the music industry."

"Of course I know that, Frank, but listen." Nancy pulls her chair closer to the table and lowers her voice. "I was thinking about auditioning for a play called *Annie Get Your Gun*. The music and lyrics were written by Irving Berlin—*the* Irving Berlin, and I just know it will be a huge hit on Broadway. Everybody says so. It would make me a star, I know it."

"You want the lead part of Annie?" Frank asks.

"Heavens no. I'm going to try out for the part of Dolly Tate. She plays Frank Butler's assistant in the play. Frank Butler is the Wild West Show's star."

"Dolly Tate, huh?"

"Yes, it would be the perfect part for me, and I know this play will be a huge hit," Nancy explains.

The waitress appears at their table and sets down a peach ice cream soda and two spoons. She takes away their empty plates.

"Would you like some of this?" Frank asks.

"No, no, but thanks."

"Well, hon, just how in the world do you expect me to get you that part?"

"That's just it, Frank. You are the only one who can help me…Well, you and maybe some of your friends."

"Some of my friends?"

"Yes, I need help from some of your friends. Like Lucky and his associates."

"Jesus, Mary, and Joseph, what are you talking about, Nancy?"

"Well, there's this woman named Lea Penman, and I happen to know she is going to try out for the part of Dolly. She's good, actually very good, and I'm afraid she's going to get the part. In fact, I'm certain she'll get it unless something terrible happens to her. I need someone to hurt her, Frank. Hurt her really bad," Nancy says.

"I—I don't know what to say, Nancy."

"Please, Frank. I'm very serious. I need help with this, and you're the only one I can turn to."

Frank thinks for a few moments. "Well, why don't you just try out for the part first? You might surprise yourself and get it. What do you think?"

"There is no way, Frank. This girl Lea is good, very good. If you saw her you'd know right away, there is no contest. In fact, I would hire her if I were judging the auditions. That's how good she is. And you know I'll pay you back, Frank. You know you won't be sorry. I'm always good about repaying favors," she says as she takes his hand in hers.

"Well, let me see what I can do. Do you have her address?"

"Yes, yes right here." Nancy opens up her purse, pulls out a piece of scrap paper, and hands it to Frank. "I just need someone to break her leg or something like that. Something that would make it impossible for her to dance or to sing. That's what I need. I don't think you'll need to kill the woman... unless you need to... The play is supposed to open in May, so I'll be auditioning soon."

"Okay, doll. I'll see what I can do for you," Frank says. He glances at the scrap of paper, then places it in his front pocket.

Frank finishes his soda, and they leave the restaurant.

*   *   *

On April 1, 1946, Nancy walks into the Imperial Theatre on Broadway to audition for the part of Dolly Tate in *Annie Get Your Gun*. She is early and watches as Lea Penman sings and dances in front of the producers of the play, who will decide if she gets the part. After a few minutes of watching, Nancy realizes she has no chance of getting the part. She could never be as good as Lea. Nancy decides not to audition at all and leaves the theatre. When she arrives home, she calls Frank.

"Frank, oh, Frank, I'm so glad I caught you. I just saw Lea Penman trying out for the part of Dolly in that play I was telling you about—you know, *Annie Get Your Gun*—and I...well I just can't compete."

"Sure you can, Nancy. You'd be great."

"No, Frank. You don't understand. I've changed my mind. I've definitely changed my mind. I'm just not that good, and Lea deserves the part. I hate to admit it, but she's perfect for it. She really is."

There is a moment of silence, then Frank shouts into the phone, "You want *her* to have the part? Well it's a little late to make that decision now, isn't it?"

"Frank, Frank, you think it's too late?"

"Well hell yes, Nancy. Everything has already been arranged."

"Then you'll just have to stop it. You need to stop it, Frank."

"Goddamn it, Nancy. You're not going to change your mind back again are you?"

"No, no, Frank, I'm certain. I think she should get the part. It would be too difficult for me physically. I just can't do it."

"Well, hang up the goddamn phone then and let me see if I can stop them from doing anything. I just hope it's not too late."

"Thanks, Frank. And thank Lucky for me, too."

"You owe me big time, doll. Big time."

"I know that, Frank, and I always repay my debts. You know I'm good for it. I'll definitely repay you."

"I know, doll. Now you need to hang up the phone."

*   *   *

"A RIP-ROARING 'ANNIE GET YOUR GUN'"

– The *New York Times*

Annie Get Your Gun opens on Broadway May 16, 1946 at the Imperial Theatre, and Lea Penman stars as Dolly Tate, Frank Butler's attentive assistant.

The role of Annie is given to Mary Martin, Nancy's co-star in *Lute Song*. But on opening night, Richard Halliday, Mary Martin's husband, attends the performance. When they return home following the premiere, he informs her, "This play is way too physically taxing. You're going to kill yourself."

Mary Martin withdraws from the Broadway play, and the lead goes to Ethel Merman.

When the time comes for the play to go on the road for its post-Broadway national tour, Ethel Merman is unwilling to do it, and Mary Martin jumps at the chance, going on tour for approximately two years and belting out the songs.

CHAPTER 24

NANCY FURTHERS
HER CAREER

February 10, 1947

ZaSu gets Nancy a role with another touring company in Chicago, this time as Susan Haggertt in *The Late Christopher Bean*. In 1947, Nancy returns to New York. She realizes she needs to get involved with more influential men to further her career, so she begins having an affair with Alfred Drake, who is known as the 'King of Broadway Musicals.' In the 1940s, he starred in numerous musicals including, *As You Like It, Two for the Show,* and *Oklahoma*. Nancy tries everything she can to stay involved in his life with the hope of moving her career along.

However, Nancy soon meets Max Allentuck, the general manager for the production of *Deep Are the Roots*. Allentuck is also known as 'Broadway Max,' and he eventually manages other shows, including *Death of a Salesman, A View from the Bridge, The Diary of Anne Frank, Look Homeward, Angel,* and *The Music Man*. Nancy decides she likes Max much more than Alfred, as Max is now the top producer in Manhattan.

Nancy initially courts Max vigorously while trying to avoid Peggy Phillips, whom she believes Max will eventually marry. Max has the ability to get her parts, so she needs to stay close. However, Max is quite serious about his Jewish religion, and Nancy's step-father, whom she adores, is a rabid anti-Semite. She decides to date other men.

Nancy has three dates with Clark Gable in New York, and then numerous men begin calling on her. One of them is Benjamin Thau, head of casting for Metro-Goldwyn-Mayer, one of the world's largest film studios. He casually mentions the possibility of a screen test in Hollywood. Nancy's mother contacts Spencer Tracy to make certain the screen test actually occurs, and Tracy, one of MGM's biggest stars in 1949, makes it happen.

Mrs. Tracy is indebted to Nancy's step-father, Dr. Loyal Davis, who is one of the top neurosurgeons in Chicago. Mrs. Tracy had taken their deaf child to see him and was told there was no cure for the child's nerve deafness. Dr. Davis told her, "You can either make a life for yourself or let this destroy you." Mrs. Tracy turned her son's deafness into a cause by starting the John Tracy Clinic and devoting her life to working with the deaf.

Nancy soon signs a contract with MGM.

CHAPTER 25

JOHN F. KENNEDY AND CHARLES LINDBERGH

May 11, 1962

"WHITE HOUSE DINNER IN HONOR OF ANDRE MALRAUX"

– The *New York Times*

On Friday, May 11, 1962, thirty years after the body of Charles Lindbergh's kidnapped infant son was found, Jackie and John Kennedy invite Anne and Charles to a White House dinner for French cultural leader Andre Malraux. Charles and Anne Lindbergh have attended other dinners at the White House over the years, and President Kennedy feels it appropriate to invite them to this event considering Charles' connection with France.

Table seating assigned, Charles Lindbergh, now sixty years old, is next to the president in the State Dining Room. Being somewhat superstitious, he always asks to be seated at table seven. Anne sits next to Vice President Johnson in the Blue Room.

"I am delighted to sit next to you, Charles. You have had quite the fascinating career," Kennedy says in his thick Boston accent.

"Yes. It has been interesting for sure," Lindbergh responds.

"Won't you join me in a Bloody Mary? I know it's a little unusual before a formal dinner, but it's my favorite and my staff makes the best. I've trained them well."

"Well, yes sir. I will join you," Lindbergh says.

Kennedy raises his hand and motions for a server to come over to their table. He orders two drinks, and the server removes Kennedy's empty glass. Within a matter of minutes, two Bloody Marys are set in front of them.

Frank Sinatra, a friend of Kennedy's, is the entertainment for this evening. Frank has his date, Marilyn Monroe, on his arm as he walks over to the seated president. Marilyn's hair is blonde and shoulder-length with a slight wave. Her lips and nails are painted bright red, and her black eyeliner extends just beyond the corners of her eyes. The small mole on her left cheek has been accentuated with the touch of a black pencil. She is wearing a low-cut sequined silver gown with long white gloves and a diamond choker necklace. Her diamond chandelier earrings dangle and sparkle as she moves her head.

"Mr. President," Sinatra says, "I don't know whether or not you've met my friend, the fine actress Miss Marilyn Monroe."

President Kennedy turns his head to look behind him, then he and Charles Lindbergh stand up quickly, their chairs almost tipping over. They turn around to face the couple.

"Why Miss Monroe," President Kennedy gushes, "it is such a pleasure to meet you, and I must say, you really are beautiful." He takes her gloved hand, lifts it, and gently kisses it. "I loved your performance in the movie *Gentlemen Prefer*

Blondes, oh, and I also loved *How to Marry a Millionaire*. You were fantastic in both." They stand looking at each other for a moment.

Jackie Kennedy, wearing a strapless pink Oleg Cassini evening gown and elbow-length white satin gloves, has remained seated. She turns her head for a moment and glares at Kennedy. He's been staring at Marilyn, and when he looks around the room he notices guests from the surrounding tables watching him.

"Oh," says Kennedy, "and this is my friend, Mr. Charles Lindbergh."

"It's a pleasure to meet you, Mr. Lindbergh," Marilyn says in a breathy voice. "You flew that plane to Paris a long time ago, didn't you?"

"Yes, ma'am. Yes I did. Quite a while ago," Lindbergh nods and stares.

"Oh, and—and, of course, this is my wife, Ja-Jackie," Kennedy stutters. Jackie remains seated, turns her head slightly in the direction of Miss Monroe, and nods.

"Have you known Mr. Sinatra a long time, Miss Monroe?" Kennedy asks and winks.

"Oh, my, yes. Quite a while. Oh, and please call me Marilyn."

"Certainly, Marilyn. Well, we're looking forward to Mr. Sinatra's performance tonight," Kennedy says.

"I think one of the songs he's going to perform is 'Blue Skies.'" She turns to look at Sinatra. "Isn't that right, Frank? 'Blue Skies'?"

"Yes, dear, that's right."

She turns back to face Kennedy. "He said it's one of your favorites. Is that correct, Mr. President?"

"Why, yes. I love that song. Yes, I just love it. Well, that's great."

"And our friend Buddy Rich over there is going to be leading the orchestra," Marilyn says and smiles.

"I know I'm looking forward to the entertainment tonight," Lindbergh says.

A waiter standing at the front of the room rings a bell three times.

"Marilyn, dear," Sinatra says, "we must take our seats. Dinner is about to be served."

The president bows his head. "It was a real pleasure meeting you, Marilyn." He leans close to her ear and whispers, "You look ravishing. I'll call you soon."

Marilyn blushes. "Why thank you, Mr. President. It was wonderful meeting you, too. And Mr. Lindbergh, it was real nice meeting you."

Marilyn and Sinatra walk to the adjacent table to find their seats, while Charles and Kennedy sit back down. Kennedy watches as Marilyn walks away and takes her seat.

Kennedy leans over to Charles. "Oh my God, is she the hottest thing you've ever seen? Gorgeous, simply gorgeous," he whispers, shaking his head.

"Yes, Mr. President. She is beautiful. She looks like a movie star."

"Of course she looks like a movie star. She *is* a movie star."

The salad is served. They eat in silence for a few minutes, then Kennedy begins, "Charles, I asked Henry Kissinger over there if he wanted to sit next to you, but he declined."

"Of course. I'm not surprised." Lindbergh smiles and nods his head.

"Oh, and there's Rabbi Feinstein over there," Kennedy says as he points in the direction of the next table. "He and Bishop

O'Keefe are going to give this evening's invocation. I also asked the rabbi if he would like to sit next to you this evening. He declined as well."

"Mr. President, I—" Lindbergh begins.

Kennedy smiles and places his hand on Lindbergh's arm. "Oh, Charles, you know I'm just kidding with you. Of course you know my father, Joseph, was an active admirer of Hitler, and still is today. He is hated by the Jews, and rightfully so. Yes, even today he is fanatically anti-Semitic."

"Yes sir. I realize your father and I have similar views," Lindbergh says.

"You know, Charles," Kennedy says, "it's not just my father who shares your views. You and I have a lot more in common than you may think. My father not only hates the Jews, but he hates the Blacks, too, and really everyone else who is not a good, wealthy, white Catholic boy. Hell, my father was also a strong supporter of Joe McCarthy, and my brother, Robert, served on McCarthy's subcommittee.

"It is interesting to me, Charles," President Kennedy continues with a slight slur in his voice, "that you were perceived as such an amazing hero at one time, with the success of your flight and all, and then with the horrible loss of your son, Charles. You were once one of the most admired individuals in the world…and you lost all of that goodwill once you began pushing your bigoted conspiracies to keep America from fighting Hitler."

"I realize that, sir," says Lindbergh, "but that is what I believed, and still believe. We should never have gotten involved in the war. The Jews still control the wealth of this country. They own and influence our newspapers, televisions, radio stations, and movies…actually all forms of communication."

There are a few moments of silence, then Kennedy continues, "Yes, Charles, I have to agree with you. You know the apple doesn't fall far from the tree, and one ends up believing what he is taught by his parents. But there is one big difference between us. My family and I obviously had better advisors— better public relation advisors, you know? They have always provided us with the finest speech writers. Those individuals who are at the top of their field. Yes, you should have gotten a better speech writer, Charles. A writer who would have made you more acceptable to the public…A writer who would have allowed you to keep your heroic status."

Lindbergh sits back in his chair and looks quizzically at the president.

"Believe me, Charles," Kennedy continues, "I have the best writers in the world. All Jewish writers. Yes, my whole family uses Jews to write their speeches. I can bring the audience to tears just by reading a few of their words. You just missed out, Lindbergh. You didn't have good advisors. A great speech writer makes all the difference. I should know. 'Ask not what your country can do for you; ask what you can do for your country.' After all, how great a line was that?"

Lindbergh nods his head. "Obviously you are correct, sir. Great writers. I can see why the people love you."

"Of course they do. And do you think I would ever send my children to an integrated school? Never. It's the speechwriters. They make me look great. They make me look like I care."

Charles looks at him and continues eating his dinner.

"Even Martin Luther King uses a Jewish speech writer, for heaven's sake. He uses Stanley Levison, a Jewish lawyer from New York." Kennedy pauses for a moment, then leans in close to Lindbergh and whispers in his ear, "J. Edgar thinks Levison is a commie."

Kennedy straightens up in his chair. "Well, Charles, enough about speech writers." He finishes his drink, then catches the eye of a waiter standing a few feet away. Kennedy points to his empty glass and it is quickly replaced with a fresh Bloody Mary. Jackie turns her head, glances at the fresh drink, then gives the president a disapproving look. She resumes her conversation with Andrew Malraux, both speaking in French.

After a few moments, Kennedy clears his throat. "So, Charles, I have always been fascinated with airplanes and the history of aviation. I built many model planes when I was young. By the way, just where did the *Spirit of St. Louis* end up after you finished all your tours?"

"I flew it to Bolling Field, here in D.C., sir. They stored it in a hanger, made some repairs, then it was officially taken to the Smithsonian and put on display."

"Oh, yes that's right. I heard you flew it to Bolling after your last trip. You had flown about forty thousand miles in it by that time, is that correct?"

"Yes sir, just about forty thousand miles," Lindbergh replies.

"Do you ever go by the Smithsonian to visit your plane?" President Kennedy asks.

"No sir. I can't say that I do."

"Well, would you like to go after dinner? Actually wait, I've got an idea. Would you like to go to the hangar at Bolling Field tonight instead and show me some of the original parts of the plane? Isn't that where they dismantled it and replaced some of the worn parts with new ones before they took it to the Smithsonian? You could show me around and tell me all about your flight."

"I believe the original hangar is locked, sir. Would you like me to make some calls and see if we could view it tomorrow?"

"No, no, I don't sleep well, so if you're not too tired, let's go after dinner. I'll arrange to have someone take Anne back to your hotel, and Jackie doesn't care what I do. What do you say?"

"As I've said, sir, I believe the hangar is locked," Lindbergh says.

"Absolutely no problem," Kennedy says. "My people will open it up. I'm eager to hear about your adventure. I'll say a few words in just a minute, to welcome our guest, Andre Malraux, and after that we'll listen to the entertainment and then go. How does that sound?"

"Fine, just fine, sir," Lindbergh says.

"My main speech writer—a Jew, of course—handed my speech to me just before dinner. You'll love it. I can't wait for you to hear it," Kennedy says as he leans over toward Lindbergh and winks. "We'll leave right after the entertainment."

President Kennedy stands and gives a speech filled with humor, endearing anecdotes, and admiration for Andre Malraux. During Kennedy's speech, Lindbergh looks around at the audience and notes a few women dabbing their eyes with their handkerchiefs. He smiles and nods his head.

They listen to Frank Sinatra sing a medley of tunes, including "Blue Skies," "I'll Remember You," and "I Left my Heart in San Francisco," dedicated to the President and Mrs. Kennedy.

Following the last song, Kennedy walks over to Sinatra and shakes his hand. He then walks over to Marilyn, who is still seated at her table. Marilyn sees him approaching and stands.

The perfect lips, the whitest teeth, the brightest smile, and those magnificent breasts, he thinks.

"It was great meeting you, Marilyn. Let's get together as soon as possible. Call me," he says as he discreetly hands her a piece of paper with his private phone number written on it.

Marilyn blushes. "Of course, Mr. President. I certainly will."

"You were just wonderful," Marilyn says to Sinatra as he walks toward her.

"Of course I was wonderful. What did you expect?" Sinatra says, and they both laugh.

"Yes, Frank, you were especially good tonight," the President says as he looks at Sinatra and then Marilyn.

Sinatra nods his head, takes Marilyn's arm, and they walk toward the front doors of the State Dining Room.

CHAPTER 26

VISITING THE AIRPLANE HANGAR AT BOLLING FIELD

May 11, 1962

Two Secret Service agents accompany the president and Mr. Lindbergh as they drive to the airplane hangar at Bolling Field. The agents at first have trouble unlocking the hangar door, then experience difficulty in finding the light switches. But after a few moments, the building is brightly lit. Two Cessna 172 Skyhawks sit on the cement floor of the hangar. Windows line the upper half of the building. President Kennedy pulls his jacket tighter and shivers. "Hey, don't they have any heat in here?" he asks.

"No, I don't believe so, sir," Lindbergh replies.

As they enter, Lindbergh points to the far wall. "Oh look, Mr. President, there is part of the original tail of the *Spirit*. See, it says 'Ryan NYP' on it. And right next to it is a blade from my original propeller."

As the men walk around the hangar, Lindbergh spots a large chest in the back corner. He points to it. "That's where they placed any of the smaller original parts of my plane that had some type of damage. They replaced those parts with newer replicas before they moved her."

Lindbergh bends over and begins to sweep some of the dust off the top of the chest. He kneels down, opens the top, and begins rummaging through it.

"Well, Jesus Christ," Lindbergh shouts and stands up, holding a silver pocket watch in his hand. "I really can't believe this. I lost this watch just after I brought the plane to Bolling Field, and I've looked everywhere for it all these years. I had it with me during my flight to Paris. I really believed it brought me luck. It's unbelievable that I've found it again."

"What did you find?"

"My watch, my lucky Boy Scout pocket watch."

"Well that's wonderful," President Kennedy says. "I am really very happy for you."

"Thank you, sir. I'm in shock," Lindbergh says as he stares at the watch, then places it in his pocket.

The men walk around the hangar for 30 minutes, discussing the different destinations visited and adventures taken in the *Spirit of St. Louis.*

"Well, it's late and I'm tired, boys, so let's head back," Kennedy says.

After the hangar is locked and secured, the Secret Service men open the car doors, and Lindbergh and Kennedy climb into the back seat. Charles turns the watch over in his hands. "I can't tell you how truly amazing this is, sir. This watch has been out of my possession for over thirty years. Can you believe no one else found it? Why, that hangar has had hundreds of people and airplanes in it over the years."

"I guess no one else was looking for it," President Kennedy says.

Charles opens the watch and looks at the still fine details and colors painted on the face—the tents and trees. "Would you like to see it, sir?" he asks the president.

"Why yes. Yes I would."

Charles hands the pocket watch to President Kennedy, who admires the fine workmanship. "I must say, Charles, I've never seen anything quite like it. The details are pretty incredible. Really an amazing watch. I can see why you're so delighted to have it back. On the rim here, I see someone has inscribed all the traits of a good Boy Scout."

"Yes, it was a young Boy Scout who presented it to me just before I left for Paris. In fact, someone told me just before the little ceremony that the kid's father was some famous watch-maker from New York...Worked for Cartier or something like that...yes, something like that."

"It is a beautiful watch. Really a piece of art, Charles," Kennedy says as he hands the watch back to Lindbergh. "Did you know I was the first Boy Scout ever to become President of the United States?" Kennedy asks.

"Huh, no, I didn't know that," Lindbergh says.

"Yes, I was in Troop 2 in Bronxville, New York from 1929 to 1931 and attained the rank of Star Scout. Yes. I was a Star Scout," Kennedy announces proudly and smiles.

The men remain quiet until they reach Charles' hotel.

As Charles begins to step out of the car, he says, "President Kennedy, I would like to present you with this watch. It brought me a lot of luck just when I needed it, and I think now you will need more luck than me."

"No, no, Charles," Kennedy says. "For Heaven's sake, it has been lost to you for all these years. That's ridiculous. Keep it."

"No, I insist, sir. Please keep it as a token of our friendship and understanding. I feel I really know you better after this evening, and I truly wish you the best of luck, Mr. President," Charles says as he hands him the watch before turning and heading inside.

Kennedy quickly rolls down his window and shouts after him, "I loved my time as a Boy Scout, so thank you for this great gift."

*   *   *

Lindbergh is dropped off at 3:00 a.m. at his hotel in Washington, D.C. He attempts to quietly undress and slip into the bed, but as he gently pulls the covers around him, Anne wakes up, rolls over, and faces him.

"Where did you go tonight?" she asks.

"We went to the airplane hangar at Bolling Field to take a look at some of the old original parts from the *Spirit of St. Louis*. President Kennedy wanted to see the hangar."

"That's nice, dear," she says as she shuts her eyes.

"Anne, Anne, wait. You won't believe what I found in the hangar," he says. "Guess what I found. You won't believe it."

"I have no idea, Charles. What did you find?" she asks.

"Don't you want to guess?"

"No, Charles. It's three in the morning."

"My lucky silver Boy Scout watch. Can you believe it? After all these years. Unbelievable. Really unbelievable. I found it in a chest at the back of the hangar along with some discarded airplane parts. Can you believe no one found it and took it after all these years? That's really something, isn't it?" he asks.

"Yes, dear. That's really something." She sits up in bed and turns on the light on her nightstand. "So, now that I'm awake, let me see it."

"Oh, I don't have the watch. I gave it to the president," Charles says.

"You what? You gave it to the president? Something you'd lost for thirty years you gave to President Kennedy?" she asks.

"Yes. I think he'll need all the luck he can get, so I gave him my lucky watch."

"Well, that was very generous of you," she says as she turns off her light and lays back down, staring at the ceiling. "Charles, you want to hear something strange? About thirty years ago, I went to a fortune teller in New York to ask her about our baby. During our session, she told me you'd eventually find your watch. It was such a strange conversation. I suppose that's why I remember it. Yes, yes, and she wanted to make sure I would tell you to give the watch to a very powerful man. What a coincidence, huh? You giving the watch to President Kennedy and all. Quite a coincidence, right? Charles? Charles?"

Anne looks over at Charles. He is snoring.

CHAPTER 27

PRESIDENT KENNEDY
AND JOHN-JOHN

May 12, 1962

President Kennedy keeps the Boy Scout watch in his top desk drawer in the Oval Office, frequently opening up the case to admire the artwork. John-John, the president's son, often sits in his lap during the president's conference calls, and President Kennedy allows him to play with the shiny silver pocket watch to entertain himself.

John-John takes the watch in his hand and goes into the adjacent room while the distracted president remains on his conference call. Later that day, a nanny finds the watch on the floor, and, mistaking it for one of John-John's toys, places it in a toy box in his bedroom.

In the late afternoon, Edward Clark, a reporter for the *New York Times Magazine* arrives at the White House to interview the president. The interview takes place in the Oval Office.

"Mr. President, I must say, it is an honor to meet you. I, as well as your adoring public, have been extremely impressed with the accomplishments you've been able to achieve during your first term in office. To what do you attribute your success?"

"Well, Edward, I have very knowledgeable individuals comprising my cabinet, and we have certainly tried to reach across the aisle to work with many of our astute Republicans. We all want the same things, after all, and that is for the American people to be safe, healthy, and free from hunger. They should be able to afford a comfortable life and enjoy and preserve our magnificent land. Some members of my administration are particularly talented when it comes to passing bills and pushing various issues through congress. Why, I couldn't ask for anyone more gifted than Stewart Udall."

"Your Secretary of the Interior?"

"Yes. And Arthur Goldberg, my Secretary of Labor. Oh, and Abraham Ribicoff, my Secretary of Health, Education, and Welfare, all brilliant men. Actually, all of the individuals I have hand-picked for my cabinet are ideal for their positions. And, of course, you know how much I depend upon my brother, Bobby. We have discussions late into the night, almost every night, about the future we see for America."

"Mr. President, I plan to list some of your accomplishments thus far in your term for the article, which will be published in the *Times* this coming Sunday. Would you mind listening to this list to see if you'd like to add anything?"

"No, not at all. Please proceed."

"Well, here is what I have: increased unemployment benefits, aid to cities to improve housing and transportation, the water pollution control act to protect rivers and streams, the soaring growth of membership in the Peace Corp, the increase of social security benefits and the minimum wage, and, sir, perhaps the most important of all, your skill in averting nuclear war through negotiations with Soviet leader Nikita Khrushchev."

"Yes, yes, Mr. Clark, that pretty well sums it up."

President Kennedy, not a superstitious man, is surprised at how much he has been able to accomplish since Charles Lindbergh gave him the Boy Scout pocket watch. But it's just a coincidence, he tells himself. Yes, just a nice, convenient coincidence.

"Well, that's all I need, sir," Mr. Clark says, "and again, it has been an honor to meet you. Thank you for your time." The men stand up and shake hands, and the reporter leaves the Oval Office.

President Kennedy sits at his desk, opens his top drawer, and realizes the silver pocket watch is missing. He finds his son, John-John, now almost three years old, in the boy's bedroom.

"John-John, sweetheart, come here for a moment. Your daddy wants to ask you something. Come sit in my lap, my big boy."

John-John crawls onto his father's lap.

"John-John," the president asks, "do you remember playing with a silver watch earlier today in my office while I was on the telephone?"

John-John looks at his father and shakes his head.

"A silver watch, a shiny silver watch, remember? I keep it in my desk drawer, and you like to play with it," the president explains.

There is a moment's pause, and the president is hopeful. John-John shakes his head.

"Well okay, then," President Kennedy says, and he lets his son slowly slide off his lap.

"President Kennedy," the English nanny says. "I believe I overheard you talking about a silver watch just now. Is that correct, sir?"

"Yes, Olivia, that's correct."

"Well, I am so sorry, Mr. President, but earlier today I picked up a silver object off the floor and placed it in John-John's toy box. It must have been the watch you're looking for. I thought it was one of his toys. I will go and get it for you right away."

"Oh thank God. Why that's wonderful, Olivia. Yes, please bring it to me now."

After a few minutes, Olivia brings President Kennedy the pocket watch. He takes it, goes back to his desk in the Oval Office, sits down, and opens the case. After admiring it for a few moments, he decides to no longer keep the watch in his desk drawer, as it will be too tempting for John-John. "I'll keep it in my bedroom," he says to himself.

CHAPTER 28

MARILYN MONROE
AND KENNEDY

May 13, 1963

M arilyn Monroe has stayed the night as a guest in President Kennedy's bedroom at the White House. At 5:00 a.m. a Secret Service agent awakens her and instructs her to get dressed and leave the sleeping president's bedroom. She asks for some privacy while she dresses. When she finishes, she notices a silver pocket watch on the president's dresser, picks up the watch, and opens it. She admires the fine details, then closes the watch and places it back on the president's dresser. When she walks out of the president's bedroom, the Secret Service is waiting to escort her to the rear entrance of the White House.

A private plane takes Marilyn back to Los Angeles.

At 3:00 on May 13, five dozen long-stem red roses are delivered to Marilyn's recently purchased home, a Spanish hacienda in Brentwood, Los Angeles. Secluded and private, the 2300-square-foot home is a single story with a red tiled roof, an attached garage, and a guest house. 'Last night was perfect,' is written on the card. There is no signature.

Marilyn calls President Kennedy's private line.

"Hello, Jack. I just wanted to let you know how much I love the beautiful roses. My entire house smells wonderful. How have you been?"

"I'm fine, Marilyn, and I'm glad you like the roses."

"You sound like you're in a rush, Jack."

"Well, of course I am. I'm just about to go into another meeting. I'll talk to you later."

The next day, Marilyn tries calling the president's private line. There is no answer. She calls the White House operator and is informed the president is in a meeting and cannot be disturbed. She leaves a message for him to call her. He does not.

CHAPTER 29

THE DEMOCRATIC
FUNDRAISING GALA

May 19, 1962

"HAPPY BIRTHDAY, MR. PRESIDENT!"

– National Enquirer

A fundraising gala for the Democratic Party takes place at Madison Square Garden with just over 15,000 people in attendance. Jacqueline Kennedy decides not to attend the event and instead spends the day at the Loudoun Horse Show with her children, John-John and Caroline.

Entertainment for the gala includes, among others, Peggy Lee, Mike Nichols, Diahann Carroll, Jimmy Durante, Shirley MacLaine, Bobby Darin, Maria Callas, Jack Benny, Ella Fitzgerald, Harry Belafonte, Henry Fonda, and Marilyn Monroe.

Backstage, at 8:30 p.m., Marilyn Monroe begins to get dressed for her performance that evening. She's been rehearsing her act—which has been staged and produced by Broadway composer and lyricist Richard Adler and choreographed by Carol Haney—repeatedly over the last few days.

She has difficulty getting into her dress, and because it is so tight, she decides to wear nothing underneath it. The dress, designed by Jean Louis, is sheer, flesh-colored, and made of marquisette fabric with 2,500 shimmering rhinestones. She looks at herself in the mirror and touches up her lipstick. Marilyn's white ermine fur coat is draped over the couch. She sits down carefully in a chair and waits for someone to knock on her door to let her know it's time to take the stage. She is nervous, and her heart is racing.

At 9:00, Peter Lawford, John Kennedy's brother-in-law, knocks on the dressing room door, then enters her dressing room. He sees her sitting in a chair, her head bent down with the palms of her hands covering her eyes.

"Okay, Marilyn," he says, "you're up. We're ready for you."

"Not just yet, Peter. I'm just too nervous. I'll forget my lines, and besides, I don't think I can walk."

"Sure you can. You'll be great. Those are all your friends out there," he says.

"No, no, they're not my friends. They're waiting for me to fail. I just don't think I can do this."

"Oh my God, Marilyn. They are all waiting for you."

"Peter, I'm sorry, I'm so sorry, but I just don't think I can do this."

Peter pauses for a moment, then reaches into his pocket. "Here, doll. I want you to take a couple of these. They're very mild and they'll relax you. You're just nervous, and this is what you need. Just take two." He pours her a glass of water, then shakes two pills out of the bottle and hands them to her.

"I already took something at home," she says.

"Well that doesn't matter. You're still nervous, aren't you? Here, take these. They'll just take the edge off."

"Sure, sure. Okay," she says as she takes the pills from him. "Just give me a few more minutes."

"I'll be back in about thirty minutes to get you, so be ready," Peter says.

"I will be," Marilyn says nodding her head.

Forty-five minutes later, Peter Lawford knocks on her dressing room door, then enters. "Okay, doll. Let's get this show on the road." He notices Marilyn's tear-streaked face. "Oh, no. This will never do. This will never do, my dear. You are supposed to be the main attraction tonight…the great surprise. This will never do. What in the world is wrong?"

"I just can't, Peter. I've thought it over, and I just can't. I will embarrass the president and myself. They'll all hate me," she says.

"Nonsense. Nonsense, woman. They'll love you."

"Oh, Peter, please try to understand," she says, sobbing. "Look at my hands, they're shaking. I won't be able to do it."

"Listen to me. You have no choice. You *will* go out there. I am going to give you two more of these pills, and you're going to take them, understand? You really have no choice in the matter. Do you understand what I'm saying? Good God, woman, you were supposed to be out there an hour ago."

She nods her head, takes the pills from his hand, and swallows them.

"Marilyn, I am going to return in twenty minutes. Let those pills do their work. I want to make certain you are ready. I will accept no excuse. You *will* be ready. I will see you then," he says and leaves the room.

After twenty minutes, Peter Lawford returns. Marilyn has touched up her makeup and calmed down. Peter helps her stand, although she wobbles a bit, then catches her balance.

Lawford looks at the back of her dress, finishes zipping it, pats her on her behind, and then wraps the white ermine fur coat around her shoulders.

"Ready, doll?"

"Yes, Peter," she says in a slurred voice. Peter places his arm around her waist for support. They leave the dressing room and head for the stage of Madison Square Garden.

Three times during the evening, Peter Lawford introduces Marilyn to the crowd, but she still doesn't appear on stage. The guests soon believe his announcements are part of a comedy skit and laugh appropriately after each announcement. When Marilyn does finally appear, he introduces her as 'the late Marilyn Monroe.'

Marilyn hesitates at first, then walks onto the stage. The room darkens, and a single spotlight shines on her. She slowly peels off her white ermine fur coat, revealing the dress, and the audience gasps.

Accompanied by jazz pianist Hank Jones, and in a low, sultry voice, Marilyn sings the traditional "Happy Birthday" song, substituting the words 'Mr. President' for his name.

An enormous birthday cake is presented to the president as he walks onto the stage.

"I can now retire from politics after having had 'Happy Birthday' sung to me in such a sweet, wholesome way," he says.

The audience laughs.

CHAPTER 30

MARILYN AND HOLLYWOOD

May 31, 1962

Nancy Davis Reagan, now a Hollywood actress, and married to Ronald since 1952, has invited Marilyn for dinner this evening at the Polo Lounge in the Beverly Hills Hotel.

The women arrive at 6:30, and as they are escorted to their table, they glance at the familiar photograph behind the bar which depicts Will Rogers and Darryl F. Zanuck, two lounge regulars, playing polo.

"I love that picture," Nancy says.

"Me, too."

Nancy is wearing a pink Chanel suit with a matching bag, while Marilyn is dressed more casually in loose-fitting tan pants, a white silk blouse, and a red scarf.

Nancy looks up at the candy-striped ceiling of the restaurant and then glances at the forest green walls. "I don't know how they get away with these colors in here," she says to Marilyn, "but they do seem to work somehow."

"I like the colors," Marilyn says, looking around. "They kind of relax me."

Both women sit down.

"Oh look, isn't that Bettie Davis over there?" Nancy asks. "Don't turn around. I think it's her. I hear she's making a movie called *What Ever Happened to Baby Jane*. I think she might be a little too old to make movies."

Marilyn smiles.

"Well, almost happy birthday, young lady!" Nancy exclaims. "You do look beautiful, my dear, but far too thin. Are they not letting you eat on the movie sets these days? Why, your blouse and your trousers are just hanging off of you. Are you feeling alright?"

The waiter comes over, hands them menus, and pours water into their glasses. "Good evening, ladies, and welcome to the Polo Lounge. Would you like something else to drink?"

"Yes," Marilyn says, "I would like some champagne."

"And you, ma'am?" the waiter asks as he looks at Nancy.

"Nothing for me, thank you. Water will be fine."

"And would you ladies like to order dinner now or wait a bit?"

"I'll have the McCarthy salad," Marilyn says.

"Well that sounds good," Nancy says. "I'll have the same, except please leave off the cheese, the bacon, and the dressing."

"Very good," the waiter says. "I will have those ready for you soon."

Their waiter leaves the table, and a different waiter sets a basket of bread and butter, and the famous flatbread, on the well-starched white tablecloth. He refills Nancy's water glass.

"Nancy, I realize I've lost a little weight, but I just don't seem to have any appetite."

"Well, have you seen a doctor? I know a good doctor I could recommend."

"No, I don't think I need a doctor," Marilyn says. "I've been having a little trouble with a man I've been seeing."

"Oh, what kind of trouble? And who are you seeing?" Nancy asks as she leans in toward the table.

"Just this man. He is pretty involved in politics. I love him, and I know he loves me, but for some reason he won't take my calls. He won't see me. I want to go to his house, but I'm afraid his staff won't let me in."

"His staff won't let you in? Well that doesn't sound right, and he must be fairly wealthy to have a staff. You think he's instructed his staff not to let you in?"

"Well, maybe," Marilyn says. "He's married, unfortunately, and I don't know if his wife even knows about us."

"He's married? Oh dear Lord, no," Nancy says. Marilyn nods her head, and tears begin to form.

The waiter brings the two salads and sets them in front of the women. He then places a glass of champagne in front of Marilyn. Marilyn picks up the glass and drinks half of it, and Nancy looks at her disapprovingly.

"Nancy, I know I'm drinking too much and taking too many pills, but please don't judge me. I'm very lonely, and I have sworn to the Secret Service that I won't talk to anyone about this. Oh, wait, please forget I just said that. You have to forget I just said that. You will, won't you?"

"Of course, Marilyn. I didn't hear a thing."

The women sit in silence for a moment.

"Nancy, you have been so nice to me. In fact, I consider you my only friend."

"Oh my goodness, Marilyn, you have so many friends."

"No. No, I really don't. Not close friends. Not friends I can confide in."

"Well, you know I'll do anything to help you. Is there anything I can do?" Nancy asks.

"No. I've gotten myself into this terrible mess."

The waiter walks over to their table and looks at the untouched salads. "Is everything alright? Would anyone like any fresh pepper on their salad?" Marilyn looks down at her lap and shakes her head.

"No, no thank you. We won't be needing anything," Nancy replies.

The waiter walks away from the table.

"Thank you for listening to me and to my silly problems. I just don't know what to do," Marilyn says.

"Oh, *I* know," Nancy says. "Ronnie and I will get you a date with a bachelor we both know and adore. He will definitely help you forget your current crush. He's very handsome. Will you let me do that for you?"

"Nancy, I can't date anyone else. I've already been divorced three times, for heaven's sake, and I'm in love with this man. Besides, most men don't want to get to know me. They think I'm a shallow, dumb blonde...a floozy...and I can't shake that image."

"Marilyn, don't say that. You have a brilliant mind. Why, as soon as they talk with you for a few minutes, they'll know you are neither a dumb blonde nor a floozy."

"Believe me, they don't want to do any talking."

Nancy nods her head and begins to eat her salad. "Marilyn, you're not touching your food."

"I'm just not very hungry."

A couple from the next table has been staring at Marilyn, and finally they stand up and walk over to her table. "Miss Monroe, would you mind terribly giving us your autograph?"

Their waiter appears and approaches the couple. "I'm sorry, but we don't want to bother the other guests, now, do we?" he says as he escorts the couple back to their own table.

Marilyn shakes her head.

The waiter returns. "So sorry for the rude interruption. Well now, how is everything tasting? Delicious?" He notices Marilyn still has not eaten anything. "Is something wrong with the salad, ma'am? May I get you something else?"

"No, I'm fine," Marilyn says. She finishes her glass of champagne and hands it to the waiter. "I'll take another glass, please."

"Certainly, ma'am," the waiter replies, removing the empty glass and leaving the table.

"Do you really think you should be having more champagne?" Nancy asks.

"It will be my meal for the day."

"I'm worried about your drinking," Nancy says.

"Honestly, I seem to need more alcohol and pills just to get through the day lately. Just to relieve the pain. I usually sit around in my pajamas all day waiting for the phone to ring, waiting for him to call. Isn't that pathetic? Aren't I the biggest loser you know? I am such a mess. But I know he'll call. He really does love me."

Marilyn uses her napkin to wipe her eyes and blow her nose. Nancy takes a handkerchief out of her purse and hands it to Marilyn. The waiter sets a glass of champagne in front of Marilyn.

"Darling, we really need to get you out of this situation. What would you think of Ronnie and I arranging for you to be in another movie? Or what about television? Would you like to appear on television?"

"I honestly don't think I could commit to doing anything right now. But you and Ronnie have been wonderful. I know it was your influence that got me the parts in my movies, and I'll be forever grateful."

"We were happy to do so. We both think you're a fine actress."

Marilyn sips on her champagne for a few minutes. "So what would you do, Nancy? Should I threaten him and tell him I'm going to call his wife? Do you think she already knows? Should I reach out to the newspapers? But that would destroy his reputation… and he has such beautiful children. I would hate to wreck their lives."

"No, no you shouldn't do anything of the sort. I just need to get your mind off of him and get you interested in something else…or someone else," Nancy says.

"Peter Lawford and my boyfriend's brother, Robert, have told me to quit calling him," Marilyn explains. "Can you believe it? Oh…and Frank Sinatra called and told me to quit calling *him*. What nerve. He actually threatened me and told me to stop calling him. Unbelievable."

"Yes, dear, that is unbelievable, but you should really try to get some food in you. And…truthfully, Marilyn, if you are being threatened, you should probably quit contacting your gentleman friend."

"I know you're right; it's just been very difficult."

There is a few moments' pause.

"Nancy, we're such good friends. I almost don't even know how to ask you this, but could you do me a huge favor? Do you happen to have any extra sleeping pills or pain pills in your purse that you could give me?"

Nancy hesitates. "Marilyn, my sweet girl. I am the one trying to get you to *stop* taking all those pills and drinking so much alcohol. I realize the doctors here in Los Angeles are handing pills out like candy. But listen to me, if you do go see a doctor and he prescribes pills for you, just say no."

"What? Just say no? Why that's ridiculous, Nancy. Just ridiculous."

"Well, I'm sorry you feel that way, but that's what you should do."

"Easier said than done, Nancy. Easier said than done."

Marilyn starts to hand the handkerchief back to Nancy. "No, no," Nancy says, "just keep it."

The salad plates are removed, and a hefty slice of cheesecake with a candle on top along with two forks is set in front of Marilyn. The waiter lights the candle and steps away from the table.

"I thought you might like some cheesecake," Nancy says. "Would you like me to sing 'Happy Birthday'?"

"No, no, please don't. Just take this fork and help me eat this," Marilyn says, handing her the extra fork.

After a few bites of dessert, Nancy requests the bill. She pays it and then both leave The Beverly Hills Hotel.

CHAPTER 31

MARILYN CALLS NANCY

June 11, 1962

Nancy's phone rings at 2:00 a.m.

"Nancy, Nancy, are you awake?"

"Huh? Marilyn? Is that you? Is everything alright? Go back to sleep, Ronnie. It's for me. Marilyn? Are you okay?"

"I am so sorry to call you this late, but I just can't sleep."

"What time is it?"

"It's…it's around two in the morning, I think."

"Well, what's wrong, dear?" Nancy asks.

"I'm afraid Fox is going to fire me, and I am so mad at Dr. Greenson."

"Fire you? And who, again, is Dr. Greenson?"

"He's my psychiatrist, remember? And I rely on him completely. You know he gives me all my medications and helps me with all my decisions. And he's out of town. Can you believe that? Out of town when I need him the most. Just when I'm sure I'll be fired." Marilyn begins to sob. "What should I do, Nancy? What should I do?"

"Well, I don't know. Let me think here for a moment," Nancy says.

"I know," Marilyn says. "I'll call his children. I have their number. I'll call them and insist they make their father come home."

"Where is he?" Nancy asks.

"He's vacationing in Switzerland."

"And you think he should come home?"

"Yes, I certainly do. Thank you for your help, Nancy. You really are a great friend. I'm going to call his children right now."

"Well, okay, if that's what you think you should do." Before Nancy can say goodbye, she hears a dial tone.

Ralph Greenson's children notify their father about Marilyn's distressing phone call, and he decides to return home, arriving in California on June 6, furious with Marilyn for ruining his vacation. Greenson himself has had a lifelong tendency to irrational fits of anger. However, he is convinced he can persuade Marilyn to do anything, within reasonable boundaries.

CHAPTER 32

MEETING JFK AT THE BEVERLY WILSHIRE HOTEL

June 12, 1962

Marilyn picks up her phone and is relieved to finally hear from President Kennedy.

"Hello, darling. I have missed you and I've booked a suite for us at the Beverly Wilshire for tonight. Please don't disappoint me. Please say you'll meet me there."

"Jack, it's so good to hear from you. Why haven't you returned any of my calls?"

"Marilyn, you know how busy I am. Surely you understand. I just couldn't break away. But I really have missed you terribly, and I hope you'll forgive me. Won't you join me tonight? I have some surprises for you."

"I just bet you do," Marilyn says. "Well, if you're a very good boy, I guess I could clear my calendar for you."

"Well that's just wonderful. Please plan on arriving about eight. I'll be staying in the penthouse suite. My Secret Service men will know to let you in."

Marilyn arrives at 9:00 and is escorted in by Secret Service.

She sees a large bottle of champagne set in ice. She walks over, lifts the bottle, and reads the label. "Hmm...Piper Heidsieck Champagne, My favorite."

"You're late," Kennedy says.

"You knew I'd be late. But I'm worth it, aren't I?" she asks as she slowly takes off her light jacket.

"Definitely worth it," he says, walking toward her.

Kennedy takes his silver pocket watch out of his pocket and places it on top of the dresser.

"That's a beautiful watch," Marilyn says.

"Oh, thanks. It's a Boy Scout watch that Charles Lindbergh gave me," Kennedy replies.

Marilyn walks over to the dresser, picks up the watch, and opens it. "I remember seeing it in your bedroom at the White House. The painting on the face of this watch is lovely," she says. "Look at these trees and the river on the front, and look at the beautiful blue color of the water."

"I know, it's a great watch, and it keeps perfect time." Kennedy pauses for a moment. "Funny thing about the watch, though. Lindbergh believed it brought him luck, and I kind of believe that, too."

"Oh Jack," Marilyn laughs, "don't be so superstitious."

Kennedy laughs as well. "I know, pretty silly...But hey, enough talk about the watch, get over here, woman."

*   *   *

Early the next morning, Marilyn is awakened by one of Kennedy's Secret Service agents, and she again requests some privacy as she gets dressed. Just as she finishes, she glances over at the bed and sees Kennedy is still asleep. Marilyn walks over to the dresser, takes the silver pocket watch, and places it in her purse.

She opens the hotel's bedroom door and sees another Secret Service agent waiting just outside. He escorts her to a back entrance of the hotel, where a car is waiting to drive her home.

Marilyn tries calling the president's private line the morning of June 13. There is no answer. She calls the White House operator and is informed the president is in a meeting and cannot come to the phone, so she leaves a message for him to call her. He does not.

CHAPTER 33

THE LOST WATCH

June 14, 1962

Marilyn attempts once again to reach President Kennedy. "Jack, I've been trying to reach you, but you won't return my calls. Please, it's urgent. I need to speak with you."

President Kennedy returns her phone call at 10:00 a.m.

"Marilyn, you have got to quit calling me," Kennedy says. "I told you I would call you when I got a chance, but I have been overwhelmingly busy. I will call YOU, okay? You need to wait for MY call, understand? But oh, by the way, did you happen to see my silver pocket watch? I'm almost certain I placed it on the dresser at the Wilshire when we were there, and now I can't find it."

"Your what?" Marilyn asks.

"My pocket watch. It's a silver pocket watch...Remember? The Boy Scout pocket watch? Well, have you seen it?"

Marilyn hesitates. "Well, no. No, I haven't."

"Gee, it means a lot to me. I know that's silly." There is a moment's pause, then the president continues. "So you haven't seen it?"

"No. I told you, I haven't seen it."

"Well, okay then, I've got to run." He hangs up the phone.

"I love you, too," Marilyn whispers into the receiver, then gently hangs up the phone.

CHAPTER 34

JFK AND THE WHITE HOUSE

June 14, 1962

After listening to his 11:00 a.m. morning briefing, then eating turkey and cranberry sandwiches, chips, and blueberry cobbler for lunch with his brother, the president and Bobby retire to the Oval Office.

President Kennedy, wearing a crimson Harvard sweatshirt and blue jeans, sits at his desk, hunched over, writing notes on a yellow legal pad. Bobby, dressed in a white shirt with a button-down collar, black tie, and slacks, sits on the couch with his legs propped up on the coffee table. Both men are smoking cigars.

"Oh my God, Jack. I ate way too much for lunch. I'm miserable," Bobby says.

"I know. Me, too. I need to start cutting back and getting more exercise."

They sit for a few moments, then the president leans back in his chair and blows a smoke ring. "You know, Bobby, it seems to me that everything is starting to go to hell in a handbasket. Look at Viet Nam. The Viet Cong keep getting stronger, and now they've seized the capital of Phuoc Vinh. You know I've increased the number of military advisers and Special Forces in the area, and now all the college kids are beginning to protest the war."

"I know, Jack. I've heard all the rumblings. They might begin marching in the streets."

"And hey, you know that pocket watch I showed you the other day? The Boy Scout pocket watch? The one Lindbergh gave me?"

"Yes, what about it?" Bobby asks.

"I think Marilyn stole it."

"What?"

"Yes, I think Marilyn stole it from my dresser the other day. I asked her about it and she denies it, but I think she stole it."

"Jesus. Well, you'll never see that watch again," Bobby says.

"I know you're right. Goddamn it," the president says, blowing another smoke ring.

They sit for a few moments, then the president continues, "And that Black Panther Party in Oakland," he says, shaking his head. "What a nightmare that is."

"But the Panthers are still under constant police surveillance, correct?" Bobby asks. "So they can't stir up too much trouble."

"No, I think you're wrong there. I have to agree with J. Edgar on this one. They probably are the greatest threat to the internal security of our country. And Lyndon, don't get me started on Lyndon," Kennedy says, exasperated. "He never used to give me advice. Hell, he never even used to talk to me. Now he has to give me his opinion about everything. He's telling me I need to expand civil rights and spend more money on education and urban and rural development. I told him I don't need his advice."

"Jack, just tell Lyndon to back off. Tell him to act like a vice president, for God's sake, and do some ribbon cutting at some event, or travel to some foreign country or something like that," Bobby suggests.

"And Bobby, Jackie is spending all kinds of money restoring the White House and purchasing expensive pieces of art. She's buying lavish clothes. She is really out of control. I hope the press doesn't get wind of it. Oh, and to top things off, both John-John and Caroline have a fever, and they haven't been out of bed in two days."

CHAPTER 35

MARILYN MONROE AND JFK

June 21, 1962

Marilyn attempts to reach President Kennedy again. Her voice slurs as she leaves her message on the machine. "Jack, goddamn it, pick up the phone. Call me. I swear I will kill myself if you don't call." She pauses. "I will tell your wife, I swear, or the press, or both of them if you don't start returning my calls. Pick up the goddamn phone and call me."

The president does not return her call.

Beginning June 23, 1962, Marilyn takes part in a total of five photo sessions with *Vogue* magazine. The sessions with *Vogue* follow a three-day photoshoot on and around Santa Monica beach for *Cosmopolitan* magazine. Although Marilyn appears happy by all accounts to her adoring public, she continues desperately trying to contact the president—with no success.

Between July 13 and July 22, Marilyn places a total of eight telephone calls to Attorney General Robert Kennedy. He assures her that both he and his brother Jack are interested in her career and are concerned for her health. But there is never time for either of them, as he explains to her, to participate in lengthy social calls. Robert Kennedy gently but firmly discourages Marilyn from continuing her attempts to call the president.

By late July, 1962, Marilyn and Joe DiMaggio, whom she had divorced in 1961, start seeing each other again and get closer as she depends more and more on him for emotional support. They share simple suppers at her home in Los Angeles and rent bicycles to ride along San Vicente Boulevard toward the ocean.

Despite Robert Kennedy's pleas to get her to stop calling the White House, Marilyn dials Kennedy's private line on July 23 at 10:00 p.m. She thinks she hears the *click* of someone answering the phone.

"Listen to me you—" she shouts into the phone.

Then she hears: *BEEEEEEEEP.* "Please check your listing. The number you have dialed is not a working number."

"Goddamn it to hell," she shouts, slamming down the receiver.

*   *   *

Although Marilyn is having little luck where the Kennedy brothers are concerned, her movie career is going full steam ahead.

On Thursday, July 26, Marilyn is invited to be the Lawfords' guest at the new Cal-Neva Lodge in Lake Tahoe where Frank Sinatra will be performing. She readily agrees to attend and telephones Joe DiMaggio to ask him to meet her there. They keep a low profile during the entire weekend, though she does speak briefly with Dean Martin, her co-star on *Something's Got to Give.* They discuss a movie project, a comedy called *I Love Louisa.*

On Sunday evening, July 29, Marilyn returns to Los Angeles with the Lawfords, while Joe heads for San Francisco to appear in an exhibition baseball game, but also to tell his family that he and Marilyn are going to remarry. Marilyn plans a wedding date for Wednesday, August 8, in Los Angeles.

The next day, Marilyn watches a collection of excerpts from the various films of director J. Lee Thompson in Arthur Jacobs' screening room. She agrees to accept Thompson as the director of *I Love Louisa,* planned to be shot in early 1963.

CHAPTER 36

MARILYN MONROE

July 31, 1962

As Marilyn goes about preparing for her wedding, she phones Elizabeth Courtney, who comes for the final fitting of her wedding dress. That afternoon, Marilyn spends several hours calling, among others, a florist, her local wine shop, and a caterer.

The next morning, she phones the White House. The operator answers, and she asks to speak to the president. She is placed on hold for three minutes, then the operator returns to the line. "I am so sorry, Miss Monroe, President Kennedy is no longer accepting your calls."

"What? Do you know who this is?" Marilyn screams.

"Yes ma'am, I do," the operator replies.

"This is Marilyn Monroe. Did you tell the president Marilyn was calling?"

"Yes ma'am, I did."

There is a pause. "Well, did you actually speak with him personally?"

"Yes ma'am, I did."

"And he told you he didn't want to speak with me?"

"Yes ma'am, that's correct."

"Well, we'll see about that," Marilyn says.

"Yes ma'am," the operator says, then disconnects the line.

*   *   *

August 2, 1962

Marilyn is still depressed after drinking three glasses of champagne, so she takes a few pills. Her anger toward the president mounting, she picks up the phone and begins to dial.

"Hello, Jackie? This is Marilyn. Marilyn Monroe. I don't know if you remember meeting me or not," she says in a slurred voice.

"Oh, I know who you are, Marilyn."

"Oh, you do? Well that's great. Then you must know your husband is in love with me and is going to leave you. I just wanted to make certain you knew about us. Yes, he despises you and he loves me. Do you understand? And there is nothing you can do."

Silence.

"Miss Monroe, I don't know how you got my personal phone number, but I can assure you, Jack will never divorce me. And, Marilyn, try to understand, you are just one of his many play toys." Jackie pauses. "I want you to listen to me carefully, Marilyn. I am instructing you to never call my personal line again."

"You're instructing ME?" Marilyn shouts.

Jackie hangs up the phone.

*   *   *

August 3, 1962

Nancy and Marilyn arrange to have lunch at the Chateau Marmont on Sunset Boulevard. The hotel is reminiscent of old Hollywood with its dark paneling, gold accents, and large crystal chandeliers. Nancy arrives at 12:30; Marilyn, at 12:50. Nancy watches the waiter escort Marilyn from the front entrance to the table. He pulls out her chair, allowing her to sit down.

"Fashionably late as ever," Nancy says.

"Oh, Nancy, I am so sorry. I just had another fitting for my wedding dress. I have lost a little weight and they had to adjust it. Again, my apologies."

"No need to apologize," Nancy says. "I completely understand. Tell me, is there anything I can do to help with the wedding?"

"Absolutely nothing. It's going to be small, you know, since it's our second time marrying each other and all," Marilyn laughs.

"Could I help arrange for anything? Flowers, perhaps? Champagne?"

"Oh, my, no. Everything has been arranged, but thanks so much. I am delighted that you and Ronnie will be able to join us."

"We are thrilled, and I must say, Marilyn, you look very happy."

"I am happy, very happy. Very happy," Marilyn says, though her words slur slightly.

The waiter takes their orders and returns quickly to set fruit plates in front them. Marilyn asks for a glass of champagne.

"Champagne?" Nancy asks.

"I'm celebrating, Nancy. I'm celebrating."

"Oh, I see."

The women eat their fruit salads, and Marilyn asks for another glass of champagne.

Nancy looks at her with concern. "So tell me, Marilyn—you know you can tell me the truth. Have you been able to cut back on your pills? Are you still filling those prescriptions from you doctors?"

"Yes, but I only take the pills when I really need them," Marilyn replies.

"Is anything else wrong? Are you certain about this marriage, Marilyn?"

There are a few moments of silence.

"Well, it's too late now," Marilyn says as tears begin to form.

"It's never too late, darling," Nancy exclaims. "If you don't want to go through with this, then don't. People will understand, believe me. If you think you've made the wrong decision, just stop the wedding."

"It's scheduled for August 8, for God's sake. It's too late. Everyone's been invited, and everything's been ordered. What am I going to do? I still love Jack. What should I do?"

Nancy takes a handkerchief out of her purse. "Well, dear, I seem to keep losing my favorite handkerchiefs to you in restaurants now, don't I?"

Both women laugh as Marilyn blows her nose.

"I am so sorry, Nancy. I am such a fool. Joe is the right man for me. He has always supported me, always stayed by my side. I am so lucky to have him, really. I'm crazy to be having second thoughts. Forgive me. It's just the last-minute jitters. I'm sorry. Only *I* would have last-minute jitters for my second wedding. I'm just being silly."

"Of course, my dear. You've made the right decision, I'm sure," Nancy says, reaching across the table to pat Marilyn's hand.

Marilyn sits up straight. "Oh my gosh, I almost forgot." She reaches into her purse and takes out a shiny silver pocket watch. "Nancy, you have honestly been my best and most supportive friend all these years. Thank you for listening to all my ridiculous problems. I have no one else to talk to. No one else could begin to understand. So, I have this precious pocket watch I'd like to give you. It belonged to one of my good friends. I'm sorry I didn't wrap it first, but I thought it might be a nice gift for Ronnie. It's an unusual watch, and I know he's difficult to buy presents for...Maybe he will like this." She hands the watch across the table to Nancy, who turns the watch over in her hands and opens the case.

"Why, Marilyn, this is beautiful. What is all this writing along the edge?"

"It has something to do with the Boy Scouts, I believe."

"Well, I know Ronnie will love it. This is very sweet of you. Thank you."

"It's brought me a little luck, I believe...well, with work anyway, and with Joe. So I hope it brings good luck to you and to Ronnie."

The women finish lunch, walk out of the Chateau Marmont, and get in their cars. Nancy drives one block, then slams on her breaks—almost causing an accident. *Oh my goodness.* She thinks. *Years ago, that fortune teller—Madam Genova—predicted I would receive a silver pocket watch from a dear friend. How very strange.*

CHAPTER 37

MARILYN AND JOE

August 4, 1962

Joe DiMaggio has phoned Marilyn repeatedly but gotten no answer. Worried, he drives to her house, first knocking, then pounding on the front door. As he reaches into his pocket for his keys, he notices the door is already open. When he steps in, the smell of rotting food is overwhelming.

In the kitchen, Joe sees the countertops and sink filled with unwashed dishes. In the living room, he finds Marilyn lying on the couch in a white bathrobe with a purple stain on the front. She lies on her back with her head to the side, and her hair is matted and unwashed. Joe calls, "Marilyn," but she doesn't respond. As he sits down next to her, he shakes her shoulders, then pulls her up to a sitting position.

Marilyn whispers in a slurred voice, "Jack, oh Jack. I knew you would change your mind."

"Who? What are you saying, Marilyn?"

"Oh, Joe, Joe darling, it's you. I must have just dozed off," she says as she closes her eyes and attempts to lay back down.

Looking around the room, Joe sees bottles of pills on the coffee table and empty wine glasses scattered about. "I'm going to call an ambulance," he says, shaking her shoulders once more.

She opens her eyes. "No, no, no, Joe. Don't do that. I don't want the publicity. No one can know. Let's just keep this between us, huh? I'm fine, really, I'm just fine. Just a little tired," she says, her eyes closing again.

Joe picks her up and takes her into the bathroom, where he takes her robe off, then places her on the floor of the shower with her back leaning against the shower wall. When he turns on the cold water, Marilyn screams.

"Joe, Joe, turn off the damn water. I'm fine, I'm fine, I'm fine, Joe, just shut off the damn water."

After a few moments, he turns it off, and, with his arm around her waist, helps her stand. They step out of the shower, and he wraps towels around her, walks her into the bedroom, and turns down the covers. He helps Marilyn lie down, then covers her up with a blanket.

"Where is Eunice, Marilyn? Where is your housekeeper?" he asks.

"I sent her home yesterday. I just wanted to be alone for a while," she says, nodding her head with her eyes closed. "I'm okay, Joe. I'm fine, really. I just need to get some sleep so I'll be fresh for our wedding. I must have taken too many pills, Joe, and I'm so sorry. I'll be much more careful, really. Now you should go. I'm sure you have lots to do. Please, go on, really. I'll be just fine." With that, she drifts off to sleep. Joe watches her for about an hour, then cleans the kitchen and straightens the house.

He checks on Marilyn one more time and sees she is sleeping soundly. Joe leaves her home and locks the door behind him.

He then contacts Dr. Greenson, Marilyn's psychiatrist.

"I'm very concerned, Doctor. Marilyn seems more depressed than ever. She's drinking and seems to be taking even more pills."

"Well, Joe, she's probably nervous and excited about the wedding. I'll give Eunice a call and ask her to spend the night with Marilyn."

Eunice spends the night, but at 3:00 a.m. she hears a click and finds that Marilyn has locked herself in her bedroom.

"Miss Monroe, Miss Monroe," Eunice shouts through the door. "Can you hear me? Is everything alright in there?" But Marilyn does not reply.

Eunice walks outside, onto the front lawn, and, with a flashlight, peers into Marilyn's bedroom window. Marilyn is not moving. The housekeeper runs inside and calls Dr. Greenson, who arrives soon but has to enter Marilyn's bedroom by breaking a window. He rushes to Marilyn's side and feels for a pulse. There is none.

"MARILYN MONROE KILLS SELF"

– *New York Mirror*

After a brief investigation, the Los Angeles police conclude that Marilyn Monroe's death was "caused by a self-administered overdose of sedative drugs and that the mode of death is probably suicide."

*   *   *

On November 22, 1963, after their plane arrives at Love Field in Dallas, Texas for a campaign tour, Mrs. Kennedy disembarks and walks toward a fence where a crowd of well-wishers is gathered. She spends several minutes shaking hands. Jaqueline receives a bouquet of red roses from a little girl in the crowd wearing a pink ruffled dress, and she brings the bouquet to the waiting limousine. Governor John Connally and his wife, Nellie, are already seated in the open convertible as the Kennedys enter and sit behind them. Since it is no longer raining, the plastic bubble top has been left off. Vice President and Mrs. Johnson occupy another car in the motorcade. The procession leaves the airport, traveling along a ten-mile route that winds through downtown Dallas, heading to the Trade Mart where the president is scheduled to speak at a luncheon.

Crowds of excited people line the streets and wave to the Kennedys. The car turns off Main Street at Dealey Plaza around 12:30 p.m. As it passes the Texas School Book Depository, gunfire is suddenly heard.

Bullets strike the president's neck and head, and he slumps over toward Jacqueline. The governor is shot in the back.

The car speeds off to Parkland Memorial Hospital, just minutes away, but at 1:00 p.m. John F. Kennedy is pronounced dead.

"KENNEDY ASSASSINATED"

The Denver Post

In late 1963, Boy Scouts of America President Ellsworth H. Augustus and Chief Scout Executive Joseph A. Brunton Jr. write the following telegram to Jacqueline Kennedy:

The hearts of five and a half million Scouts and Scouters are saddened by the tragic death of their nation's leader and their

Honorary President. Throughout his life he carried out the Oath he took as a Boy Scout—on his honor to do his best to do his duty to God and his country. The strength and vigor of his leadership will always be an inspiration to Scout leaders and boys alike as we strive to build for the future on the heritage for which President Kennedy gave his all.

CHAPTER 38

MONIQUE LECLAIRE AND THE DETECTIVES

April 20, 1977

Two large gentlemen enter Avril's General Store. They are wearing dark blue suits and ties, both have neatly trimmed moustaches and dark hair, and each has a bulge on his left side, just under his jacket. At the counter, they notice a pair of blue jeans, with an extremely large waist band, tacked up high on the back wall behind the counter.

"What's with the jeans?" the man asks.

"Oh, we sell Levi Jeans, and the salesman gave us this pair for display. It's for a man with a ninety-five-inch waist."

"Yikes. Well, anyway, are you Mr. Nicolas Avril?" Detective Sergeant William Gardella asks.

"Yes I am, sir. What can I do for you?"

"Well, I'm Detective Sergeant William Gardella, and this is Detective John Falotico."

Detective Falotico nods. "Mr. Avril, we are looking for a Monique LeClaire. We were told we could find her at this address."

"Yes, of course. She rents the space upstairs. Why? Is she expecting you?"

"No, no, she's not expecting us," Detective Gardella says, "but we'd like to speak with her."

"Well, she might be with one of her clients, so would you mind if I just go up and check first?" Mr. Avril asks.

"No, go on ahead," Detective Falotico says.

Mr. Avril climbs the single flight of stairs to Monique's room and knocks on her door.

When it opens, he asks, "Are you with a client?"

"No, not now. What can I help you with, Mr. Avril?"

"Well, there are two detectives downstairs that want to speak with you."

"Two detectives?"

"Yes."

"Huh. Did they say what they wanted?" Monique asks as she stands in her doorway with her arms folded.

"No, they didn't tell me anything else."

"Well, okay then. Thanks Mr. Avril. Why don't you send them up?"

Mr. Avril goes back down and informs the detectives that Monique will see them. When they arrive upstairs, Monique's door is open, and they enter, surprised to see the many shelves filled with colorful bottles. They stare for a moment at the large cabinets against the wall.

"Why didn't I know this place existed?" Detective Falotico says to Monique, looking around the room.

Detective Gardella approaches Monique and holds out his hand. "Good afternoon, ma'am. I am Detective Sergeant Gardella, and this is my partner, Detective Falotico."

Detective Falotico shakes her hand.

"Good afternoon, gentlemen. What can I do for you?"

"Do you mind if we sit at your table?" Detective Gardella asks.

"No, not at all. Please have a seat."

"This is quite a place you have here, Miss LeClaire," Detective Falotico says. "Yes, quite a place."

Monique nods her head.

"Please let me tell you why we're here today," Detective Gardella says. "I'm certain you've read about this local crime spree—the man shooting people, mainly young people and couples, with a .44 caliber Bulldog revolver. You must have read about him in the paper."

"Yes, I have," says Monique.

"Well," continues Detective Gardella, "he left a handwritten letter near the bodies of Alexander Esau and Valentina Suriani, his latest victims, and we'd like you to take a look at it. We've been told you might be able to help us catch this guy."

"What's that? A letter? I'm sorry, detectives," Monique says, "but I think you've come to the wrong place. I look into the futures of individuals; I do not solve crimes. This is not what I do."

"We realize that," says Detective Falotico. "And actually we, or at least I, don't believe a fortune teller can help us find this murderer, but our chief insisted that we come talk to you. You see, Joseph Todaro Sr. told him to get you involved in the case, and, frankly, our chief does whatever Mr. Todaro asks him to do. He is really putting some pressure on him."

"Now why would he do that?" Monique asks.

"Well," Detective Gardella says, "it's quite a story. Apparently, our latest victim, Valentina Suriani, was Mr. Todaro's niece. As we understand it, Miss LeClaire, Mr. Todaro has been to see you, seeking your counsel, and was pretty impressed with your talents. Also, Mr. Todaro's sister, Carmen, hasn't gotten out of bed since all this happened to her daughter. I'm sure you can understand that."

"Yes, I'm terribly sorry for her loss. But I'm afraid I'm still unable to help you."

The detectives look at one another. "That's exactly what the chief said you'd say," Detective Falotico says. "He said if you told us that, we should plead with you to help. If it's money you need, Todaro will give it to you. He'll offer anything. Todaro told the chief 'nothing else matters' and he keeps repeating that to the chief: 'nothing else matters.' In other words, he'll do anything to catch the guy who killed his niece. He'll offer you anything. And listen, we believe this psycho will keep on killing if you don't help us."

"I don't need anything from Mr. Todaro," Monique says, "and I don't want his money."

All three sit in silence for a moment.

Detective Gardella places the letter on the table. "Will you *please* just look at this? Just look at it so I can go back and tell the chief you couldn't help us. Please, just look at it."

Monique looks at both detectives, then reluctantly reads the long, rambling letter, written in poor handwriting and filled with misspellings. In it, the killer refers to himself as 'Son of Sam,' and clearly expresses his determination to continue his killings. He taunts police for their fruitless efforts to capture him. One phrase in the letter—'me hoot it urts sonny boy'— police hypothesized was taken as a Scottish-accented version of 'my heart, it hurts, sonny boy.'

"Well, what do you think? Do you think the guy is Scottish?" Detective Falotico asks.

Monique places her palm on the letter. "No," she says, "he's definitely not Scottish, and I know for certain he will kill again—next month. He is taunting you, you realize, in this letter."

"Yes, of course we know that."

"Moreover," Monique says. "This man will kill two more couples over the next few months."

"Two? Just two more couples and then we'll catch him?" Detective Falotico asks.

"Yes. I believe so. Two more couples will be murdered."

"Do I understand what you just said? We will *catch* him? Is that what you just said? We will get him but only after he kills two more couples?" asks Detective Gardella.

Monique places her palm, once again, on the letter. "Yes. You will find him, because a patrol officer will place a ticket on his car. You will find him that way."

The detectives look at each other for a moment. Detective Falotico says, "A ticket placed on his car? Oh Jesus, woman. You actually think that information is going to help us? A ticket on his car? Oh my God. Do you realize how many tickets we give out each day? How about a little more clarity? Could you, like, give us the name of the street, or the make of the car? Jesus, lady, we need details. That is really no help at all." Detective Falotico shakes his head. "And just when is he going to get this ticket on his car? Or could you at least tell us what the ticket is for?"

Monique picks up the letter once again and stares at it. "All I can tell you…" she says. "All I can tell you is, I feel a woman who is fearful of this man will call. She will tell you the man got a ticket on his car. I can't tell you any more than that. That's all I see," says Monique.

The detectives write some notes, then get up to leave. Detective Gardella says, "Miss LeClaire, our shooter seems to seek young girls with long dark hair. Does that help you with anything?"

"No, Detective. I'm afraid not."

"Well, thank you for your assistance, Miss LeClaire. Would you please contact us if you have any more insight into these murders?" Detective Gardella asks.

"I can assure you, Detective, I will have no further insight."

"Well, may we contact you again if we think of any more questions or receive any more notes or information?" Detective Falotico asks.

Monique hesitates. "Fine. Sure. You can contact me."

Monique walks them to her front door and watches them walk down the stairs. She goes back inside and gives Jenny a call.

CHAPTER 39

MONIQUE CALLS JENNY

April 20, 1977

"Jenny, two detectives just left," Monique says.

"Two detectives? Oh my. Well what did they want?" she asks.

"They were questioning me about the recent murders here in New York. You know, the guy who kills the young couples and all…the guy who just walks up to couples and shoots them."

"What did they want with you, for heaven's sake?" Jenny asks.

"Apparently the murderer wrote a letter, and they asked me to read it, to try and help catch him."

"Were you able to detect anything from the letter?"

"Possibly a few things, but most of it was too vague, too general to actually help."

"That's very interesting, Monique. I wonder why they came to you for help."

"It's mafia related. Apparently, Joseph Todaro's niece was one of the victims," Monique explains.

"Oh my goodness. Well, that makes sense…I mean it makes sense how you are involved. Boy, the killings have frightened everyone in New York."

"Yes, I know. The letter was horrifying, Jenny. This killer really is a monster, without any remorse. I can sense he enjoys killing and will continue until he's caught. He gets a thrill from getting close to his victims and seeing their fear. He seems to be a fairly intelligent young man—severely crazy, but intelligent."

"Do you think the police will ask you to help them solve other crimes?"

"I hope not. I really wasn't able to give them anything truly helpful."

"Well, call me if you think there is anything I can do. I love you. Please take care of yourself and be careful, for goodness sake."

"I will, and I love you, too," Monique says.

"Hey, would you like to come to dinner tomorrow?" Jenny asks.

"Sure, that would be great. What can I bring?"

"Wine. Just a bottle of wine," Jenny says. "That would be perfect. Red or white, it doesn't matter. Oh, and I'll ask Joshua to join us. It will be fun."

"That sounds great. It's been a while since I've seen him. See you then."

CHAPTER 40

DINNER WITH JOSHUA

April 21, 1977

Joshua is the first to arrive for their impromptu dinner party. Jenny's drapes are open, and he can see the lights of the Chrysler building on Lexington Avenue through her large living room window. He's grown into a fine man and is now a successful surgeon. His hair is the color of salt and pepper, and he's letting his sideburns grow long.

"Welcome, welcome, welcome stranger," Jenny says, throwing her arms around him in a big hug. "Hey, what have you got there?"

"Oh, just some wine," Joshua says. "The man at the liquor store told me it was supposed to be pretty good."

"Are you still not drinking any alcohol?" she asks.

"That's right. I never touch the stuff. I learned that lesson well from my father."

"Of course. I remember. Well, I imagine it's really best that you don't drink alcohol, with your work and all. So what would you like to drink? I have soda, water, juice, milk. What sounds good to you?"

"If you have a Coke, that would be great."

"Sure, I'll get you one, and how about helping me cut up some carrots and celery for the salad?"

"I'd be happy to." Joshua follows her into the kitchen.

"So how is your work at the hospital? Staying busy?" Jenny asks while he cuts the vegetables and she opens the oven to check on the chicken.

"Oh my gosh, that smells so good. What are we having?"

"Your favorite: roasted chicken and potatoes."

"Terrific. I'm starving."

"I roasted two chickens, just to make sure there was plenty. And maybe enough for some leftovers for you to take home."

"I wouldn't count on there being any leftovers." Joshua smiles. "Oh, and you wouldn't believe how busy it is at the hospital. I'm on call now every other night."

"Oh, Joshua, that's too much. Are they planning on hiring any more cardiac surgeons?"

"Well, we're interviewing two new candidates next—"

The doorbell rings.

"Oh sweetheart, do you mind answering the door. Monique will be so happy to see you."

Jenny hears joyful screaming and laughter from the other room, and after a few minutes, Monique and Joshua enter the kitchen. She is carrying two bottles of wine.

"Well, I think we'll have enough wine for tonight," Jenny exclaims. "Why don't you two go sit down in the dining room? Oh, and Monique, would you please pour the wine? But for just you and me. And Joshua, would you fill the glasses with water and grab yourself a Coke? I was so excited to see you, I forgot to get you one. Everything is ready, so I'll start putting the food on the table. Oh and Joshua, please put the salad on the table and grab the salad dressings, too."

Jenny places the food on the table and lights the candles.

"Goodness gracious," Monique says. "Everything looks and smells so good."

"It really does, Jenny," Joshua says. "Thanks so much for inviting me. I've eaten so much Chinese takeout recently from China Inn, I'm sure I'm their most frequent customer. A home-made meal is really a treat."

"Well, I'm delighted you both could come this evening."

The food is passed around, and Joshua piles his plate high.

"So how is work, Joshua?" Monique asks. "Are you considering retiring any time soon?"

"Oh, I've thought about it, but what would I do, for Heaven's sake? I really don't have any hobbies. I don't play bridge or paint or anything, and I really don't enjoy traveling. Cardiac surgery is like a hobby for me now. I love what I do, and the patients seem to appreciate my help. Last week, in fact, one of my patients gave me an original Chagall painting. I tried to refuse it—in fact I told him I would not accept it—but he had it delivered to my home. Would either of you like to have it? It's quite impressive," Joshua asks.

"No, no, please, no more paintings. My walls are already filled with your patients' gifts. Just two months ago you gave me that original Picasso, remember?" Monique says.

"Me, too. Please, no more paintings," Jenny says. "I don't have any room on my walls, either. Though I do love the Gauguin. It's on my bedroom wall. I love looking at it before going to sleep, but I don't have any more room. Just look around, for Heaven's sake."

Joshua looks around. Original oil paintings by famous artists fill almost every square inch of wall space in Jenny's apartment. He nods his head. "Well, just think about it. Maybe one of you would like to switch out some of the art on your walls for different pieces."

"No, no. I love every piece I have," Monique says. "They all bring me great joy."

"Me, too, Joshua. I adore every piece of art you've given me," Jenny says. "I often walk around my apartment and just admire all the different paintings and think of you. What a wonderful success you've made of your life. I'm so terribly proud of you."

"Believe me, I realize my success is due to both of you."

They sit and eat for a few moments.

"Well," Joshua says, "I also have a new piece of Erté sculpture that I was just given. I tried my best to refuse that, too. Any interest?"

"No, no, no. But thanks anyway," Jenny says, laughing. "One day we'll have to donate our lovely pieces of art to a museum."

"Monique," Joshua says, "I want to thank you again for getting us tickets to Pavarotti at the Met last month. That was a real treat. I'd never heard Puccini's *La Boheme* performed so magnificently. How in the world did you get such great tickets?"

"Oh I have my connections," says Monique. "I'm pretty close to a few Italian businessmen, and they are very accommodating. Actually, some of them went to see the performance, too."

"It was unbelievably great," Joshua says. "In fact, for a few days, I couldn't get the music out of my head. I was singing it in the shower. My poor neighbors. It was such a thrill to see the performance in person."

"I'm so glad you enjoyed it, dear." Monique smiles.

"I thought the performance was absolutely wonderful, too," says Jenny. "And it was fun dressing up for the occasion.

I loved looking at everyone's gowns, and the jewelry…oh my goodness, the jewelry some of the women wore…especially some of the necklaces. Why they were stunning."

"But the clients that you see every day must wear some pretty impressive jewelry and dresses, right?" asks Monique.

"That's true, but everyone seemed to really outdo themselves when it came to dressing for the Met. The women probably dressed to impress the other women. I'm sure some of the jewelry must have come from their lockboxes at their banks for that event," Jenny says.

Everyone laughs.

"So are you dating anyone, Joshua?" Monique asks.

Both women glance at each other, and Monique winks at Jenny.

"No, no, not really," Joshua says. "I go out with one of the nurses at the hospital every once in a while to a movie or to a play, but it's nothing serious. I think she'd like to get serious… to get married, but I'm sixty-four, for Heaven's sake."

"Well, it would be nice to have a companion. It's really none of my business, but it would be nice for you to have someone to be with," Jenny says.

"You know, I probably never got married because I really never wanted to have children," Joshua explains. "My father was such a monster. I'm sure that has something to do with it."

Monique and Jenny nod their heads.

"Besides, you both are all the family I need," Joshua says. "Who could ask for a better family, really? A better support system? I love you both very much."

"We love you, too, dear," says Monique.

"And what about you two?" Joshua asks. "Why haven't either of you married after all these years?"

"Oh my, Joshua," Jenny says. "You have to remember we are able to see into the future. When these rich women come for a reading, or to see what lies ahead, they are often only seeking to know which parties they should attend or which home they should purchase. When I look into their futures, I often see their husbands as drunkards, or gamblers, many of them cheating on their wives or beating their prostitutes. And some of the men don't like to bathe, can you believe that?"

"Yikes. Do you ever inform these women about their husbands?" Joshua asks.

"No. I realize most of them already know, and the others... well, they don't want to know," Jenny says.

"I have seen the same, Joshua," Monique says. "As you know, many of my clients aren't wealthy. In fact, some are barely able to eke out a living, or they lead lives of crime. Many of them beat their wives. Why would Jenny or I want to bring that into our lives?"

"Yes, I can certainly understand," Joshua says.

They sit quietly for a few moments, then Joshua says, "Jenny, I've never asked you about Jack's father. Do you mind telling me what happened to him?"

"No, I don't mind. When Jack was very little, I told him that his father was killed when he fell off a horse," Jenny says.

"I remember Jack telling me that story," Joshua says.

"But that's not completely true. Actually, I have no idea what happened to him, Joshua, because he disappeared as soon as I told him I was pregnant. Later, when Jack was a little older, I told him the truth about his father."

They sit for a few moments.

"I'm sure that must have been rough," Joshua says.

"Yes, it was hard sometimes, but it taught me to take care of myself…and, of course, Monique has always taken good care of Jack and me."

"Oh, but surely you must know there are some wonderful men out there," Joshua says. "I know. My mother married one."

"Yes," Monique says, "your mother's *second* husband is wonderful, and I'm certain you're correct about other great men being out there. But Jenny and I are lucky enough to have been able to support ourselves comfortably all these years and to rely on each other. We don't need men to support us. And frankly, neither of us wants to take care of a man."

"Yes," says Jenny, smiling at Monique. "You are exactly right. We are very happy just to have each other…and of course we have you in our lives, Joshua…you and Jack. You two are the only men we need."

"Yes, that's right, Joshua. I feel the same way," Monique says as she reaches out and squeezes Joshua's hand.

Joshua smiles.

"Well, enough of that," Jenny says. "More chicken or potatoes, anyone? Joshua?"

"Yes, please," Joshua says as he piles a second helping onto his plate. "So what have you been up to, Monique? Any interesting clients?"

"Well, now that you ask, two police detectives came by yesterday and asked me about this man who has been killing young couples. I'm sure you've read about him in the newspaper. Last month, at a press conference, Mayor Beame announced that the same .44 Bulldog revolver was used in most of the killings, including the most recent ones. The detectives said that he seems to seek out young women with long, dark hair."

"Jesus. I can't believe the police asked you to help them find the killer. That's amazing. Of course I've read about him in the paper."

"Jenny was surprised that I was involved, too, weren't you?" Monique asks.

Jenny nods her head.

"The latest victim was tied to the mafia," Monique continues. "She was the niece of Joseph Todaro Sr., and he is one of my clients. Mr. Todaro wanted me to be involved in the case, and it seems our police chief does whatever Mr. Todaro asks him to do."

"Very interesting," Joshua says. "However, I'm a little nervous that you're helping to find this psycho killer."

"Please don't be. The only people I'll speak with are the two detectives…and both of you, of course. Anyway, the detectives brought me a letter to read that the killer wrote," Monique explains.

"He wrote a letter?"

"Yes. He left it at the scene of his latest crime. Though he sounds intelligent, there are numerous misspelled words. I wonder if he even misspelled them on purpose. There are references to the devil and to Satan, and I suspect he might be trying to throw the police off his track. I get the feeling this man loves publicity and loves to read about himself in the paper. I also believe he feels compelled to return to the scene of his crimes."

"Did you tell the police that?" Joshua asks.

"I told the police that a woman would call them about a car that received a ticket from a traffic police officer. That's how the crime will be solved."

"A ticket on her car?" asks Jenny.

"No, not her car," explains Monique. "She'll call about the killer's car."

"How will she know it's the killer's car?" Joshua asks.

"She won't," Monique says. "She will call the police and tell them a very strange man with a gun looked at her in a funny way one evening. She will tell them it was near the site of one of the shootings and that his car got a ticket."

"A ticket for what?" Jenny asks.

"I don't know, really. Maybe it will be a ticket for parking too close to a fire hydrant, or something like that," Monique says. "I didn't mention that to the police because I wasn't too sure about it. Also, in my vision, this man's car looked yellow to me, but I didn't tell them that either. Sometimes I'm very wrong when it comes to seeing colors in the future, and I didn't want to end up misleading them."

"Oh my gosh, Monique. Please be very careful," Joshua says. "So, does this mean you're going to get involved in trying to solve other crimes?"

Monique and Jenny laugh. "Hah. Jenny asked me the same question...but no. This will be my first and last attempt to help solve a crime...at least I hope it will be."

"I hope it will be her last, too," says Jenny.

After a few moments of silence, Joshua says, "Well, Jenny, that was a fantastic dinner. Thanks again."

"Please wait! I made a triple chocolate cake for dessert, and we'll have coffee."

Joshua helps take the dirty dishes into the kitchen. Plates with huge slices of soft, moist, rich chocolate cake with decadent chocolate icing are brought out, along with steaming cups of coffee.

"So how is your mother, Joshua?" Jenny asks.

"Oh, she is great. She and Harry just moved into a new apartment building. They now have a view overlooking Central Park. It's really lovely. By the way, that was the perfect job you helped mother get years ago, Jenny. It's hard to believe, but they've been married now for almost thirty years."

"I'm so happy to hear that," Jenny says.

"And how in the world is my good friend Jack?" Joshua asks. "It's been months since I've spoken with him."

"Oh, he and his family are great, and their kids are doing well," Jenny says. "I think he plans to bring them here this summer for a visit. It will be fun. I'll be sure to let you know when they're in town."

"Please do. I miss seeing him," says Joshua.

They sit eating their cake and drinking their coffee until Joshua finishes and asks for another piece of cake. Jenny brings him a massive slice, which he has no problems devouring.

Everyone helps clear the table. Jenny washes the dishes and Joshua dries them while Monique wipes the table in the dining room.

"Hey, Jenny," Joshua says. "There's something else I've been remembering lately and have been meaning to ask you about. You remember when you let me borrow that silver Boy Scout pocket watch?"

"Sure, hon," Jenny says. "Boy, that was quite a few years ago, now, wasn't it?"

"Well, what ever happened to it? You think that woman's husband still has the watch?"

"No, Joshua, I don't. I remember placing a spell on two watches that day, and I rarely cast spells. Monique is the expert in that department. As I recall, the woman wanted a good luck charm placed on the watches for her son and husband, and I used a good luck spell that I had heard Monique cast in Louisiana many years earlier.

"The spell didn't work initially, and when I think back on it, I just might have left out a sentence or two, or maybe I said the sentences out of order. Regardless, the spell didn't go quite as smoothly as I had hoped, so, along with the 'good luck' charm, a little 'bad luck' followed."

Monique joins them in the kitchen and helps dry the dishes.

"What do you mean a little bad luck followed?" Joshua asks.

"Well, as soon as I finished casting the spell on the watches," Jenny explains, "I realized it was not just a simple spell of good luck. The spell would compel the owners of the watches to take care of them and keep them close, but to complicate things even more, the spell directed each watch to travel until it found its rightful owner. I am still able to visualize the watches every once in a while because I placed the spell on them. I know they are still seeking their destiny, their final owners."

"Do you know who the final owners will be?" Joshua asks.

"No, dear, I sure don't," Jenny says.

"Yes," Monique says, "that spell turned out very strangely. Jenny and I have discussed it, and I told her that particular spell should only have been cast at night, and only during a new moon, when the stars are brightest. It's also a spell meant for people and not objects. That's why we believe it took on a life of its own."

"Very interesting," Joshua says, nodding his head, "very interesting."

The dishes are finished, and Jenny walks her guests to her front door. "I am so sorry there are no leftovers, Joshua."

"Oh my God, that was the best meal I've had in years. And can you believe I polished off the rest of that cake? I'm just sorry I made such a pig of myself. Thanks so much for inviting me," Joshua says as he gives Jenny a big hug. "I love you."

"I love you, too," says Jenny. "Oh, and I've been meaning to tell you all night, the sweater you're wearing is beautiful. That color of blue is perfect for you."

"Well, it better be," Joshua says. "You bought me this sweater for my birthday last year."

"Oh my, yes, of course," Jenny laughs. "Well, it does look great. I have fabulous taste, don't I?"

"Yes you do," Joshua laughs.

Monique and Jenny hug goodbye. "I'll talk to you tomorrow," Monique says to Jenny. "This was a lot of fun."

CHAPTER 41

THE DETECTIVE RETURNS

June 1, 1977

"Miss LeClaire, may I please speak with you?" Detective Falotico calls from the other side of Monique's door.

She hesitates for a moment. "Detective, I have already told you all I know."

"I realize that," he says, "but we received another letter, and I'd like you to take a look at it."

"I am with a client now—but could you come back in thirty minutes?"

"Thank you, Miss LeClaire. Yes, I'll return then."

After a while, and after seeing a young woman walking down the stairs, he returns to Monique's apartment.

"Miss LeClaire, we just received a letter written by the man claiming to be the .44 Caliber Shooter. It was sent to Jimmy Breslin, the *Daily News* columnist," Detective Falotico explains, handing her an envelope.

"Come on in," she says as she examines the envelope.

On the back, neatly hand-printed in four precisely centered lines are the words:

Blood and Family
Darkness and Death
Absolute Depravity

.44

The letter is signed 'Son of Sam' with a sketched-out logo beneath the signature that combines several symbols. Monique places it flat on the table, and her fingertips glide over the writing.

"You should publish his letter in the newspaper, Detective. Our killer loves publicity, and I feel that he often returns to the scenes of his crimes. When he becomes active again, he will, perhaps, make a mistake. Other than his car getting a ticket, and a woman contacting you about a suspicious man, I cannot see any more details. Somehow, you'll need to connect her call and the ticket to finally capture him."

"Again, Miss LeClaire, I am grateful for your insight, and I pray that it will help us, but remember, please, how many thousands of tickets are placed on cars…And after we publish this letter—that's *if* the chief allows us to publish it—we will probably get thousands of calls with tips about this killer. You understand that, don't you?"

"Yes, Detective, I understand very well," Monique says.

"So you are still not able to tell us a make of car, or when the ticket will be given or what the ticket will be for?" the detective asks.

"No sir. I cannot."

They both sit in silence at the table for a few moments.

"Well, at least it appears you have some hope that he will be captured."

Monique nods her head, and he leaves.

The *New York Daily News* publishes the letter a week later—after agreeing to withhold portions of the text—and Jimmy Breslin urges the killer to surrender. The article explains that the shooting victims to date have had long, dark hair, which causes thousands of women in New York to acquire short cuts or dye their hair a bright color. Beauty supply stores have trouble meeting the demand for wigs. The article in the *New York Daily News* makes that day's paper the highest-selling edition of the *Daily News* to date; more than 1.1 million copies are sold. Police receive thousands of tips, all of which prove useless.

Sal Lupo, a twenty-year-old mechanic's helper, and Judy Placido, a seventeen-year-old recent high school graduate, are shot by Son of Sam around 3:00 a.m. on June 26, when three gunshots blast through the parked car in Bayside, Queens. A witness provides a partial plate number of the license on the killer's car

CHAPTER 42

THE DETECTIVE AND MONIQUE LECLAIRE

June 30, 1977

Detective Gardella calls Monique. "Miss LeClaire, we have *not* gotten a phone call from a woman about a suspicious man with a ticket on his car."

"She will phone you," replies Monique.

They both hang up.

One month later, on July 31, Stacy Moskowitz and Robert Violante, both twenty years old, are in Violante's car in the neighborhood of Bath Beach, on their first date. A man approaches the car and fires four rounds into it, striking both victims in the head.

August 2, 1977

Detective Gardella calls Monique again. "Miss LeClaire, we *have still not received* a phone call from a woman about a suspicious man with a ticket on his car. Are you still certain that will occur?"

"She will phone you," replies Monique.

They both hang up.

August 8, 1977

Detective Gardella calls Monique yet again. "Miss LeClaire, sorry to bother you again, but we *have still not received* a phone call from a woman about a suspicious man with a ticket on his car. Do you still believe she will call us?"

"She will phone you," replies Monique.

They both hang up.

CHAPTER 43

THE REPORT

August 9, 1977

"Hello, is this the police station?"

"Yes it is, ma'am. What can I help you with?"

"Well, my name is Cacilia Davis, and I'd like to report something."

"What is it you'd like to report?"

"Well, actually, I'd like to speak to the detective who is working on that killer case—you know, the Son of Sam case. I saw something suspicious and I'd like to report it."

"Let me transfer you, ma'am." *Click*

"Detective Gardella. How may I help you?"

"Hello, Detective. My name is Cacilia Davis and I'd like to report something."

"Okay, ma'am, go right ahead."

"Do you have a paper and pencil handy?" she asks.

"Yes ma'am, I sure do."

"Well okay, then. Four days ago, I was walking my dog near the scene of the Moskowitz and Violante shooting. I live near there. You know where that is, right?"

"Yes ma'am."

"Well, a uniformed policeman ticketed a car parked near a fire hydrant. Soon after he left, a young man walked past me, near the ticketed car. He looked at the car and then just stood there and stared at me. He was holding some type of dark object in his hand."

"Dark object? What do you mean 'dark object'?" Detective Gardella asks.

"Well, I'm pretty sure it was a gun. I ran home and heard shots firing on the street behind me. I don't know why I waited four days before calling, but I just kept thinking about it and finally decided it might be important."

"Let me get this straight, Miss Davis. It is Miss Davis, correct?"

"Yes sir, that's correct."

"You saw a suspicious man with a gun near the crime scene, and he was looking at a car that was getting a ticket on August 5th?"

"Yes. That's right."

"Well, okay then. I have the information. Thank you for calling." Detective Gardella immediately notifies Detective Falotico.

The police investigate cars that were ticketed in the area on the night of August 5, and David Berkowitz's 1970 four-door yellow Ford Galaxie is among the cars police discover.

The next day, August 10, 1977, police investigate Berkowitz's car, which is parked outside his apartment building at 35 Pine Street in Yonkers. They see a rifle in the back seat, search the car, and find a duffel bag filled with ammunition and maps of the crime scenes. Police wait for Berkowitz to leave his apartment, avoiding the risk of a violent encounter in the building. They are also awaiting approval of a search warrant, worried that their search might be challenged in court.

The initial search of the vehicle is based on the rifle visible in the back seat, although possession of such a rifle is legal in New York State and requires no special permit. The warrant still has not arrived when Berkowitz exits his apartment building at 10:00 p.m. and enters his car. Detective John Falotico approaches the driver's side of the car and points his gun close to Berkowitz's temple, while Detective Sergeant William Gardella points his gun from the passenger's side.

Berkowitz looks at them both, smiles, and then states flatly, "Well, you got me."

"Now that I've got you," Detective Falotico says to the suspect, "who have I got?"

"You know," Berkowitz says in a soft sweet voice.

"No I don't. You tell me."

Berkowitz turns his head and says, "I'm Sam."

"You're Sam? Sam who?"

"Sam. David Berkowitz."

A paper bag containing a .44-caliber Bulldog revolver is found next to Berkowitz in his car. The ballistics match the gun used in the shootings.

"BERKOWITZ CHARGED IN 'SAM' CASE, ORDERED HELD FOR MENTAL TESTS"

– The *New York Times*

CHAPTER 44

MONIQUE AT
MR. AVRIL'S STORE

August 11, 1977

Monique walks into Avril's General Store early in the morning, when Mr. Avril is still turning on the lights.

"Monique," he says, "a young man came by just now and left this for you." He hands her a small, rectangular, red leather box.

"Do you know who he was?" she asks.

"No. He didn't look familiar."

Monique takes the box with her upstairs, and as soon as she unlocks the apartment door, she rushes to answer the ringing phone.

"Good morning, Miss LeClaire. This is Detective Falotico. We got him. You were right. A woman called describing a man who frightened her, and she told us she saw a policeman ticketing his car."

"Of course. I knew she would call," Monique says.

"Well, I want to thank you for all your help...and I was wondering, would you be willing to help us again?"

She hesitates for a moment. "Thank you, Detective, but I don't think so. Have a good day," she says. With the red leather box still in her hand, she opens it, to find a card:

Thank you, Miss LeClaire
Joseph Todaro, Sr.

Underneath the card is an Art Deco style Cartier onyx wristwatch, set with both round and baguette diamonds.

CHAPTER 45

RONALD AND
NANCY REAGAN

February 3, 1979

After Ronald Reagan is elected governor of California, he becomes involved with the Boy Scouts of America and is active with the Golden Empire Council, whose mission is to instill values in young people and prepare them to make ethical choices during their lifetimes. The council's values are based on character, citizenship, and personal fitness, and they are found in the Scout Oath and Law. Reagan serves on the council's advisory board.

Nancy has had the silver Boy Scout watch hidden in her closet for quite a while, and she checks on it periodically. For his birthday on February 6, 1979, she gives the watch to Ronnie, as it just might have more significance for him now. She informs him Marilyn Monroe gave her the watch, quite a while ago, as a gift, and that Marilyn believed it brought her luck, so Ronnie should keep it with him at all times.

The following day Nancy twists her ankle on a rock in her backyard. Her physician wraps the ankle in a bandage and tells her to place ice on it, and keep it elevated for a week until the swelling goes down.

In November 1980, Ronald Reagan is elected President of the United States and is sworn into office in January, 1981. Nancy's wardrobe soon consists of dresses, gowns, and suits made by luxury designers, including James Galanos, Bill Blass, and Oscar de la Renta. The white, hand-beaded, one-shoulder Galanos dress she wears to the inaugural ball costs $10,000, and the overall price of her inaugural wardrobe is $25,000.

Ronald and Nancy, now the First Lady, move into the White House, and Nancy soon begins much-needed repairs, as it has fallen into a state of disrepair following years of neglect. Mrs. Reagan directs a major renovation of several White House rooms, including all of the second and third floors and rooms adjacent to the Oval Office, such as the press briefing room. The renovation includes repainting walls, refinishing floors, repairing fireplaces, and replacing eroding pipes.

Nancy orders a new state china service for the White House since the last full service was ordered by the Truman administration in the 1940s. She works with Lenox, the primary porcelain manufacturer in America, and chooses a design pattern of an etched gold band bordering scarlet- and cream-colored ivory plates with a raised presidential seal etched in gold in the center. The cost of a single place setting is nearly $1,000, and the full china service totals $209,508. It is used for the first time on February 4, 1982. Although the china is paid for by private donations, its purchase generates quite a controversy, as it was ordered during an economic recession. Furthermore, this purchase coincides with Ronald's administration proposing school lunch regulations that will allow ketchup to be counted as a vegetable.

CHAPTER 46

LEONORE ANNENBERG'S BIRTHDAY PARTY

February 20, 1981

Nancy Reagan, accompanied by two Secret Service men, flies to California to attend a birthday party for her good friend, Leonore Annenberg, at the Musso and Frank Grill on Hollywood Boulevard. Other socialites in attendance include Mary Jane Wick and Betsy Bloomingdale. Because of Nancy's Industry connections, the women are seated in a separate room of the restaurant—a private space reserved for its star-studded clientele. With a lunch of lobster and crab to go along with their Long Island iced teas and martinis, a fortune teller has been hired for entertainment. Nancy is thrilled, as she has had an interest in astrology and mysticism for many years, which was piqued when she had a brief session with Madam Genova.

When "Happy Birthday" has been sung and the cake is about to be served, the fortune teller appears and stands in front of their table, looking carefully at each of the women. She is tall, thin, looks to be in her mid-forties, and is wearing a bright, loose-fitting yellow dress. Her long, curly red hair is wild, going in every direction, and a headband stretches across the middle of her forehead.

The women stare at her for a moment, then laugh nervously, quickly glancing at each other.

"Well good afternoon, Miss Carmine," Mary Jane says. "Please forgive us for laughing, as we might have had a little too much to drink. But we are all very eager to learn what you have to tell us today, isn't that right, ladies?"

"I know I am," Leonore says.

"And me, too. I want to know what my future has in store," Betsy says, then laughs.

Miss Carmine's expression remains serious, and she nods her head.

Mary Jane introduces Miss Carmine to all the other women while they move to a larger round table to listen to the predictions of their fortune teller, bringing their drinks with them. Betsy Bloomingdale asks to go first.

Miss Carmine sits on one side of the large round table, which is bare except for the women's drinks, while the four women sit on the other side, chairs drawn close to one another.

Betsy giggles. "Miss Carmine, will my husband kill me for buying another mink coat?" The other women laugh.

"Wait, wait," Mary Jane says, "am I going to get the diamond necklace that I want for my birthday?"

The women laugh and snort, but they soon realize Miss Carmine is not smiling.

"Okay, ladies, let's settle down," Leonore says to the other women. "I'm so sorry, Miss Carmine. Again, I apologize. We were just having some fun. We'll be good now, we promise. Won't we, ladies?"

The women nod their heads.

"Have you been telling fortunes for a long time, Miss Carmine?" Betsy asks.

"Yes, for many years."

"Are most of your followers from around here?" Leonore asks.

"Yes, they are."

"Oh, do you happen to know Joan Quigley?" Nancy asks.

"Yes, I've met her a few times," Miss Carmine says. "Many of her clients, I believe, are now from Hollywood or are involved in politics." Miss Carmine looks down, picks up her oversized brown purse from the floor, and places it in her lap.

"Miss Carmine, just one more question if you don't mind," Nancy says. "Have you ever heard of a woman named Madam Genova?"

Miss Carmine looks up and stares at Nancy. "Who? Who were you asking about?"

"She calls herself 'Madam Genova,'" Nancy says. "At least I'm pretty sure that's what she told me her name was. It's been quite a few years since I've seen her. I remember being quite impressed with her predictions."

"Yes. I know her. She works in New York. We speak to each other every once in a while. I admire her talent and occasionally seek her advice."

"It's amazing how you fortune tellers know each other," Mary Jane says.

Miss Carmine nods and takes a deck of seventy-eight tarot cards out of her purse. Each card has its own intricate imagery and symbolism, portrayed in elaborate colors. She cuts the deck by dividing it into several piles and then combines the cards into one deck again.

Miss Carmine clears her throat and then sits up straight in her chair. "This afternoon I will begin by reading a tarot card for each of you. After I have finished with the tarot card readings, I will take each of you aside and read your palm."

The women nod.

"Now ladies, I don't know if you've ever been to a tarot card reading or not, but these cards are meant to tap into your own intuition and wisdom so you can start taking positive steps toward a brighter future." The women look at each other, smile, and nod. "These cards represent our thoughts, feelings, experiences, and beliefs. Some of them represent a temporary kind of energy that affects your life at the moment. Other cards will illuminate a path forward, and still others will prompt you to reflect on your life's broader lessons. Alright then. Is everyone ready? We'll begin with you, Mrs. Bloomingdale. I want you to shuffle the cards, place them in a stack, and turn over the card on top of the deck."

Betsy does as requested and turns over the top card, The High Priestess. She looks anxiously at Miss Carmine for an interpretation.

The fortune teller looks into Betsy's eyes. "My, you have turned an interesting card. The High Priestess is a card of mystery and stillness. You must retreat and reflect upon a recent situation. You must trust your inner instincts to guide you through it. Have you been as honest as you could have been? Things around you are not what they appear."

"Oh my," says Betsy. "Not as they appear? Well, I guess not. I should look twenty years older, but thank God for my wonderful plastic surgeon."

The women laugh. Miss Carmine does not.

"The High Priestess card also informs me of your love of fine clothes," Miss Carmine says.

"Well Heaven knows that's true, Betsy," Nancy says as the women continue to laugh.

"Miss Bloomingdale," Miss Carmine says, "it also appears you love to host dinner parties and fundraisers and pay great attention to the details of both. Do you feel that's accurate?"

"Why yes, yes I do. I think that's a perfect description of me," Betsy says.

"Mrs. Annenberg, I believe you're next. Would you please shuffle the deck and turn over the top card?"

Leonore does so. She turns over The Hanged Man.

"Oh my," says Leonore. "This must mean something dreadful is going to happen."

"No, not at all," explains Miss Carmine. "This card represents self-sacrifice. You must have made many sacrifices in your life—for your husbands, perhaps?"

"Why, yes. Yes, I have. Your reading is very accurate, my dear."

"I see you made great sacrifices for two of your husbands as well as for your current husband," Miss Carmine says.

Leonore blushes. "Yes, I have made sacrifices for all three."

"Your sacrifices, I would like you to know, Mrs. Annenberg, will bring you fame and fortune. You and your current husband will become known as great philanthropists, donating money to schools, charitable causes, and to the arts. Your third marriage will bring you only joy."

"Well, that is wonderful news. Thank you," says Leonore.

"Mrs. Reagan, I believe you are next. Would you please shuffle the deck and turn over the top card?"

Nancy does. She turns over The Empress.

"Ahh…The Empress," Miss Carmine says.

"Well, that's me for certain," Nancy laughs. "Ronnie treats me like an empress."

"The Empress, Mrs. Reagan, represents a mother figure, a creator, and a nurturer. Is that who you feel you are?"

"Why yes. Yes. Definitely. I do try to nurture people, especially Ronnie." She laughs.

"The Empress also denotes the love of fine clothes and beautiful surroundings. A word of warning about The Empress, however: often those individuals who are ruled by The Empress tend to follow the advice of others to a fault. I don't know exactly how that fits in with your life, Mrs. Reagan, but perhaps you know, or you will soon know."

"Why that's very interesting, Miss Carmine. Very interesting," Nancy says.

"And, Mrs. Wick, I believe you are next," Miss Carmine says as she hands over the deck of tarot cards.

Mary Jane Wick shuffles the cards and turns over the top one.

"Ahh, I see you have drawn The Magician," Miss Carmine says. "This card is associated with skill, diplomacy, subtlety, and self-confidence. I see you as being very successful, especially in the skill of fundraising."

"Oh my, Miss Carmine. I hope you are correct."

The women laugh. Miss Carmine does not.

"Those individuals who are ruled by The Magician are very talented. You are able to make the holidays magical, and friends and family will all look forward to spending them with you each year. Your fundraising, with the guidance of The Magician, will be largely devoted to the theater, where magicians love to perform, and also to land conservation. Your legacy in life will be your amazing ability to raise funds for worthy causes."

"So many of the things you just said are very accurate. I am really amazed at your talent, Miss Carmine," Mary Jane says.

Following the tarot card readings, Miss Carmine takes each woman aside to a smaller table to afford her some privacy while reading the group's palms. Leonore is told she will live a long, happy, and wealthy life. When she reads Nancy's palm, she is told of many glamorous dinner parties where she will wear amazing couture gowns and there will be powerful individuals in attendance. Mary Jane Wick is told she will be happily married far longer than any of her friends.

Betsy Bloomingdale is the last to have her palm read.

"Please hand me your right palm, Mrs. Bloomingdale." Betsy does. "I am going to interpret your life line, which is here, and the other lines of your palm—your wisdom line, love line, fate line, and marriage line," Miss Carmine explains to Betsy, pointing out the individual lines on her palm.

Betsy notices a concerned look on Miss Carmine's face as she examines her palm. She leans in close to Betsy's ear and whispers, "I'm sorry to tell you, but I fear your husband is quite ill. It has something to do with his voice. He will not be alive in two years. And after his death, his mistress will plague you."

"What? What did you say to me?" asks Betsy.

"Your husband is very ill," Miss Carmine says in a low voice, "and you will have trouble with his mistress following his death."

"Why, that's ridiculous," Betsy says as she stands up and walks away from the small table.

"Is anything wrong?" Leonore asks.

"No, no, nothing. It's just time for me to get going," Betsy says. "I think I just had a little too much to drink. It's been lovely, girls, but my driver is outside and I'm going to head out. It was a wonderful birthday party."

Betsy does not look back as she rushes toward the restaurant's exit.

"Do you think she's alright?" Leonore asks Nancy.

"Why yes, I'm sure she's fine."

Miss Carmine gathers up her cards and places them in her purse. Mary Jane pays her for her services, and all the women leave the restaurant.

*   *   *

When Betsy arrives home, she slams the front door, throws her purse on the couch, and storms into her husband's office. "You son of a bitch! You have ruined my life. Everyone knows about your affair with Vicki Morgan. Even the goddamn fortune teller at today's birthday party knows about her!"

Betsy believed her husband's affair had been well hidden from the public eye.

In 1969, Betsy's husband, Alfred Bloomingdale, then fifty-four years of age, began an affair with seventeen-year-old Vicki Morgan, whom he met at a restaurant on the Sunset Strip. In 1973, Betsy told him to break off the relationship, and Alfred complied with the request. He had provided Vicki with a lavish lifestyle over the years, including a substantial allowance, extravagant jewelry, and a luxurious apartment.

Soon after the affair ended, Vicki Morgan spiraled into poverty and depression. By 1979, she had been through three marriages and had become a drug addict. She entered rehabilitation and met a man also in treatment by the name of Marvin Pancoast. They vowed to live together after their treatment was complete.

*   *   *

In 1982, Alfred Bloomingdale is diagnosed with terminal throat cancer and tells Vicki he has only months to live. On February 12, 1982, he dictates two letters that spell out continued support for her, 'in the event of my incapacitation or absence.' Humiliated, Betsy finds out about the letters and promised payments, and, as Alfred lays dying, cancels the payments in June, 1982.

Alfred Bloomingdale dies of throat cancer on August 23, 1982. Following his death, Vicki Morgan hires the famous palimony attorney Marvin Mitchelson to file an eleven-million-dollar lawsuit against the Bloomingdale estate for financial compensation as Bloomingdale's mistress. Sordid details, including allegations of sado-masochistic activities, are revealed in the headlines:

"BLOOMINGDALE RIDES AND WHIPS NAKED PROSTITUTES"

– New York Post

"ALFRED S. BLOOMINGDALE - THE REAL MARQUIS DE SADE"

– The Washington Post

"ALFRED GAGS THEM, THEN THE FUN BEGINS"

– National Enquirer

Soon after the palimony lawsuit is filed, Morgan learns that Mitchelson had dinner and a meeting with President Ronald Reagan and his wife Nancy, who is close friends with Betsy Bloomingdale. Morgan loses trust in Mitchelson, fires him, and instead, hires attorney Robert Steinberg. During the trial, Morgan refers to a letter in which Alfred Bloomindale says he will give her $240,000.

In 1982, Vicki Morgan is awarded $40,000 in the palimony suit. The amount of the award is contested; however, the lawsuit is largely dismissed in 1983.

That same year, Vicki Morgan moves into an apartment with Marvin Pancoast and returns to work in the sex trade. After living together for only three weeks, on July 7, 1983, Pancoast beats Vicki to death with a baseball bat.

In December 1984, a jury awards the Morgan estate the remaining $200,000.

CHAPTER 47

THE ASSASSINATION ATTEMPT
OF RONALD REAGAN

March 30, 1981

President Reagan has just finished meeting with labor representatives at the Washington Hilton Hotel and is walking with his entourage to his limousine. He takes his silver pocket watch out of his front pants pocket to check the time, but the watch begins to vibrate and falls out of the president's hand. He bends down to retrieve it just when John Hinckley Jr., a troubled twenty-five-year-old man, fires six shots at him. Hinckley's bullets hit Reagan and three of his attendants. White House Press Secretary, James Brady, is shot in the head and critically wounded. Secret Service agent Timothy McCarthy is shot in the side, and District of Columbia policeman Thomas Delahanty is shot in the neck. After firing the shots, Hinckley is overpowered and pinned against a wall. President Reagan, unaware he's been shot, is shoved into his limousine by a Secret Service agent and rushed to George Washington University Hospital.

Just prior to going into the operating room, the president says, "Please tell me you're Republicans." Reagan's surgery lasts two hours, and afterwards he is listed in stable and then in good condition.

While in the hospital, the president explains to Nancy that he was bent over, picking up his pocket watch, which had fallen onto the sidewalk, when the shooting began. Ronald tells Nancy his doctors informed him that if he had not been bending over, he would have been shot in the heart and would certainly not be alive.

"Well Ronnie, it sounds to me like the watch just might have saved your life."

"Yes, Mommy. I think you're right."

CHAPTER 48

JOAN QUIGLEY AND
NANCY REAGAN

April 15, 1981

After graduating from Vassar College, Joan Quigley writes an astrology column for *Seventeen* magazine. From 1972 to 1985, Miss Quigley appears as a regular guest on the syndicated talk show of her client, Merv Griffin. A thin, quick-witted woman with blonde hair worn in the classic bouffant style, she is the ideal guest for daytime television.

Merv Griffin informs Nancy Reagan that his astrologer, Miss Quigley, has guided his decisions through the last ten years and has been very accurate in her predictions. He attributes his successful life to her, and, at his suggestion, Nancy contacts her.

"Hello, Miss Quigley, I'm not certain if you will remember me, but we met one time on the set of *The Merv Griffin Show* quite a few years ago now. This is Nancy Reagan. I hope you don't mind my calling you. Merv was kind enough to give me your telephone number. You don't mind that he shared it with me, do you?"

"Oh, Mrs. Reagan, of course not. And yes, I remember you. I understand your husband has just recently been released from the hospital."

"Yes, that's true. It was horrible, absolutely horrible. Now I am just petrified of even thinking of letting him leave the White House. Miss Quigley, I know Merv trusts you and relies on your predictions."

"Yes, he does."

"Do you believe you could have foreseen, and possibly prevented, the assassination attempt on my husband?" Nancy asks.

There is a moment's pause, then Joan responds, "Yes, of course I could have prevented it. If I had consulted my charts, I definitely could have prevented it."

"Really? Actually prevented it? Why that's remarkable, Joan, just remarkable."

"Yes," Joan replies. "My charts are always accurate."

"Well, would you mind terribly, then, allowing me to become one of your clients? Nothing more can happen to my Ronnie, absolutely nothing more. Neither of us could survive it."

"Of course, Mrs. Reagan. We must keep him safe at all cost. That's the most important thing. I would be happy to help you and President Reagan," she responds.

"This would have to be our secret, of course," Nancy says. "I used to consult Jeane Dixon and was fairly satisfied with her guidance. I also met once with a marvelous fortune teller in New York years ago. She was really amazing. However, I don't even know if she is still in business…But you have been highly recommended, and I'm grateful that you will help us through these dangerous times. Very few people can understand what it's like to have your husband shot and almost die, and then to have him constantly exposed to enormous crowds, tens of thousands of people, any one of whom might be a lunatic with a gun."

"Oh, my dear, of course I understand," Joan says. "I would like to explain, however, that Jeane and I are quite different in our techniques and predictions. I do political astrology, which means I chart full moons, new moons, eclipses, and cycle charts of the major planets to predict the political decisions and influences in Washington. By the way, Mrs. Reagan, do you remember the name of the fortune teller you met with in New York?" Joan asks.

"Why, yes. Her name was Madam Genova. Have you heard of her? Do you happen to know her?" Nancy asks.

"Yes, yes I do. I respect her abilities and think she is quite talented. We speak with each other periodically," Joan says.

There are a few moments of silence. "Do you happen to know whether or not Madam Genova is still working with clients?" Nancy asks.

After a short pause, Joan replies, "No, I don't know."

The silence continues, then Nancy says, "Well Joan, I am delighted to be one of your clients. I know we can work well together."

"Mrs. Reagan, I, too, think we will work together beautifully. I don't know if you're aware of this or not, but I worked on the president's campaign in 1980 because he had the most brilliant horoscope I'd ever seen. Your husband could have been a great general. His sun is in the mid-heaven, so his stars are very lucky for our country."

"Why, Joan, that's wonderful to know, very reassuring."

"Yes, Mrs. Reagan, we must protect the president at all costs. If you listen to my guidance, I will make certain you both are kept safe."

"Joan, I will be paying you through a third party, just to ensure our privacy," Nancy explains. "I would like to consult with you on the phone, initially at least, every week—actually, whenever I need your assistance. I can assure you that you will be well compensated. I could give you a retainer of, say, $3,000 each month? Would that be satisfactory to you?"

"I will do whatever I can to assist you, Mrs. Reagan," Joan replies. "Why don't we plan to speak on Saturday afternoons? Then I will be able to help with the president's schedule."

"Wonderful. I will call you at three o'clock next Saturday," Nancy informs Joan. "The president has a press conference coming up soon, and I want to make certain it goes smoothly."

"Of course, Mrs. Reagan. I will wait for your call on Saturday."

"Oh wait, Joan, what if I happen to need to speak with you during the week?"

"That will be fine. But if I have to reschedule one of my current clients or need to spend more time reviewing my charts for you and the president, I will have to charge you extra. Do you understand?"

"Yes, Joan. I understand."

CHAPTER 49

NANCY'S CALL TO JOAN

April 18, 1981

"Joan, this is Nancy."

"Mrs. Reagan, thank you for being so prompt."

"Oh, of course. I am always prompt and will expect you to be the same."

Silence.

"Well, let's begin," says Joan. "I will need some details from you first. When and where were you born, and do you happen to know the exact time of your birth?"

"I was born on July 6, 1921, in New York City. I believe it was at three o'clock in the morning," Nancy says.

"Oh my goodness, you and I have the same birthday."

"Now that is a strange coincidence, isn't it?" Nancy says. "Perhaps I was destined to have you as my astrologer."

"Yes, Mrs. Reagan, I believe that's true," Joan replies. "And when was the president born?"

"He was born on February 6, 1911, in Tampico, Illinois. He was born at five fifteen in the afternoon. It may seem strange that I would know that, but Jeane Dixon needed the same information."

"Astrology, as you probably already know, Mrs. Reagan, must incorporate the cosmos. The Earth, the individual person, and the environment must be viewed as a single organism, and all of these aspects correlate with one another," Joan explains. "Cycles that change in the universe are reflective of similar cycles observed on Earth and within the individual. Mathematical relationships of energy which manifest in numbers, visual angles, shapes, and sounds are all connected within a pattern of proportion. My use of astrology incorporates the constellations, through which the Sun, Moon, and planets move on their journeys across the sky. My charts reveal the impact of the twelve signs of the zodiac.

"So I see you were born under the sign of Cancer and the president was born under the sign of Aquarius. Very interesting. You rule the moon, and President Reagan rules Saturn. You are probably aware of this, but the president has the traits of wisdom, stability, and persistence. He runs some risk of accident, disease, and bad luck. We know this is true because of his recent assassination attempt, now don't we?"

"Yes, I suppose that's true," Nancy answers.

"Your nature, Mrs. Reagan, is associated with wandering. I am able to see that you love to travel. Is that true?"

"Oh, my, yes. I do love to travel, that's correct."

"I can see clearly now that I will be able to help you schedule all of your husband's events in order to keep him safe. It is imperative that you call me every week to go over his schedule. I will study my charts and let you know just when the planets are in their correct orbit and the zodiac signs are aligned.

"And regarding the president's upcoming press conference, Mrs. Reagan, be certain the death of Eddie Sauter and the minor league baseball game between the Rochester Red Wings and the Pawtucket Red Sox are both mentioned at the beginning of his speech."

"Oh my goodness, Eddie Sautor? The great jazz composer died?" Nancy asks.

"Not yet. Just be certain the president mentions it in his speech next week."

"Well, sure…sure. I'll make certain he mentions it…and the baseball thing," says Nancy. "Let me write this all down. Oh, and there is one more thing, Joan. I was given a silver pocket watch by a dear friend years ago. She told me it brought her great luck. I gave the pocket watch as a gift to the president just before he was elected, so I have to think it might just do what my friend said it does."

Nancy pauses for a moment and then continues. "And I know you might think this is silly, but I also think it saved his life during the assassination attempt. Would you mind terribly taking a look at it and letting me know what you think?"

"I'd be glad to look at it for you."

"Wonderful. I'll have my secretary drop it off at your home," Nancy says.

*   *   *

While Joan waits for Mrs. Reagan's secretary to deliver the pocket watch, she sits at her kitchen table looking around at the outdated room. *I remember when I used to be happy with my avocado green oven and refrigerator*, she thinks to herself. *They just don't seem to go with the flowered wallpaper anymore.* She is interrupted by the doorbell.

After retrieving the package, Joan returns to her kitchen table, unwraps the package, and examines the silver pocket watch with the aid of her round, brass magnifying glass.

The initials 'HTJ' are engraved on the inside of the casing. After a few moments she feels a slight vibration, then the watch becomes very warm—too warm to hold. She drops it on the table and studies it for another hour. Joan calls the First Lady.

CHAPTER 50

JOAN'S CALL TO NANCY

April 18, 1981

"Hello Nancy? This is Joan."

"Well good evening, Joan. It's unusual for you to call me, especially this late. Is anything wrong?"

"Mrs. Reagan, I know we don't usually speak with each other during the week or in the evening, but it was important that I call. It's regarding the pocket watch you sent over. I've studied it carefully. It...it's a beautiful watch indeed, finely made with the most exquisite materials. But I feel a very powerful spell was placed on this watch many years ago. Although I was not able to discern the exact spell, I sense the watch has had both a blessing and a curse placed upon it, and I don't believe either spell can be removed. Also, and I know this must sound strange, but the watch seems to be seeking something. My best advice is to keep the watch close. I sense if you do, it will provide some luck; however, if it is lost or abandoned, I fear there may be serious consequences."

"Oh my goodness. Why, you're frightening me, Joan. And I'm trying to understand just what you're telling me.

A blessing and a curse? And what do you mean by 'conse-quences'?" Nancy asks.

"You know I am able to see and predict most things; how-ever, this watch has such a powerful aura, like a soul longing for something...And I realize that sounds bizarre, something mechanical having a soul. I am just not able to tell you exactly what the spell means. I do feel luck emanating from the watch, but I also sense the presence of harm. Again, I would advise keeping it close."

"Well harm is the last thing I want happening to Ronnie and me. I'll have to get rid of the watch."

"I strongly recommend against that, Mrs. Reagan. You should not get rid of the watch."

There are a few moments of silence.

"Joan, thank you for calling and for letting me know. I'll have my secretary pick up the watch tomorrow, and I'll make sure the president takes good care of it and keeps it close."

CHAPTER 51

THE WHITE HOUSE DINNER

April 19, 1981

"I told the chef to make macaroni and cheese for dinner tonight," Nancy says, throwing her hands up in frustration. "That's what the president wants, macaroni and cheese. How difficult could that be?"

"I apologize, ma'am," the butler says. "I know we had our sous-chef go to two different supermarkets trying to find the correct cheese, but neither had it. I apologize, ma'am."

"Well, for God's sake, Lawrence, don't let it happen again," Nancy says.

"Yes ma'am," Lawrence says. "Oh, and I have one request for you."

"Yes, what is it?" Nancy asks.

"If you could give us a little more notice about what you'd like for dinner, well, that would be very helpful. Sometimes two hours just isn't enough."

"What? What did you say to me, Lawrence?"

"Nothing, ma'am."

"No, tell me. What did you say to me?"

"I just wanted to mention, ma'am, that sometimes we need a little more time to find the proper ingredients for a specific dish that you or the president may desire, so if you could give us a little more time to find them, the kitchen staff would greatly appreciate it."

Nancy puts her silverware down on her plate and sits up straight. "Lawrence, do you know who I am?"

President Reagan cowers and lowers his head a little closer to his dinner plate. He continues eating.

"Yes ma'am," Lawrence says.

"Well, who am I?"

"You're the First Lady, ma'am. The First Lady of the White House."

"And do you know what that means, Lawrence?" Nancy asks.

"Yes ma'am."

"What does that mean?"

"It means you can have any meal you would like."

"Yes. That's correct. And do I need to give you more time to find ingredients?"

"No ma'am, I suppose not. I apologize for being so rude."

"That's correct. And that is all, Lawrence. Please leave the room. I don't want to see any more of you this evening."

After all the dishes are served, Nancy requests that the rest of the waitstaff leave the room.

"Well, I hope we don't have any more sass from that young man," Nancy says to the president.

"I don't think we will."

"If we do, if I hear one more sassy word coming from his mouth, he'll be gone. I think he'll be very easy to replace. In fact, I might just replace him anyway. What do you think, Ronnie?"

"Anything you'd like to do, I am fine with, Mommy."

"Oh, and Ronnie, I need to talk to you about something. You know Ron is going to be performing in another ballet soon. We've never gone to see him, and I think we should."

"When will he be prancing around on the stage?" the president asks.

"Now Ronnie, you probably shouldn't say things like that. You can say that to me, of course, when we're alone, but don't say it where the staff can hear you. You know there are a couple of queer individuals who work in the White House. Actually, my newest decorator is a queer man."

"Well, as long as they stay in the closet, I don't mind so much. But prancing around on a stage? Isn't that kind of announcing it to the world?"

"What does it really matter?" Nancy asks.

"It matters because I have very conservative friends, and very Christian supporters."

"Oh Ronnie. The world already knows Ron is strange. He's an atheist, for God's sake. So what if he's queer? I know, I'll ask Joan what we should do. His performance is on May eighteenth. Joan will let us know what to do."

"Well, Mommy, I think it's a mistake for us to attend, but whatever you say, I'll do."

"By the way, do you have your pocket watch with you?" Nancy asks. "I had someone pick it up from Joan's house today. She said it was important for you to keep it with you at all times."

"Yes, Mommy. I have it right here in my pocket, just like you told me to do."

CHAPTER 52

NANCY SEEKS JOAN'S ADVICE

May 1, 1981

"Joan, as you probably know, our son Ron has always been a strange boy. When he was twelve years old, he informed us he was an atheist and said he would no longer attend church services. And then he got kicked out of school…Anyway, that's another story."

"Is that why you are calling? I don't quite understand," Joan says.

"No, no. I just need your advice. I don't know if you've read much about our son or heard much about him, but he dropped out of Yale about five years ago to become a ballet dancer…of all things, a ballet dancer. Can you imagine? Well, you probably can't. Anyway, he dances with the Joffrey II Dancers, which is apparently a troupe for beginning dancers, but that's beside the point. The president and I have never attended any of his performances…that is, any of his ballet performances, and he has one coming up very soon. With how many very conservative friends we have, we are quite embarrassed, as you can imagine, that our son has chosen that profession. What do you think we should do? Should we attend?" Nancy asks.

"Let me examine my charts. When is the performance scheduled to take place?"

"May eighteenth. It will be on May eighteenth at the Lisner Auditorium," Nancy says.

"Well, let me look closely at my charts and I will call you back," Joan says.

Two hours later, Joan calls Nancy. "My charts tell me that you and the president should attend—you should show your support. Your lack of support, I see in my charts, appears to be worse in the eyes of the general public than acknowledging you have a queer son."

"A queer son? Who said anything about a queer son?" Nancy asks.

There are a few moments of silence.

"You should attend the performance, Mrs. Reagan," Joan says.

"Well, okay then, I'll get tickets for us. I certainly hope your charts are correct."

"I'm certain they are."

CHAPTER 53

NANCY REAGAN

July 11, 1981

"Joan, today my question for you is, what is the best time for Ronnie to begin his press conference on Tuesday? It's very important that he make a good impression on the press."

"Ahh," Joan says. "Let me look carefully at my charts. It might take me a moment. Let me see here."

"At exactly seven oh three p.m., Mars will just be completing its orbit around the sun and the timing will be perfect. He must begin his speech then. However, he must complete his speech by exactly eight ten p.m., which means he must leave the East Room at that time. The East Room will be full, and the men from the press will still be asking questions, but he must be told not to take any more questions after eight ten."

*   *   *

July 14, 1981

Nancy accompanies the president to the entrance of the East Room. "I love you, Ronnie," she says.

"I love you, too, Mommy."

"Do you have your lucky pocket watch with you?" Nancy asks.

"Of course," he says, placing his hand over his left front pants pocket.

"Good luck, sweetheart," Nancy says as she watches him enter the room.

The Deputy White House Press Secretary Larry Speakes introduces the president to the members of the press, and he begins his speech at exactly 7:03 p.m.

President Reagan gives a soft-spoken speech and discusses world politics along with comments about Joe Montana getting married, John McEnroe and Chris Evert winning their matches at Wimbledon, and his nomination of Sandra Day O'Connor for Supreme Court Justice. He answers a few questions and leaves the East Room of the White House promptly at 8:10 p.m.

The next morning, Nancy reads the newspaper and finds that the press has labeled her husband 'The Great Communicator.'

CHAPTER 54

NANCY'S WEEKLY CALL
TO JOAN

May 1982

"Good morning, Mrs. Reagan. I have looked at my charts today and I see some very exciting news ahead."

"Exciting news? Well, what do your charts say? Is Ronnie safe? Oh, and when should I schedule Air Force One to take off this afternoon?"

"Let me see here now. When the moon is in the Seventh House and Jupiter aligns with Mars, then peace will guide the planets and love will steer the stars. It looks like it's the dawning of Aquarius."

"The dawning of what?" Nancy asks.

"The dawning of Aquarius. You remember that your husband was born under the sign of Aquarius, correct?"

"Well, yes. Yes, of course," Nancy replies.

"I see harmony and understanding…oh, and sympathy and trust abounding. Today you will not hear any falsehoods or derisions, and you will only see golden living dreams of visions. Your mind will be liberated with your own thoughts."

"Oh, my, well that does sound like good news," Nancy says. "But what did you say about the moon being in the Seventh House, or something like that?"

"Why, yes, that's exactly what I said."

"That...that sounds quite familiar...That phrase...It sounds familiar to me, like I've heard it before. I'm almost certain I've heard that phrase before," Nancy says.

"Mrs. Reagan, I have told you in the past that when something sounds familiar, it must be true, haven't I?"

"Well, yes, yes, you're correct."

"Perhaps you have heard these words from the spirits that surround us," Joan explains. "If that's so, it's a very good sign— an assurance that what I am telling you, what I am predicting, will come true. My charts are very accurate. Today they indicate Saturn is approaching too close to the sun, and some significantly disruptive individuals with strong influence in the White House must be severely disciplined. It shows they must be fired. You will know who they are, however, you must pose as the president's devoted wife, someone who cares nothing about policy or politics. Nevertheless, you must plan carefully and ensure their departure as soon as you detect their malicious influence...And have the president's plane take off at exactly two twenty-nine p.m. today."

CHAPTER 55

THE DISMISSALS

June 5, 1982

"Mrs. Reagan, the past two days' cosmic weather feels like it has been ramping up to the intensity of tonight's moon. Mars will be in conjunction with Aries. The months ahead may host some cathartic outbursts of anger that feel like they have been building up for some time. This catharsis may be ultimately healing and pressure-relieving, but it could also inadvertently cause some of us to say things we'll later regret. Anger is real, and often justified, yet there are compassionate ways to handle it. You will need to be wary of those that attempt to harm you and the president, especially those who work closely with you," Joan advises.

Over the next few years, Nancy proceeds to fire or manipulate a resignation for:

- Her chief of staff, Peter McCoy, for not changing her negative public image.
- Assistant to the President, Joe Canzeri, for double billing two expense-account dinners to the White House

and the Republican National Committee and accepting a below-market home loan from banking friends.

- Secretary of State, Alexander Haig, for being too excitable and always demanding priority seating on Air Force One.

- U.S. Ambassador to Great Britain, John Louis, for being absent from London during the Falklands War.

- White House photographer, Karl Schumacher, for double-exposing a roll of film containing photos of Frank Sinatra that she had wanted to give to the *Washington Post*.

- Secretary of Interior, James Watt, for being too politically conservative and for banning the Beach Boys from singing on the Mall.

- Mona Charen, for not being subservient enough.

- Secretary of Interior, William P. Clark, for being too politically conservative and not acceptable to Mike Deaver.

- U.S. Ambassador to Austria, Helene von Damm, for showing too much cleavage and for having too many husbands.

- Press Secretary, Jennifer Hirshberg, for being too pretty and drawing more press coverage than she does.

Numerous other firings for minor misdeeds follow, and the entire White House staff realizes it is the First Lady they must kowtow to in order to keep their jobs.

CHAPTER 56

THE MISGUIDED TRIP
TO BERGEN-BELSEN

May 1, 1985

The president and his staff make plans to attend the Economic Summit in Bonn, Germany, and there soon follows a news release stating President Reagan plans to visit the little cemetery in Bitburg, West Germany as a side excursion.

The president decides against making a ceremonial trip to a German concentration camp because Nancy views such a trip as 'too negative and depressing.'

Reagan promises instead to visit a cemetery, which Henkel, the leader of the White House advance team, has checked out. Within the cemetery, however, are the graves of forty-nine Nazi storm troopers. Even after the president is informed, he insists on honoring the site and is widely condemned for his insensitivity to the Holocaust. Jewish groups in the United States, Europe, and the Soviet Union demonstrate against him. Many World War II veterans return their medals.

Reagan responds by stating, "We have to put the past behind us. The soldiers buried in Bitburg were victims, just as surely as the victims in the concentration camps."

But this statement only provokes further bursts of outrage, including two resolutions introduced in the House of Representatives asking him not to visit the cemetery, coupled with a similar resolution signed by fifty-three senators.

Reagan, who fancies himself a hero to the Jewish people, cannot understand the outrage.

Elie Wiesel, who grew up in the death camps and lost his parents in Auschwitz, accepts the Congressional Gold Medal of Achievement from Reagan in April, then pleads with him on national television not to lend his presence to the German military cemetery.

Nancy is furious at Wiesel for shaming her husband in public, but she, too, pleads with him to cancel the trip to the cemetery because the polls show that a majority of Americans disapprove of the president's decision to lay a wreath at Bitburg. This is the first great crisis in the Reagan presidency. Reagan's approval rating plummets in the polls.

Nancy tries to salvage something out of the mess and plans a side trip to the concentration camp at Bergen-Belsen, where Anne Frank died.

The First Lady insists that the timing of their visits to the concentration camp and to the small German cemetery be synchronized with the stars. Joan Quigley is consulted and a revised schedule is submitted. Joan tells Nancy that the trip to Bergen-Belsen must be made at 11:45 a.m. on May 5, 1985, because of "the positive position of the planets." She says she picked 2:45 p.m. for the eight-minute ceremony at Bitburg because her charts of the zodiac indicated that "the moon and

Saturn were in the third house, while Neptune, on the angle of the chart, veiled the occasion and dimmed it."

Just prior to stepping onto Air Force One, Nancy asks Ronnie whether or not he has his silver pocket watch with him. He does.

The newspapers and magazines feature cover photographs of the president laying a wreath at Bergen-Belsen, not at Bitburg, which reinforces the First Lady's faith in her astrologer, who claimed she would "fix up the Bitburg thing."

CHAPTER 57

THE WHITE HOUSE

October 20, 1986

William Henkel is in charge of the White House advance team, and has input on all scheduling decisions, meaning he knows about Nancy's astrologer.

Every weekend, Henkel is paged on his beeper, indicating that Nancy is trying to reach him and is ready to discuss the president's schedule. She sits in her cabin at Camp David with a phone in each hand—Joan Quigley on one, Henkel on the other—and they begin charting the president's upcoming events. Nancy proceeds on a day-by-day, hour-by-hour basis, sometimes fine-tuning arrivals and departures to the minute. She receives the advanced activities from Henkel and relays them to Quigley, who checks each date on her zodiac chart to see whether the stars predict a good or a bad day for the president. On the 'bad' days, he is not to leave the White House, because, according to Joan, he could be harmed. Then Henkel has to propose alternate dates. The three of them go back and forth for hours, with Henkel keeping scrupulous notes of each session so he can avoid "the threat days where you have to be careful" and capitalize on "the good days—the okay-to-travel days."

"Mommy, I wish you wouldn't keep doing these consultations with Joan Quigley. It might look very odd if it comes out in the press," the president warns. "But if it makes you feel better, go ahead and do it."

CHAPTER 58

THE LOSS OF THE SILVER
POCKET WATCH

November 1, 1986

"Ronnie, I haven't seen your Boy Scout pocket watch in a while. Where did you put it?" Nancy asks.

"My what, Mommy? You haven't seen what in a while?"

"Your Boy Scout pocket watch. Your pocket watch. Remember, that silver watch with the beautiful painting inside? Where is it?"

"A watch? What watch? I don't know what you're talking about," the president says.

"You've lost the watch? That beautiful watch? Oh, Ronnie. I'd help you look, but I have a call with Joan in fifteen minutes."

CHAPTER 59

NANCY'S CALL WITH JOAN

November 1, 1986

"Hello, Nancy. I'm sorry to inform you, but the news on the horizon, I'm afraid, is not looking good."

"Well what's wrong? What do you see? What can we do, Joan?"

"I see the moon is attracting Pluto at ten a.m. By mid-day, Venus will leave passionate and dramatic Leo to enter earthy, analytical Virgo. Venus, the planet of love and attraction, will be in receptive Virgo until December twenty-seventh. Until then, we may be working on refining our balance and tuning back into our health routines. We may also be perfecting our communications in our relationships and putting to order any unrealistic expectations. However, I feel some very bad news will arrive in the next forty-eight hours. Unfortunately, Mrs. Reagan, the pull from the moon is so strong we are helpless against its force."

"Joan," Nancy says, "the president has lost his watch."

"He's what?" asks Joan.

"His watch, he's lost his silver pocket watch. I just found out about it."

Silence.

"That is terrible news," Joan says. "Have you asked your staff to look for it?"

"Yes. I have just screamed at them to find it. They know they *must* find it. I have even gone so far as to offer a large reward. But so far, no luck."

CHAPTER 60

PREPARING TO MEET MIKHAIL GORBACHEV

November 2, 1986

Nancy and the White House Staff begin to notice the president's mental health deteriorating. He forgets to put in his hearing aids, cannot find his glasses, and looks tired and bewildered. The president flounders his way through responses and fumbles with his notes. Oftentimes he is at an uncharacteristic loss for words.

Nancy believes seeking an arms-control summit with Soviet leader Mikhail Gorbachev will bolster the president's declining reputation in his second term.

When the president's aides give him a detailed agenda for his first meeting with Gorbachev, Reagan does not look at it.

"Have you shown this to Nancy?" he asks.

"No sir," the aide replies.

"Well," Reagan says, "get back to me after she's approved it."

CHAPTER 61

THE IRAN-CONTRA AFFAIR

March 17, 1988

Nancy and Ronald get ready for bed in their master bedroom suite on the second floor of the White House. Nancy places cold cream on her face while sitting at her dressing table dressed in her blue satin nightgown and matching robe. Ronald is in bed reading *Time* magazine.

"I just can't believe all those lies that have been uncovered and published in that Beirut newspaper," Nancy says.

"What newspaper?"

"You know, the Beirut newspaper, *Al Shiraa*. And the scheme William Casey confessed to being involved in during today's Daily Briefing. You remember, the article about the arms shipments and McFarlane's Iran visit."

"Oh yes, Mommy. But I wouldn't worry about it. It's all so complicated, I'm certain everyone will forget about it soon and we'll move on."

"Move on? I don't think so, Ronnie. This whole mess could easily be blown out of proportion."

"Oh, Mommy, you worry too much. This whole incident will be back page news by next week."

"I really don't think so, Ronnie. If Donald Regan ever gets questioned about this," Nancy warns, "you are in big trouble. He attends all of your daily national security briefings, and he knows far too much. And goddamn it, Ronnie, he writes everything down. I'm terribly afraid he will end up confessing to your role in the cover up. He'll tell the world you were involved in the shipment of missiles to Iran."

The article in *Al Shiraa* revealed a clandestine plot carried out by the Reagan administration. Americans were being held hostage by Hezbollah, an ally of Iran, in Lebanon. The Reagan Administration and CIA Director William Casey along with the National Security Council Advisor, Oliver North, secretly arranged for an arms-for-hostage deal with one of its bitterest enemies in the Middle East, Iran.

As part of the negotiations, Israel sold weapons from the U.S. to Iran—which had been designated a State Sponsor of Terrorism in 1984 and subjected to an arms embargo—in exchange for the release of the American hostages.

Following the release of the hostages, North and Casey began funneling the profits from the arms sales into another illegal venture, a secret plan to support the Contras—the militants in Nicaragua which opposed the communist Sandinistas. This act was in direct defiance of the Boland Amendments, which Congress had passed from 1982 to 1984, specifically prohibiting the U.S. from supporting the Contras.

Following the publication of the article in *Al Shiraa*, Oliver North destroys pertinent documents, and Attorney General Edwin Meese admits that profits from the weapons sales were sent to aid the Contras. National Security Advisor John Poindexter resigns, and President Reagan fires Oliver North. Congressional investigations soon follow. Widespread criticism and outrage over the scheme force President Reagan to apologize on national television on March 4, 1987, and the president's approval rating falls to 44%.

Nancy is beside herself. *What happened to that goddamned lucky watch?* she wonders.

CHAPTER 62

JOAN'S WARNING

May 3, 1988

" Mrs. Reagan, I thought I should call you. Unfortunately, I see more trouble ahead. In the middle to late afternoon, the moon in headstrong Aries forms another square aspect, this time with Pluto in authoritative Capricorn. The heated lunar moon clashes with the planet of immense change, and transformation and emotional power struggles may erupt to the surface near the end of the workday. This square aspect may trigger a conflict with someone in your life or be experienced as an inner dialogue of unease and frustration."

*　　*　　*

"ASTROLOGY IN THE WHITE HOUSE"

– *Time*

Donald Regan serves as White House Chief of Staff under President Reagan from 1985 to 1987, but after numerous battles with Nancy over decisions she has made on behalf of the president, including the Iran-Contra affair, he is forced to leave D.C. and return to New York.

In May of 1988, White House spokesman Marlin Fitzwater announces at a press conference that First Lady Nancy Reagan has consulted an astrologer on the president's travel and scheduling plans.

He sets the tone for this announcement at the White House briefing, which he begins by saying that he will "take your first question at exactly 12:33 and a half." After responding to seventy questions on the issue, Fitzwater concludes the briefing by reading the horoscope of Donald Regan in *The Washington Post* on February 27, 1987—the day he was forced out under pressure from the First Lady and replaced by Howard H. Baker Jr.

The horoscope for Regan, whose zodiac sign is Sagittarius, reads, "You'll complete assignment. A burden will be lifted from your shoulders. You will grasp spiritual meanings. Events occur which place you on more solid emotional, financial ground. Be confident."

Asked whether he believes in astrology, the divorced Fitzwater says, "Only when it agrees with my preconceived thought—I'll believe it when it says I'm destined to meet a beautiful woman and fall in love and become rich."

*   *   *

January 14, 1989

"Joan, I hate to even ask, everything has been so dismal lately, but what is in store for the president and me over the next week? What plans should we make?"

"Well, I'm afraid you are correct, Nancy," Joan replies. "There is not much good news ahead. I have consulted all my charts and see the fiery moon is in a challenging aspect to Jupiter. It may highlight some early morning frustrations or impatience with the realities of delayed progress.

"Late tonight, the moon will make its last appearance before leaving fiery Aries, forming a square with Saturn in disciplined Capricorn. Saturn is the planet of limitations, and Capricorn is the sign of building structures. After two days of hot-button topics and frustrations, tonight's square challenges us to form new emotional boundaries to reign in potential reactivity. Many of us feel frustrated and on the defensive, but tonight we face the ways that we may have to let our emotional fires burn out of control. The moon, void of a true course, begins moving erratically until Monday morning. You will feel great anger and great loss over the next week, I'm afraid."

CHAPTER 63

GETTING READY TO LEAVE THE WHITE HOUSE

January 18, 1989

Nancy Reagan walks aimlessly around the China Room, stopping to gaze at the various patterns of china and mumbling to herself. President Reagan quietly walks up beside her and touches her arm.

She is startled.

"So here's where you are. I couldn't find you. Come on, Mommy, let's go," he says.

A Secret Service Agent watches discreetly, ten feet away.

CHAPTER 64

G.H.W. BUSH BECOMES PRESIDENT

January 21, 1989

President George H.W. Bush, the 41st President of the United States, is sworn into office on Friday, January 20, 1989. The next day, the Reagans' furniture, clothing, and personal items are quickly and efficiently removed from the White House.

Barbara Bush, the new First Lady, supervises her family's move into the residence. "Millie, Millie, come here. Come over here. Leave those men alone. You are right in the way and you're going to get hurt. Come over here, sweet girl. Oh you are such a good girl."

The small tan and white dog trots over to Barbara.

"That's a fine-lookin' dog you've got there, ma'am. What kind is she?" the mover asks.

"She's an English Springer Spaniel, and thank you. She's my love," Barbara says, bending down and patting Millie on the head.

Barbara continues to supervise the placement of the various pieces of furniture as they are arranged in the different rooms of the White House. When she walks into the Oval Office Study—the small working space immediately across from the Oval Office—she notices Millie sniffing at something behind a large bookcase. Barbara picks Millie up, moves her out of the way, and looks to see what Millie has found. She sees a shiny object on the floor behind the bookcase and is able to push the large piece of furniture slightly away from the wall, giving her just enough room to reach behind it and retrieve the object.

It's a silver pocket watch. She opens it, sees the tents, trees, and river painted on the face, then examines the letters on the dials and on the rim and recognizes it as a Boy Scout watch.

CHAPTER 65

BREAKFAST
AT THE WHITE HOUSE

January 22, 1989

B arbara and George sit across from each other at the long dining room table reading articles from the newspapers stacked neatly in front of them. Millie is asleep at Barbara's feet.

The White House staff serves them breakfast at 8:00. Steaming coffee presented in tall white china mugs and ice-cold orange juice in fine crystal stemware are placed on the neatly pressed linen tablecloth. Barbara is served first—a stack of buttermilk pancakes with a large dollop of butter on top and maple syrup dripping over the sides; for George, a plate of thickly cut bacon, scrambled eggs, and biscuits slathered with butter and honey.

Three waiters, all in well-starched uniforms, stand against the wall, facing the table and waiting for orders while trying not to intrude.

George looks up from his newspaper. "Hey, Bar. I need you to do me a favor. Jeb is arriving around three to watch the Super Bowl with me. Gee, I hope he's not going to be late.

Anyway, I made a bet with him. I've taken the 49ers and given him ten points."

"He's not staying in Miami to watch the game?"

"Heck no. Miami's going to be a nightmare...crazy town. He's getting out of Dodge."

"Well, that's nice. Is Columba coming with him?"

"No, she's staying in Florida. You think giving him ten points is risky?" George asks. "I thought so at first, but I really think the 49ers will beat the Bengals. Bill Walsh is great, and *Joe Montana*? I know Joe won't let me down. I love that guy. Hey, maybe we should invite him to the White House for dinner. What do you think? That would really be something."

"Invite who?"

"Joe, Joe Montana," he says.

"Sure, sure, we'll invite him," Barbara replies.

"So, anyway, will you make sure the tamales, chili, and the fajitas—oh, yes, and the guacamole and everything else is ready tonight around five? Jesus, I hope the tamales turn out okay. This is the first time the chef is making them, so fingers crossed. Right? Anyway, the food needs to be good and hot. Would you take care of that, hon?"

"Of course, dear. I'll make sure the food is perfect. Oh, George, I almost forgot to give you this." Barbara takes the silver watch out of her shirt pocket. "Look what I found in the Oval Office Study yesterday. It's a Boy Scout watch. Isn't it lovely?" She opens the watch.

George looks up from his newspaper. "Yes, yes, very lovely."

"Weren't you a Cub Scout about a thousand years ago?" she asks.

"Yes, well it wasn't quite a thousand years ago."

"So, do you like the watch? Are you going to keep it?"

"Sure, sure, Bar. Listen, I'm really focused here on this article about Joe Montana right now. Why don't you just put the watch in the dresser drawer in our bedroom?"

"Okay, George." She places the watch back in her skirt pocket, and both return to their newspapers.

"It just seems I like this watch a little more than you do," Barbara says under her breath.

"Sure, Bar, sure, anything you say," he says as he continues to read his paper.

Barbara begins reading an article in the *New York Times* about Nelson Mandela and apartheid in South Africa. Mandela remains in Victor Verster Prison in the Western Cape of South Africa. She learns Mandela has been in prison now for almost twenty-six years, sentenced to life for conspiring to overthrow the government. He was moved to Victor Verster Prison from Pollsmore Prison due to a diagnosis of tuberculosis that was exacerbated by the damp conditions in his cell. According to the article, he is now permitted visitors.

"George," says Barbara, "maybe you should send someone to South Africa to visit with Nelson Mandela. It would certainly be a nice gesture, and it would make you look like you support him and his cause. It would be very good for your image."

"That's a good idea, Bar," he says, still reading the paper.

"George, George, are you listening to me? Did you hear what I just said?"

"Yes, yes, something about Mandela, isn't that right?"

"Yes, that's correct George. Sometimes I think Millie listens to me more than you do, don't you, sweet girl?" she says as she bends down to pet Millie.

"George, listen to me for a moment. I think you should send someone to South Africa to visit with him. Please stop reading the newspaper and listen to me. Here is what Mandela said about the Boy Scouts in South Africa according to this article: 'In 1976, the South Africa Scout Association took the courageous and unprecedented step of defying an unjust system and opened its doors to all young South Africans in a single united association.' Isn't that a coincidence, finding the Boy Scout watch and then finding this article? Do you think it's a sign?"

"Do I think it's a what?"

"A sign, George. A sign. I think this is a sign that you should send someone to South Africa and give the Boy Scout watch to Mandela. Heaven knows he would appreciate it more than you. Yes, that's just what you should do. Have someone give him the watch. It would probably be the nicest thing he has while he's in prison."

"Sure, Bar, sure. I'll do that." George sets his paper down. "In fact, I'll make you a deal. If you make sure the food is good and hot this evening for the Super Bowl for me and Jeb, I'll send someone to that prison in Africa. Oh, and be sure to test the tamales before they serve them. If they're terrible, for God's sake, just don't let them serve them."

There is a moment's pause.

"Aw hell, Bar, just have someone order five dozen pork tamales from Ninfa's in Houston, and get them here before the game starts. I don't want to embarrass myself in front of Jeb. Oh, but let's tell him our chef made the tamales."

"Well, thank goodness it's still early, George. I'll make sure the tamales are ordered now and that they'll be flown here, hot and fresh, by late this afternoon."

CHAPTER 66

PRESIDENT BUSH
PHONES JAMES BAKER

January 24, 1989

James Baker, a tall, thin, athletic man, has known the Bush family for many years and, in fact, was a regular tennis partner of George H.W. Bush at the Houston Country Club in the late 1950s. Rarely seen in clothes other than a suit and tie—except, of course, when he is playing tennis—Baker has lived a privileged life, attending The Hill School and Princeton University before serving in the United States Marine Corps.

As he served as White House Chief of Staff and United States Secretary of the Treasury under President Ronald Reagan, President Bush has appointed him the Secretary of State of his newly formed Cabinet.

President Bush sits at his desk in the Oval office and makes a call, instructing the White House operator to get James Baker on the line. Barbara sits in a chair, facing him, on the other side of his desk.

"Hey, James old man, how's it goin' this morning?" President Bush asks as he winks at Barbara.

"Oh, you know, Mr. President, I'm still trying to resolve the ongoing Arab-Israeli dispute."

"Yes, yes. Who knows if that will ever get resolved…But hey, James. I want you to drop that problem for a while and go on a trip for me. I want you to visit Africa."

"Africa? Where in Africa?"

"Actually, I want you to go to a prison over there in South Africa," the president explains. "In the Western Cape of South Africa is a prison called Victor Verster, and Nelson Mandela is incarcerated there. I want you to visit him and give him a gift from me. I want to show him our support."

There are a few moments of silence.

"Sir, might I offer a slightly different approach?" James asks. "I certainly don't want to offend you, but don't you think a letter of support from you would be equally and as delightfully received?"

"No, James. I don't. I think you need to go there and speak to the man in person."

"Mr. President, I'm certain you're aware that there are many demonstrations, unruly crowds, many unhappy people in South Africa now. It's actually quite a dangerous part of the world. Sir, revolutions are occurring there. White people and, of course, Black people are being murdered. Surely you wouldn't want to see me go into a situation like that, correct!"

"You should plan to leave no later than early February. I'll have my secretary drop off the gift for Mandela in your office, and the White House will take care of calling the prison to let them know you're coming."

A short pause.

"Why, yes, yes, of course, sir. I serve at the pleasure of the president," Baker says.

George H.W. Bush hangs up the phone. "Well, Bar, it's done. Baker is going to South Africa in early February to meet with Mandela."

"Thank you, George." She stands up, walks over to him, kisses him on the cheek, and walks out of the room.

*   *   *

Soon after the watch has been taken from the White House, Barbara Bush is diagnosed with Graves' disease—an overactive thyroid ailment—and soon after that, President Bush is informed he has the same disease.

The economy of the United States begins to suffer and slips fully into a recession in 1990. The unemployment rate rises from 5.9 percent in 1989 to 7.8 percent. Over a million blue-collar jobs are lost, as well as 200,000 white-collar jobs. The federal deficit rises from $152.1 billion to $220 billion—a threefold increase since 1980.

CHAPTER 67

JAMES BAKER'S VISIT
TO SOUTH AFRICA

February 2, 1989

Following a turbulent eighteen-hour flight, stopping once in Germany for refueling, James Baker steps off the private plane and onto the tarmac. A black limousine is waiting to drive him to the home of the American Ambassador to South Africa, Edward Joseph Perkins.

It is warm in the car, so he begins to open the windows. Immediately, he hears two loud cracks. "Oh, Jesus, are those gunshots?" he asks the limousine driver.

"Why yes, sir. I believe that's what you're hearing," the driver replies. "Would you like some water, sir?"

"Yes, yes, water would be great."

"It is located just inside that compartment in front of you. Do you see it?" the driver asks.

"Yes. I do." James begins pouring himself some water when he hears another volley of loud pops outside his window.

"Oh, my Lord, that's automatic rifle fire, isn't it?"

"Yes, sir. Might I suggest rolling up your window? They are bulletproof."

James Baker rolls up his window and drinks some water. "I never should have made this trip," he says to himself as he shakes his head. "I was so worried I might catch yellow fever, or typhoid fever, or hepatitis…Now it's more likely I'll catch a bullet." Three armored personnel carriers in a convoy pass them on the main street, which is lined with numerous piles of garbage and stacks of burning tires. "How much longer until we arrive at the ambassador's home?" Baker asks.

"Just about thirty minutes, sir."

He sees a white policeman holding a snarling Doberman Pinscher on a short leash and hears loud screaming coming from a woman. He looks around but doesn't see her.

After thirty long minutes, they arrive at the ambassador's home. Edward Joseph Perkins, a large Black man with a professional linebacker's physique and very short hair, has the official title of 'Ambassador Extraordinary and Plenipotentiary.' Brightly colored flowers fill the large, lush garden encircling the front of the three-story red brick home. The ambassador, dressed in a dark suit and bright blue tie, and his wife, who wears a full-length emerald gown with a long gold chain necklace, stand in front of the home, along with one of their servants, ready to greet the Secretary of State. Following appropriate introductions, the servant takes Mr. Baker's bags and shows him to his room at the top of the stairs.

Ambassador Perkins' staff has prepared the bedroom for the Secretary of State, appropriately laying out the finest towels, soaps, and linens. James unpacks, washes up briefly, and walks downstairs to dinner.

Over the past twenty-four hours, the ambassador's kitchen staff has worked feverishly preparing a special formal dinner for the American Secretary of State, with a menu pre-approved by the White House. Ambassador Perkins has also invited the Minister of Justice, Kobie Coetsee, to join the dinner party. Prior to dinner, introductions are made, then everyone is seated in the dining room.

A large flower arrangement is removed from the center of the table prior to the meal. Wine is poured. The servants walk behind each guest with platters of food, placing small portions of the various dishes on the guests' plates. When the servants finish, they stand with their backs against the wall so they can monitor the table, and fill glasses with wine and water as needed.

James Baker, having not eaten even a bite of food all day, eats everything on his plate, then asks politely for second portions. "Edward," James says, "this meal is delicious. Is this steak from local farmers? And what about this dish?" James points to long, slender, fried items on his plate. "Is this some sort of green bean that you've fried and served with curry?"

"I am delighted you like it, James. I wanted to introduce you to some of our local meat and produce this evening." Edward begins pointing at the different items on his own plate. "Yes, everything you have eaten tonight, from the meat to the vegetables, is from local farmers. We are quite fortunate, aren't we?"

"Yes, yes," James nods, "everything was just delicious." He drinks a full glass of water, but then his stomach rumbles slightly, and he feels the room getting quite warm.

"Mr. Baker, would you like some more steak?" the server standing behind him asks.

"Oh, no, no. Just some more water."

He drinks more water, and his stomach rumbles more loudly, after which, he releases a large amount of flatulence. The smell of rotten eggs fills the air. James looks around the table, pretending to seek the person who passed the gas.

"Perhaps we should all go into the living room for some dessert and coffee," Ambassador Perkins suggests, standing up and moving away from the group.

"Thank you, Edward, but it's been a long day, and I'd better get some sleep before my meeting with Mr. Mandela tomorrow. Your hospitality has been just wonderful."

"Oh, of course, James. But wouldn't you like some dessert and coffee before you retire?"

"No, no," James says, feeling a sharp stomach cramp. He gasps slightly, then looks to see if anyone has noticed. "I should really just go up to bed."

"James, the Minister of Justice and I would like to take a few minutes to help prepare you for your meeting with Mandela tomorrow. I feel it's quite important," says Edward. "For example, it would be nice if you were able to say a few polite phrases in Afrikaans."

James, still at the table, feels his stomach cramp subsiding. He wipes his forehead. "Certainly, Edward, I'm sure you're right, and coffee and dessert sound fine. Oh and by the way, I've already tried to memorize a few phrases in Afrikaans."

James and the minister follow the ambassador into the living room. Strong coffee and a South African pumpkin tart are served, then cigars are handed around.

James lets out a loud burp. "Oh my goodness, excuse me. I don't know where that came from."

"James," the Minister of Justice says, "tomorrow you will be asked to remove all items from your pockets before going into Victor Verster Prison. I advise you to have no sharp objects, not even a small knife, in your pocket."

"Of course, of course not," James replies. "My visit with Mr. Mandela will be quite short. I just want to give him greetings and support from President Bush, and a gift."

"A gift? I don't think you'll be able to give him anything," Ambassador Perkins says.

"It's just a watch," James explains. He takes a bite of the tart. "And the gift has already been cleared by—" James grabs his stomach as a cramp racks him. Sweat breaks out on his forehead, and he turns pale. He quickly places the plate with the unfinished tart on the nearby coffee table, while the fork slides off the plate and lands on the floor. He makes no attempt to pick it up.

Minister Coetsee, standing next to James, hears his stomach rumble, and says, "James, you don't look well. Are you alright?"

"I need to go to my bedroom, now," James shouts, turning around, running out of the room, and bounding up to his bedroom.

"Do you think he's alright?" Minister Coetsee asks Ambassador Perkins.

"I'm sure he'll be fine in the morning. Maybe the water didn't agree with him."

CHAPTER 68

THE VISIT TO VICTOR VERSTER PRISON

Friday, February 3, 1989

The limousine arrives at the prison at 10:00 a.m. James, weak and eager to get home, has already packed his bags, and the driver has placed his things in the trunk in anticipation of going directly to the airport after the visit with Mr. Mandela.

A military entourage greets James Baker as he arrives, and escorts him into a large, well-lit room. The floor is cement, and the walls are made of stacked light green cinder blocks. The smell of sweat, urine, and feces infuses the air.

A large Black man in a tan uniform with a baton and silver handcuffs hanging from his belt stands up from behind a table. He approaches the visiting party. "Mr. Baker, welcome. We are expecting you. Let me notify the warden of your arrival."

The guard picks up the phone and speaks with someone, then hangs up the receiver. "Please wait here one moment, as the warden and deputy warden would like to escort you to Mr. Mandela's room," he says.

Within a few moments, two white gentlemen in uniform appear. Introductions are made, and James is taken to the warden's house where Nelson Mandela is staying.

"Please take all the time you need to speak with Mr. Mandela," the warden says.

"Thank you. I won't be here long."

Mandela has his own cook, who greets James and asks him if he would prefer coffee or tea.

"Tea, please," he replies.

The cook escorts James into a large room where Mandela sits at a desk, facing him, with two large South African men standing on either side. The man to Mandela's right is wearing prison clothes: a dark blue top and matching long blue pants, identical to the clothes Mandela is wearing. The man standing to his left wears a bright red and green African print short-sleeve shirt and tan pants, along with a string of long black beads around his neck, a gold ring in his nose, and a red bandana tied around his forehead, hiding most of his thick, curly black hair. There are parallel scars, each about two inches in length, on the man's left arm, approximately twenty of them, extending from his wrist to his elbow.

James bows slightly at the waist and says, "*Hallo, ek is James Baker van die Verenigde State.*" (Hello, I am James Baker from the United States.) "*Ek het groete gebring van ons president, George Bush.*" (I have come bringing greetings from our president, George Bush.) "*Hy, en almal in die Verenigde State, hoop dat jy binnekort vry sal wees.*" (He, along with everyone else in the United States, hopes you will be free soon.)

"*End it is al die Afrikaans wat ek week hoe om te praa.*" (And that is all the Afrikaans I know how to speak.) James smiles and again bows from the waist.

"I am quite impressed with your Afrikaans," Mandela says in excellent English. "Very good, very good indeed. Now I would like to introduce you to my friends here, Madula Abadu," he says as he motions to his right, "and Dolami Macumba," as he nods to his left. "Mr. Macumba here is the prison doctor. He has taken good care of me over the years with his various herbs and potions," Mandela says, and he smiles. "He is what you Americans would call, perhaps, a medicine man."

Dolami Macumba leans down toward Mandela's ear and whispers, "*Moenie hom vertrou nie. Hy lyk baie agterdogtig.*" (Do not trust him. He looks very suspicious.)

Madula Abadu says loudly, "*Hy kan waarskynlik niks goeds doen nie. Pasop hierdie vreemdeling. Die Amerikaanse regering het nog nooit ons anti-apartheidsbeweging ondersteun nie.*" (He is probably up to no good. Beware this stranger. The United States government has never supported our anti-apartheid movement.)

"They are both saying they welcome you today and are delighted you have been sent by your government to visit with me," Mandela says with a smile.

"Your English is excellent, Mr. Mandela. I would like you to know President Bush supports your efforts; however, he seeks a peaceful resolution to apartheid, not a violent one."

"I can assure you, Mr. Baker, not a single political organization in our country, inside and outside parliament, can ever compare with the African National Congress in its total commitment to peace. However, if we are forced to resort to violence, it is because there is no other alternative whatsoever," Mandela says.

"I understand, and I appreciate your spending time with me this morning. The President of the United States would like me to present you with this gift, a watch. He has read that you are fond of the Boy Scouts of South Africa, so President Bush wanted to present you with this gift of a fine silver American Boy Scout pocket watch." James takes the wrapped gift out of his coat pocket and hands it to Mandela.

Mandela opens the gift, then pries open the watch with his fingernail. "Why, this is beautiful. The painting on the face is so exquisite, and the colors are so sharp. Thank you, and please thank your president for me."

"I certainly will, and Mr. Mandela, if they ever release you from prison, which we surely hope they will do soon, we sincerely hope you will grant us the pleasure of a visit to the White House. It would be a great honor to have you as our guest."

Mandela nods and smiles, still gazing at the watch. He hands the watch to Dolami Macumba.

"*Wat dink jy, Dolami?*" (What do you think, Dolami?)

Dolami places the watch in the palm of his right hand and closes his fingers around it. With his eyes closed he says, "*Madiba, dit is 'n baie kragtige horlosie. Dit is duidelik dat die witman nie die krag van hierdie horlosie ken nie. Daar is baie jare gelede 'n betowering daarop geplaas. Ek voel dat daar 'n betowering of geluk daarop geplaas word. 'N Betowering wat nie verander kan word nie. Hierdie dwaas weet nie wat hy vir ons gegee het nie, ek is seker daarvan. Ek is seker hierdie horlosie sal u geluk gee. Dit sal u toelaat om vry te word. U sal regoor die wêreld as 'n held erken word.*" (Madiba, this is a very powerful watch. It is obvious the white man does not know the power of this watch. I feel a spell of power or luck has been placed upon it, many years ago, and it cannot be altered. This fool does not know what he has given you, I am certain of that. This watch will bring you luck, and will allow you to become free. You will be recognized as a hero throughout the world.)

"What did he say?" James asks Mandela.

"He said he likes the watch."

*   *   *

Frederik Willem de Klerk is elected State President of South Africa and begins serving his term on August 15, 1989. Following the fall of the Berlin Wall, the newly elected president calls his cabinet together to debate legalizing the African National Committee (ANC) and freeing Mandela.

Members of the ANC doubt there will be any significant change with the new administration; however, they are surprised when de Klerk addresses the South African people on February 2, 1990:

"I will be introducing plans, during my time in office, for sweeping reforms of our political system. A number of currently banned political parties, including the ANC and the Communist Party of South Africa, will be legalized. I do want to emphasize, however, that this does not constitute an endorsement of their socialist economic policies nor of the violent actions carried out by their members. From this day forward, all those imprisoned solely for belonging to a banned organization, including Nelson Mandela, will now be released."

"SOUTH AFRICA'S NEW ERA: MANDELA FREED, URGES STEP-UP IN PRESSURE TO END WHITE RULE"

– The *New York Times*

Mandela is freed from prison on February 11, 1990 and receives a formal invitation from President Bush to visit the White House. Arrangements are made for the visit to occur on June 25. Nelson Mandela, his wife Winnie, and his entire delegation are invited.

On June 10, Winnie Mandela shows her husband articles in *Vanity Fair* and in *Ebony* magazines containing interviews with Barack Obama, a young American Black man whose reputation is becoming well known. Mandela learns Obama seeks a degree in law as a vehicle to facilitate better community organization and activism.

At the end of his first year at Harvard Law School, Obama is selected as an editor of the *Harvard Law Review* based on his grades and a writing competition. In February 1990, his second year at Harvard, he is elected president of the Harvard Law Review—a full-time volunteer position, functioning as editor-in-chief and supervising the law review's staff of eighty editors. Obama's election as the first Black president of the law review is widely publicized.

The more he reads about Obama, the more Mandela views him as a younger version of himself, with many of the same goals and desires for his people. He decides to give him the silver pocket watch and arranges to meet with Obama before he meets with President George H.W. Bush and Barbara Bush in Washington, D.C.

CHAPTER 69

MANDELA'S VISIT TO THE UNITED STATES

June 20, 1990

Nelson Mandela visits two cities, New York and Boston, before arriving in Washington, D.C. While in Boston, he arranges to have a private lunch with Barack Obama in his room at the Boston Harbor Hotel.

Three separate tables have been placed in Mandela's hotel living room: a small dining table set with fine linens, sterling silverware, china and crystal; a large rectangular table filled with an elaborate spread of cheese, bread, fruit, meats, and salads; and another small table with various desserts and coffee. When Barack arrives, water glasses are filled, wine is poured, and then Mandela requests privacy, politely asking the servers to leave the room, as he and Obama will serve themselves.

Compliments are shared between the men and common desires and goals are discussed.

After the men have dessert and coffee, Obama prepares to leave, but Mandela says, "Please stay seated a moment longer. I want to give you something." Mandela takes a watch out of his dresser drawer. "Mr. Obama, I was given this watch a few months ago as a gift. The individual who gave it to me did not recognize its worth. I was told by a man whom I trust completely that this watch had a spell placed upon it many years ago. A spell to impart luck."

"A spell you say? A spell to impart luck?" Obama nods his head and smiles.

"Yes, the watch is imbued with a charm of great luck. I know this must sound foolish to you, like some strange African superstition, and I, too, had my doubts. But soon after I was given this watch, Barack, I was freed from prison. Do you understand? After twenty-seven years in prison, I was a free man." Mandela pauses, looks down at his lap, and closes his eyes. After a few seconds, he raises his head and looks directly at Obama.

"I am familiar with your goals, son, and I see myself in you. We both have the same desires for our people, the same love for them, and we share the same struggles. As I am an old man now, I wish to pass the torch to you. You are the hope for our people and for the next generation, and our hope for justice in the world. Please keep this watch close to your heart, and never lose it. May it bring you the amazing luck it has brought me," Mandela says.

"I would be honored to accept this watch. Thank you for thinking of me. I agree, Mr. Mandela, our goals are the same. Please be assured I will treasure this gift, as I can use all the luck I can get." Barack Obama smiles and leaves.

Nelson Mandela begins to get ready for his flight to Washington, D.C.

CHAPTER 70

MANDELA VISITS WASHINGTON, D.C.

June 25, 1990

Following breakfast with President Bush and Secretary of State James Baker, the president and Mr. Mandela speak at a podium on the south lawn of the White House and discuss their desire for the removal of apartheid and the introduction of a nonracial democracy in South Africa. Mandela thanks the American people and the president for their encouragement and support. He asks the president to maintain the United States' sanctions. Because of these, South Africa has made much progress in addressing its problems.

President Bush speaks of his desire for a non-violent approach to the ending of apartheid.

"As long as my government is prepared to talk," Mandela replies, "to maintain channels of open communication between itself and the people it governs, there is no question. There will be no violence whatsoever. However, when my government decides to ban the political organizations of the oppressed, or if they do not allow any free political activity, no matter how peaceful and nonviolent, the people will have no alternative but to resort to violence."

"We share the goal of true democracy and dismantling, once and for all, the vestiges of apartheid, a system that based the rights and freedoms of citizenship on the color of one's skin," says President Bush.

CHAPTER 71

THE DEMOCRATIC NATIONAL CONVENTION

July 27, 2004

The tall, thin, handsome man leans against the wall, taking a long drag off of his cigarette. He reaches into his pants pocket and takes out his pocket watch. 9:40 p.m. Then, closing the watch and placing it back in his pocket, he thinks, *I must be the luckiest man in the world. A young African-American Senator from the State of Illinois, asked to give the keynote address at the Democratic National Convention. Unbelievable, really unbelievable.*

The periodic roar of the crowd just on the other side of the curtain is deafening.

The 1964 song "Keep on Pushing" by The Impressions begins to play, then he feels a tap on his shoulder.

"We're ready for you, Senator."

He looks for an ashtray, sees none, takes one more drag, and then hands his lit cigarette to a surprised member of the stage crew. He walks onto the stage to thunderous applause.

"Thank you so much. Thank you so much. Thank you. Thank you. Thank you so much. Thank you so much. Thank you. Thank you. Thank you, Dick Durbin. You make us all proud. On behalf of the great State of Illinois, crossroads of a nation, Land of Lincoln, let me express my deepest gratitude for the privilege of addressing this convention."

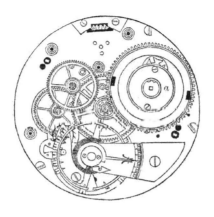

The Journey of the
Brass Boy Scout

Pocket Watch

CHAPTER 72

RICHARD T. JAMES

Richard T. James, now thirty-six years old, believes his extreme good fortune in life began when he received a Boy Scout pocket watch, a gift from his father, the famous watchmaker, for his fifteenth birthday. His mother told him the watch would bring him luck.

When Richard was in high school, he was involved in a car crash. Two individuals were killed, and one lost the use of his legs, but Richard escaped without a scratch. And that is not the only accident from which he's walked away unscathed.

Over the years, Richard has received accolades that were a complete surprise to him. He was astonished, for example, when he won a national spelling contest and a national chess tournament in the same year.

So, not knowing if the watch truly brings him luck, Richard keeps it safely in his pants pocket every day. The watch is the first thing he checks when he wakes up and the last thing he looks at before he goes to sleep.

In 1943, Richard tries to develop a way to suspend sensitive shipboard instruments aboard naval vessels and experiments with tension springs. He accidentally drops one and observes how the spring keeps moving after it hits the ground. The idea for a toy is born.

In 1944, Richard's wife, Betty, leafs through the dictionary and comes up with the word 'Slinky.' The couple makes four hundred of the 'Slinky' toys and convinces Gimbels department store in Philadelphia to display some, moving on a ramp, for the Christmas season in 1945. The first models completely sell out in ninety minutes at the price of one dollar each.

The toy soon becomes an amazing success, and a multimillion-dollar business is born.

*   *   *

May 3, 1958

"Throw the ball to me. To me," Jeanne screams, waving her arms in the air. "You always throw it to Howard. Throw it to me. I'll catch it this time."

"No, no," Howard shouts across the large field. "She can't catch anything. Throw it to me or we'll lose the game for sure."

This is the fourth visit Richard and Betty James have made, along with their six children, to the Mount Washington Hotel in Bretton Woods, New Hampshire. This morning, they play touch football in the pristine meadow on the expansive grounds. The hotel is located at the northern end of Crawford Notch, six miles east of the village of Twin Mountain along U.S. Route 302. The Mount Washington Hotel is a summer escape for residents of Boston, New York, and Philadelphia.

Richard's children have grown bored of hiking to the nearby ski lodge and touring the gardens, so, during breakfast, Richard suggested playing football in the meadow, just a half mile from the hotel's main building. Richard procured a football from the front desk and rented bicycles for them to ride to the meadow.

Although still in pretty good shape for a thirty-eight-year-old man, after three hours of running, chasing, and nursing a few twisted knees and fingers, Richard stops the game and gathers the family. They head back to the hotel for lunch.

Arriving back at the hotel, everyone goes to their room to change clothes, and they all meet in the dining room at twelve noon. The children order grilled cheese sandwiches, and Betty and Richard order chicken salad sandwiches. Richard pats his right pants pocket, out of habit, to feel for the watch. It's not there. His heart begins to race

"What's wrong, dear? You look pale. Is something wrong with your sandwich?" Betty asks.

"No, no, nothing is wrong with my sandwich," Richard says as he pats the empty pockets of his shirt and pants.

"Is something the matter, then?" she continues.

All the children look in Richard's direction.

"No. Nothing is wrong. I need to run up to our room for a minute."

Richard jumps up from his chair in the dining room and hurriedly walks to their room. Frantically, he searches through the pockets of the pants he wore during this morning's football game. No watch. Then, he opens the closet, and pats down all of the pockets. No watch. Even after opening every drawer, examining each piece of clothing, running his hands across the bottoms and back surfaces of each drawer, he's bereft. No watch.

After ten minutes, Richard returns to the dining room, attempting to remain calm. A few beads of sweat appear on his forehead. His family has remained at the table. "Hey, have any of you kids seen my pocket watch?" They all shake their heads.

"Betty, Betty, have you seen my watch?"

"Well, no, dear. I haven't seen it since last night on your nightstand."

"Oh yes, that's right. It was on my nightstand last night. It must still be there. I need to go look." Richard turns around and walks back to his hotel room.

"Is Father alright?" Jeanne asks.

"Yes, I'm sure your father is fine."

When Betty returns to their room, she sees all the drawers have been opened, and the clothes from the drawers and the closet have been removed and all tossed in various jumbled piles on the floor and the bed.

"Oh my God, what is wrong, Richard? What are you doing?"

"I'm looking for my watch, Betty! I can't find my watch!"

"Well, Richard, I'm sure it's here somewhere. Do you remember where you last saw it?"

"Jesus, Betty. If I remembered, I could find it. Just help me look for it."

"I told you I last saw it on your nightstand. Did you look in the drawer of the nightstand?"

"Of course I did. I looked in every drawer, in every pocket of every piece of our clothing, under the bed. I've torn the bathroom apart looking. It's nowhere to be found. You must help me find it. What am I going to do?" he says with tears in his eyes.

"Please calm down, Richard. We'll find it, I'm sure. Just give me a few moments."

"I promised I would never lose it," Richard explains.

"Promised whom?" she asks.

"My mother. I promised my mother I would never lose it."

"Oh, Richard," says Betty, "it's going to be fine. I'm sure we'll find it."

Betty begins picking up the clothes from the floor and placing the various items back into the drawers and closet as she checks each pocket. After thirty minutes, they have no luck finding the watch.

Richard calls the front desk to see if a watch has been found. No one has turned in a watch.

Richard phones each of his children to ask them again if they've seen the watch. None have seen it recently. He tells them to carefully search their rooms.

Richard returns to the dining room. Though it is closed, he convinces the manager to open it so he can look to see if his watch is there. Chairs are pulled away from tables, curtains are opened wide so the carpet underneath can be thoroughly examined, and Richard and a few waiters get down on their knees to look under tables. Kitchen garbage cans are emptied onto the floor and their contents examined. Every inch of the floor in the restaurant is inspected. But after a thorough search, no watch is found. Richard asks the hotel manager to question the maids, as he now believes his watch may have been stolen. The manager informs Richard that in the many years the hotel has been open, no item has ever been stolen from a guest. Richard doesn't care. He wants all the staff questioned regardless of the hotel's reputation. The manager states he will comply with the request.

As Richard lies in bed that evening, going over the day's events, he decides to gather his family at first daylight to search the meadow where they played football earlier in the day. Surely his watch must be there. He calls the front desk and arranges for eight bicycles to be ready by 6:30 the next morning.

At 6:00 a.m., Richard awakens his family and instructs them to be downstairs in thirty minutes. The bicycles are ready and waiting for them. After numerous complaints about not getting any breakfast, the family members leave on their bikes for the meadow. From 6:45 a.m. until 5:00 p.m., they meticulously search for the watch. At 5:00, Betty convinces Richard that the children are starving, and she and the children get on their bikes and head back to the hotel. Richard stays in the meadow looking for the watch until almost dark, then finally gets on his bike and goes back.

The following day, Richard gathers ten volunteers from the hotel staff, agreeing to pay them $100 each if they will spend the day searching the meadow for the brass pocket watch. In addition, if the watch is found, he will pay them an extra $500. The hotel management is not happy, as now they are short-staffed for maids, bellmen, and cooks. Various bottles, earrings, handkerchiefs, and a wallet are found in the meadow, but no watch.

Richard begs his family to make another outing to the meadow, but Betty refuses on their behalf.

Two days later, Betty and the children pack their belongings and go back home to Philadelphia.

Richard remains at the Mount Washington Hotel for another month, spending the majority of each day searching the meadow for his watch. On day thirty, early in the morning, Richard sees the manager, Mr. Williamson, in the lobby and takes him aside.

Mr. Williamson has been employed by the hotel for the past fifteen years, and he prides himself in maintaining excellent posture, dressing impeccably, providing the finest of services for his guests, and always keeping his composure.

"Mr. Williamson, good morning, sir," Richard says in a cheery tone. Mr. Williamson smells alcohol on his breath.

Mr. Williamson nods his head politely and smiles. "Good morning, Mr. James."

"I've been thinking," Mr. James says. "I would like a list of all the names and addresses of the guests who were staying here during the week my family and I did, just about a month ago. Remember? My wife and our six children stayed here for a week. Surely you remember."

"Of course I do, Mr. James."

"Well...well, one of your guests must have picked up my watch and taken it home, possibly by mistake. I will write each of your guests. Yes, I will do that. I will write each of your guests, describing my watch and asking them to return it to me. I'll even offer a handsome reward if they have it."

Mr. Williamson hesitates. "I am sorry, Mr. James. I am unable to provide you with that information."

"Listen to me, Mr. Williamson. Listen to me carefully. After living in your hotel for a month, the least you can do is give me that list."

"Again, Mr. James, as I've said, it is not possible to do that. Our guest list is considered private information."

Richard steps closer to Mr. Williamson and suddenly grabs him by his lapels. "I must have that list; do you hear me? I must have that list," he insists.

Mr. Williamson peels Richard's hands from his jacket and steps back while flattening the lapels with the palms of his hands. Richard steps backward, almost losing his balance.

"Mr. James. It appears you have been drinking. Let me have someone escort you back to your room."

"Hey, just wait a minute. Just wait a minute. Please listen to me, Mr. Williamson," Richard says in a whisper. "I'm sorry I grabbed you. That was wrong of me. If it's money you want,

I'll give you five thousand dollars for that list. No one needs to know. It will be just between you and me, I promise, but I really must have that list. Understand?"

Mr. Williamson nods and motions for a nearby bellboy, who escorts Mr. James back to his room.

An hour later, a hotel security guard knocks on Mr. James' door, informing him to pack his belongings and leave the hotel that day. He is officially banned from ever returning to the Mount Washington Hotel or its surrounding property.

When Richard arrives home, Betty almost doesn't recognize him, as he is unshaven and has lost more than thirty pounds. He is a completely different man—angry and obsessed, talking about his lost watch to anyone who will listen.

Richard attempts, numerous times, to convince Betty to go back to the Mount Washington Hotel to search for his watch, but she refuses. He then begs his older children. They, too, refuse.

Richard joins the local Evangelical Church. With a donation of $20,000 and enough prayer, they assure him, his watch will certainly be found. In 1960, Richard leaves his family and moves to Bolivia to join Wycliffe Bible Translators.

'Slinky' is no longer a multimillion-dollar business, as sales of the toy rapidly decline. Betty takes over managing the business, as well as raising the family's six children, until James Industries, Inc. is taken over by Poof Products of Plymouth, Michigan.

Richard dies of a heart attack in 1974 in Bolivia, never having found his beloved watch.

Betty is inducted into the Toy Industry Hall of Fame in 2001.

CHAPTER 73

JIM LOVELL FINDS A WATCH

May 26, 1961

Born in 1928, in Cleveland Ohio, James Arthur Lovell Jr. has always had an interest in rocketry and airplanes. Even as a child, it was all he could talk about with his fellow Boy Scouts.

In 1952, following his graduation from the Naval Academy, Jim marries his high school sweetheart, Marilyn Lillie Gerlach.

After years of training as a naval aviator and test pilot, in January, 1958, Lovell enters a six-month test pilot training course at the Naval Air Test Center in Patuxent River, Maryland. Two of his classmates are Pete Conrad and Wally Schirra. Lovell graduates first in his class. Later that year, Lovell, Conrad, and Schirra are among 110 military test pilots selected as potential astronaut candidates for Project Mercury. Shirra goes on to become a test pilot of the Mercury Seven, though Lovell and Conrad fail to make the cut for medical reasons. Lovell has a temporarily high bilirubin level in his blood.

In May of 1961, Jim Lovell has just completed Aviation Safety School at the University of Southern California. As a surprise, his wife, Marilyn, arranges a combination graduation gift and thirty-third birthday gift for her husband. She makes plans for a vacation at the famous Mount Washington Hotel in New Hampshire. As they drive the winding roads and finally approach the Mount Washington hotel, they admire the snow-capped mountains in the distance.

They pass the well-groomed golf course and arrive at the front entrance of the hotel. A bellhop greets them at their car and assists in taking their luggage into the hotel's grand lobby. After checking in, the couple heads toward their assigned room.

As soon as they enter their suite, they are captivated by the beautiful sweeping views of the lush green surroundings. Giant northern white pine trees and rolling hills surround the hotel.

"Why, this is really amazing, isn't it Jim?" Marilyn asks.

"Yes, it certainly is…really beautiful."

"Jim, you won't believe the bathroom," she yells. "It's all marble. Even the floors are marble. And the fixtures are gold. Jim, you really have to see this."

Jim sticks his head into the bathroom and looks around. "Yeah, it's really something alright."

After he walks back into the bedroom, he takes more clothes out of his suitcase and hangs them in the closet. When he finishes unpacking, he places his empty suitcase in the back corner of the closet. Marilyn, too, finishes unpacking, placing her clothes in the dresser and hanging up her clothes. She looks at herself in the dresser mirror and realizes she is missing an earring.

"Jim, I seem to have lost one of my favorite earrings. We have to stop everything. I really need to find it."

"Well, where do you remember having it last?" he asks.

"Where do I remember having it last? Well, if I knew that…I…I'm almost positive I had both earrings on when

I was checking out the bathroom...or maybe not. Surely, I would have noticed then if one was missing. Please help me find it. It must be around here somewhere."

They both search the drawers, floors, and bathroom of their suite and are about to give up when Jim checks the closet one more time.

As he removes the empty suitcase from the closet, a piece of jagged metal on the bottom of the suitcase catches the carpet and pulls it away from the floorboards. Jim bends down to unhook the suitcase, but something shiny catches his eye. He pulls the loose carpet back and sees a brass pocket watch beneath it. He picks it up, pries it open with his fingernail, and is surprised to find tents, pine trees, and a river painted on its face. As he examines the watch more closely, he notices the traits of a Boy Scout printed around the rim. He gently winds the watch, and it begins to tick.

"Jim, I found my earring. It fell into my skirt pocket," Marilyn yells from the living room.

"Hey Marilyn," Jim says, "look what I found. A Boy Scout watch. It's in pretty good condition, too."

He shows her the watch. "Isn't it great? I love it. Do you think I should I keep it? I found it in the closet over there, just under the carpet."

"Why it's beautiful, Jim," she says. "Maybe it's been in there for a long time. Why don't you go to the front desk and inquire if anyone has lost it?"

"That's a good idea," he says.

They decide to go on a hike, so they get ready and head down to the lobby.

"Excuse me, may I speak to the manager?" Jim asks the gentleman behind the desk.

"Of course, sir. Is anything wrong? Anything I can do to assist you?"

"No, no, everything is great. I just need to speak with the manager."

"Yes sir. I'll get him for you right away. One moment, please."

Soon the manager appears wearing a name tag which reads, 'Mr. Nelson Goldberg.'

"Good afternoon, Mr. Lovell. I am Mr. Goldberg, the manager of this fine hotel. I hope you are enjoying your time with us. How may I assist you?"

Jim takes the watch out of his pocket. "I found this watch in our room. It was in the corner of our closet, hidden under the carpet," he explains, handing the watch to Mr. Goldberg.

Mr. Goldberg examines the watch. "Well, this is a fine watch, indeed," he says.

"Has anyone reported a missing watch?" Jim asks.

"Well, no, not that I am aware of, but there was a change of staff and ownership of the hotel a few years ago, so let's see if someone at the front desk knows if there has been an inquiry."

After asking numerous hotel staff, he finds no one has reported a lost watch.

"I'll just put it in a drawer in my office," Mr. Goldberg says as he turns to leave.

"Wait, Mr. Goldberg," Jim says. "If you don't mind, sir, I would like to hold on to the watch and give you my contact information. Then, if anyone does inquire, I will be happy to send them the watch. Would that be alright?"

Mr. Goldberg looks at Jim for a moment. "Well, that's rather unusual, but of course, Mr. Lovell. I'm sure that will be fine."

Mr. Goldberg hands the watch back to Jim along with a piece of paper and a pen. "I am sure we have your contact information at the front desk, Mr. Lovell, but why don't you write it down here, too?"

Jim thanks Mr. Goldberg and then places the watch in his front pants pocket.

"Oh, Mr. Goldberg," Jim says, "I almost forgot. My wife and I are just about to go on a hike. Do you have any maps of the trails around here?"

"Of course. Let me get one for you."

"Here it is," he says as he unfolds it. "You are right here, Mr. Lovell," he says, pointing to a specific area on the map. "I would suggest taking this trail. It's just about two miles long and you're guaranteed to see some spectacular sites."

Marilyn and Jim leave the hotel by one of the back doors. They walk past the tennis courts, where they observe employees of the hotel staff sweeping leaves off the court's surface. The employees stop their sweeping and nod politely at the couple as they pass.

"Boy, all of their staff members are so well trained, aren't they?" Jim asks. Marilyn smiles.

They begin their hike and soon see a large deer with a spectacular rack of antlers just in front of them, standing in the middle of their path. They stop. The deer turns and stares at them. No one moves for a few seconds, then the deer walks gracefully to the other side of the path and eventually disappears into the thick forest. Marilyn and Jim take a few steps but stop when they hear rustling in the bushes. Four small deer quickly dart across the same path, attempting to catch up to the adult.

"Oh my God," Jim says, "can you believe that?"

"It was magical, just magical. We were almost run over by some baby deer." She laughs.

As they continue their walk. Jim stops and takes the watch out of his pocket. "We'd better turn around. It will be almost dark by the time we get back to the hotel."

The watch suddenly begins to vibrate so hard, it falls out of Jim's hand and onto the forest floor. As he bends down to pick it up, something whizzes over his head...Then a loud *crack*. He stands to see a deep hole in the tree directly behind him where a bullet has just embedded itself, causing the faintest smell of burning wood. Marilyn and Jim look at the bullet hole, then at each other, eyes wide, mouths open.

"Oh, Jesus," Jim says. "I was almost killed. Marilyn, someone almost killed me."

Jim places his hand over his uninjured temple, then looks around. "HEY, STOP SHOOTING. THERE ARE PEOPLE HERE." He continues looking around, then quickly grabs Marilyn's wrist and pulls her back behind the tree.

As they crouch down, Jim yells again, "STOP SHOOTING. STOP SHOOTING." He looks around again. "There must be a hunter around here, Marilyn."

Jim listens but doesn't hear any more rifle fire. He looks at Marilyn and shakes his head. "Jesus, oh Jesus."

"Well, we're okay," Marilyn says. "We're both okay now. Let's just get back to the hotel. Jim, Jim, are you listening to me? Do you want to sit here a bit or head back to the hotel? Jim, are you listening?"

"Yes, yes, I'm listening," Jim says.

Jim still has the watch in his hand. He looks at it once again and places it back in his pants pocket.

"Do you want to stay here for a minute?" Marilyn asks again.

"Stay here? Jesus Christ. Someone is around here with a *rifle*, Marilyn. I was almost killed. We can't stay here, but if we run, the hunter might think we're animals and shoot at us again. But…we really need to get out of here."

In unison, they say, "Let's go."

They run back in the direction of the hotel, as fast as they can, but after ten minutes, Marilyn says, gasping for air, "Jim…Jim…I have to…I have to stop. I have to stop and catch my…catch my breath."

They stop. Marilyn bends forward, placing her hands just above her knees.

"Are you okay, Marilyn?"

"Yes, yes. I'm fine. I…I just need to…rest for a moment," she says, taking deep breaths.

"I was very lucky back there, Marilyn. Very lucky."

"Yes, you were, Jim," she says with her head still down.

"If I hadn't bent down to pick up this watch, I would be dead. Do you realize that?"

"Yes, dear, I do."

Jim places his hand against his pocket. The metal of the watch feels unusually warm. "This watch saved my life," he says softly to himself.

After a few minutes, Jim asks, "Are you feeling any better? Ready to head back? The hotel's not very far, now."

"Yes, I'm fine."

*   *   *

In 1962, NASA needs a second group of astronauts for the Gemini and Apollo programs. Jim applies a second time and is accepted into NASA Astronaut Group 2. He is selected as backup pilot for Gemini 4, which puts him in position for his first space flight, three missions later.

CHAPTER 74

GEMINI 7

December 4, 1965

Gemini 7 is launched from Cape Kennedy with only two crew members: Command Pilot Frank F. Borman II and Pilot James A. Lovell, Jr., the first space flight for both men. The flight's objective is to evaluate the effects of fourteen days in orbit on the crew and spacecraft, twice the length of time anyone has been in space. The official patch for the flight features an Olympic torch, symbolizing the marathon-like length of the mission.

Three days into the mission, Marilyn is allowed to have a very brief conversation with her husband at Houston's Mission Control Center:

"Marilyn, Marilyn, can you hear me?"

"Yes, I can hear you fine, Jim."

"How are you and the kids getting along?"

"Everyone is just fine here, but of course we miss you and love you. How are you doing? Is everything okay?"

"Oh, my, yes. We're doing well...except we had on these awful spacesuits and were just sweating up a storm up here. Frank and I finally got permission to take them off. Imagine trying to take off a spacesuit in an area the size of the front seat of our car."

"Goodness, Jim, I can't even imagine."

"Yes, it was exhausting. We must have both lost five pounds by the time we were through with that exercise, but we're much more comfortable now."

"Oh I'm so glad to hear it. Listen, Jim, they're giving me a signal to get off this line. I miss you, and I'm sending you all my love and all the children's love. We are so very proud of you, sweetheart."

On day five of the flight, Jim speaks with Marilyn once again and tells her things are going well, except for some leaking urine collection containers—also that various crumbs from cookies escaped during eating and are now floating around in the cabin.

"I am worried about the reentry, Jim," Marilyn says.

"Oh, darling, don't worry," Jim says. "I have my lucky watch with me."

"Of course," she says. "Your lucky watch. Now I feel so much better."

On day eleven of the flight, some of the thrusters stop working. On the twelfth day, the fuel cells start to give only partial power, but Gemini 7's batteries are strong enough to sustain it for the remainder of the flight.

Gemini lands safely on December 18, 1965. The recovery ship USS *Wasp* picks them up shortly after they splash down.

Gemini 7 holds the record for the longest spaceflight duration for the next five years. The fourteen-day flight sets an endurance record of 206 orbits around Earth.

CHAPTER 75

GEMINI 12

October 25, 1966

After putting their three children to bed, Marilyn, seven months pregnant, and Jim Lovell sit at their kitchen table drinking coffee. Tomorrow, Jim will enter his pre-flight quarantine in preparation for the Gemini 12 launch.

"I don't know why, Jim," Marilyn says, "but I'm a little more nervous about this flight than I was about the last one."

"You know I'll be fine, Marilyn. Everyone has spent so much time checking and rechecking everything...It will all be just fine. And remember, it will be a shorter flight than the last one. I'm just sorry I can't be with you now, with your pregnancy and all."

"Jim," Marilyn says, taking his hand, "please don't worry about me and the children. We'll be fine. Everyone is looking after us. I'll miss you terribly. I miss you so much now just thinking about it...but I know I'll be talking with you frequently. I just, for some reason, am concerned about the flight."

"Everything will be fine," he reassures her.

"Susan has been acting up in school recently," Marilyn says. "She was sent to the principal's office today."

"What happened?" he asks.

"Well, when the principal started talking to her, she started crying and said she didn't want her daddy to leave. But he calmed her down and sent her back to class."

"I realize what I'm doing is very hard on you and the children," Jim says.

"Oh Jesus, I don't know what's wrong with me. I shouldn't have told you about what happened to Susan today. I've honestly tried to prepare the children, and myself, really, for the mission. I just want you to know how much we all love you and that we really are proud of you."

"I love you, too, Marilyn," he says as he kisses her.

"Well, now is probably not the best time to mention this," Jim says, "but I updated my life insurance policy, so if anything does happen, just contact Jamie Powell. Also, the electric and water bills have been paid for this month. Oh, and you have access to our bank account, and um—is there anything I'm forgetting? Oh yes, a copy of my will is in our silver lockbox in the bedroom closet, and Larry Goodman also has a copy. I know you're aware of all this, but I just want to remind you about everything."

Marilyn nods her head, and tears begin to flow down her cheeks. "Jim, please don't pay any attention to me. It's just that my hormones are out of control with this baby and all. I know everything will be great."

Jim puts his arms around her shoulders and kisses her on the neck. "There is nothing better than knowing you love me. That's the only thing I need."

Marilyn stands up, and they walk into their bedroom.

CHAPTER 76

THE LAUNCH OF GEMINI 12

November 11, 1966

Gemini 12 launches from Cape Kennedy with a crew of two: Commander James A. Lovell, Jr. and Pilot Edwin E. "Buzz" Aldren Jr. The objective of this mission is to prove humans can work safely and effectively outside a spacecraft. In preparation for the Gemini 12 flight, Lovell and Aldren have spent extensive time training underwater, which becomes a common technique for future space-walk simulations.

Gemini 12 was designed to perform five unique exercises: rendezvous and dock with the Agena target vehicle, conduct three extra-vehicular activity (EVA) operations, conduct a tethered station keeping exercise, perform docked maneuvers using the Agena propulsion system to change orbit, and demonstrate an automatic reentry.

On day three, a docking with Agena must be performed manually using the onboard computer and charts due to the failure of a piece of radar equipment. An engine on board experiences a drop in turbopump speed lasting about two and a half seconds, after which the pump returns to normal.

Following Gemini 12's reentry, and during its sixty-third orbit, the crew attempts to fire the propulsion system, but a stuck fuel valve prevents the engine from starting. Pump components heat and melt, and ground controllers are unable to start the engine during the orbit.

The spacecraft water supply is not working as it should, forcing the astronauts to reduce their fluid intake on the last day of the mission. Lovell develops a mild case of pinkeye.

From the viewing room overlooking the control room, Marilyn sees Jim looking at his lucky Boy Scout watch. She smiles and shakes her head.

The capsule is controlled on reentry by computer and splashes down 4.8 kilometers from its target. The crew is taken aboard the aircraft carrier USS *Wasp*.

The Gemini 12 flight paves the way for future Apollo missions and helps NASA reach their goal of getting a man on the moon by the end of the decade.

CHAPTER 77

CHAOS IN 1968

November 10

Walter Cronkite, anchor of *The CBS Evening News*, often cited as 'the most trusted man in America,' hosts a one-hour television program, *The Walter Cronkite Special*, watched by millions of Americans. It is described in *TV Guide* as, 'Walter Cronkite reviews significant events from 1968.'

It opens with the Beatles song, "A Day in the Life," playing the first line: "I read the news today...oh boy," and as the music fades out, Cronkite begins: "And ladies and gentlemen, what a year it has been." Television film clips from the year are presented with commentary, including:

March 31

As the war in Viet Nam is escalating and anti-war marches are occurring in large cities and on college campuses, President Johnson announces, "I shall not seek, and I will not accept, the nomination of my party for another term as your president."

April 4

Wailing men and women, of every color, of every age, rich and poor alike, appear as the tragic news of Dr. Martin Luther King Jr.'s death spreads across the country. King, an American clergyman and civil rights leader, has been fatally shot at the Lorraine Motel in Memphis, Tennessee, by James Earl Ray, a fugitive from the Missouri State Penitentiary. News clips are shown of Dr. King being rushed to St. Joseph's Hospital, where he dies at 7:05 p.m., and of huge race riots, breaking out in cities across the United States in the wake of his death.

June 5

Bobby Kennedy, a Democratic presidential candidate, is shot and mortally wounded by twenty-four-year-old Sirhan Sirhan at the Ambassador Hotel in Los Angeles. He is pronounced dead on June 6, about twenty-six hours after he was shot, and the world is shocked and saddened by a second Kennedy assassination.

July 25

Pope Paul VI stuns Catholics around the world with his announcement of *Humanae Vitae*, a papal letter sent to all bishops of the Roman Catholic Church, in which he forcefully reaffirms the church's previously stated position on the use of artificial birth control, calling it 'intrinsically wrong.'

September 7

A group of women, led by the New York Radical Women, gather outside Boardwalk Hall in Atlantic City, New Jersey, to protest the Miss America Pageant being broadcast live inside.

October 16

During the Olympics in Mexico City, Tommie Smith and John Carlos, two African-American athletes, each raise a black-gloved fist in protest when receiving their medals during the playing of "The Star-Spangled Banner." The athletes are expelled from the Olympic Games. Cronkite explains the situation to his television audience, shaking his head in disbelief at the harsh punishment the young men received.

November 5

Richard Nixon and Spiro Agnew capture the White House with less than 44% of the popular vote.

Cronkite ends his program on a somber note. "During these chaotic times, what can possibly bring humanity together? We can all do better than this." He pauses, takes off his glasses, looks straight into the camera, and says, "And that's the way it is, on Sunday, November 10, 1968."

CHAPTER 78

APOLLO 8

November 30, 1968

The United States' claim to world superiority in the areas of military and economic power and advanced technology is threatened in the late 1950s and early 1960s, during which time it is engaged in the Cold War with the Soviet Union.

On October 4, 1957, the Soviet Union launches Sputnik 1, the first artificial satellite. Its unexpected success stokes fears of Soviet domination around the world. The United States' Apollo 8 mission is designed to combat the Soviet Union's early success.

Citizens from all walks of life support the Apollo 8 mission, and tens of thousands of spectators turn out the morning of the launch, including two Supreme Court justices and aviation pioneer Charles Lindbergh. The *New York Times* calls Apollo 8 'the most fantastic voyage of all times.'

"For Heaven's sake, Jim, you'd think I'd be an old pro at saying goodbye to you before these flights, right?" Marilyn says as she brings two steaming cups of coffee to the table. Both are still dressed in pajamas, robes, and house slippers, and Marilyn wears spongy pink curlers in her hair. "But I don't think I'll ever get used to your leaving," she says.

"You always get nervous before these flights, Marilyn. Everything will be fine."

"I know I do," she says. "I just can't help it. I think little Jeffery may be coming down with a cold, so please don't go and kiss him goodnight."

"Does he have a fever?" Jim asks.

"No, just a little congestion…maybe an earache. He keeps tugging at his ears."

"Poor guy, but yes, I'll keep my distance. I can't believe quarantine begins tomorrow."

"Well, I'll hold the fort here until you return," Marilyn says.

"You know, I won't be gone that long this time, honey. Oh, and Marilyn, we're going to be reading from the Bible on Christmas Eve during this flight, and it's going to be televised to the nation. We're lugging a TV camera up there, though Borman at first refused to take it onboard. It weighs twelve pounds and we're cutting out everything that weighs practically anything just to decrease the weight we're carrying. Even extra meals, which weigh only ounces, are being nixed."

"Twelve pounds? Yikes. That does seem pretty heavy. I hope it will be worth it."

"Well, we'll see, I guess," Jim says.

"Reading from the Bible is a great idea for your Christmas Eve telecast," Marilyn says. "Have you decided what passage you're going to read?"

"No, we're debating it. NASA just told us to find something appropriate to read. Maybe from Genesis, because it's the foundation of so many religions and Christians are really the minority compared to other religions around the world. We don't want to insult anyone, and NASA believes this Christmas Eve we could have the largest audience ever to listen to a human voice."

"I know you'll pick just the right verses," Marilyn says as tears begin to form in her eyes. "What is *wrong* with me, Jim? I'm an astronaut's wife for Heaven's sake. I should be braver than this."

Jim reaches for her hand and holds it. "Listen to me, when we start to read from the Bible, please know that I'll be thinking of you and the kids. You are always in my heart, and you are the love of my life. I am the luckiest man in the world to share my life with you."

Marilyn nods her head, then wipes her eyes and composes herself. "Speaking of luck, I know I shouldn't even question this, but you'll have your Boy Scout watch with you?"

"Of course," Jim says, smiling. "It was the first thing I put in my bag."

"You know, Jim, I'm not superstitious at all, but I am happy that you will be taking it with you."

They both laugh, get up from the table, and begin cleaning the breakfast dishes.

The Apollo 8 crew consists of Frank F. Borman, II, Commander; James A. Lovell Jr., Command Module Pilot; and William A. Anders, Lunar Module Pilot. This is Borman's second flight in space, Lovell's third, and Anders' first flight.

Just prior to the launch, the crew hauls the weighty TV camera into the space capsule in anticipation of performing their six live broadcasts. The Apollo 8 launches on December 21, 1968, from Cape Kennedy.

Just eighteen hours after launch, Borman falls ill with vomiting and diarrhea, a major problem for Apollo 8. After getting some sleep, he feels better, but as a precaution, the other crewmembers radio Earth on a private channel to explain their predicament.

CHAPTER 79

APOLLO 8, CHRISTMAS EVE

December 24, 1968

Prior to the Christmas Eve broadcast, the astronauts become the first humans to see the dark side of the moon. That same evening, Marilyn walks out of her home on Lazywood Lane in Timber Cove with her children. It is a cool and balmy night in Florida, and in just a few minutes the astronauts' broadcast is set to begin. "Look up to the moon, children," she says. "Look up to the moon and wave at your brave father. Maybe he can see us down here if we all wave."

They do, and Marilyn whispers, "Hello darling. We all love you very much. Merry Christmas." She turns and takes the children back into her home at 9:25. The television is already tuned in to the news, as the program produced by the astronauts is about to begin.

The astronauts have decided to read the first ten verses from the Genesis creation narrative from the King James Bible. Borman gets the primetime broadcast started by saying the crew will take the audience with it through a lunar sunset.

Astronaut Lovell comments, "The vast loneliness of the moon is awe inspiring, and it makes you realize just what you have back there on Earth."

After showing the audience live pictures of the moon and Earth from space, Bill Anders begins by stating, "We are now approaching lunar sunrise, and for all the people back on Earth, the crew of Apollo 8 has a message that we would like to send to you." Anders begins to read his selected section from Genesis: "In the beginning God created the Heaven and the Earth. And the earth was without form, and void; and darkness was upon the face of the deep. And the Spirit of God moved upon the face of the waters. And God said, Let there be light: and there was light."

Jim Lovell speaks next, and just before he begins, Marilyn notices he is checking his Boy Scout watch and returning it to a pocket on his spacesuit. "And God called the light Day, and the darkness he called Night. And the evening and the morning were the first day." After Lovell finishes reading his section, Borman continues and completes the passages from Genesis.

Concluding the broadcast, Borman says, "And from the crew of Apollo 8, we close with good night, good luck, a Merry Christmas, and God bless all of you, all of you on the good Earth."

It is the most watched television transmission ever.

Following the astronauts' Christmas Eve broadcast, Madalyn Murry O'Hair, founder of American Atheists, responds by suing the United States government, alleging violations of the First Amendment. The direct appeal to the Supreme Court is eventually dismissed for lack of jurisdiction.

On Christmas morning, mission control waits anxiously for word that Apollo 8's engine burn to leave the lunar orbit has worked. After receiving confirmation, Lovell radios, "Roger, please be informed there is a Santa Claus."

The crew splashes down in the Pacific on December 27.

The three astronauts are the first to reach the moon, orbit it, and return, the first to witness and photograph an Earthrise, and the first to escape the gravity of a celestial body.

Apollo 8 paves the way for Apollo 11 to fulfill President John F. Kennedy's goal of landing a man on the moon before the end of the 1960s.

CHAPTER 80

APOLLO 13

April 1, 1970

The astronauts sit in the confined space of the mockup of their capsule and rehearse their assigned duties. After a pause, Lovell begins discussing his Boy Scout pocket watch.

"I swear, Lovell, if you tell me that story about your lucky Boy Scout pocket watch one more time," Mattingly says, "I think I just might kill you."

"Oh have I mentioned my watch to you before, Commander Mattingly?" Lovell asks, smiling. "Did I tell you where I found it? Have I actually shown it to you? Would you like to see it?" He laughs and reaches toward his pocket.

"Really, Lovell, I swear, I am sick of hearing about it," Mattingly says.

"Oh, alright then. I'll stop…for a while at least. But did I tell you I'm taking it aboard the Apollo 13 flight with us?"

"Oh good Lord, no," Mattingly replies. "I don't mind if you take it, just please, for heaven's sake, don't talk about it anymore."

"You both sound like an old married couple," Haise comments.

They all laugh.

Just days before the scheduled liftoff of Apollo 13, Ken Mattingly is exposed to German measles by backup crewmember Charles Duke. Jack Swigert replaces him on the mission.

Apollo 13 launches on time at 2:13 p.m. EST on April 11 with Jim Lovell as Mission Commander, Jack Swigert as Command Module Pilot, and Fred Haise as the Lunar Module Pilot. The crew settles in for their three-day trip to the Fra Mauro crater. Soon after liftoff, the second-stage center engine shuts down about two minutes early.

Because the major television networks believe there is no public interest in watching the flight, they do not carry the broadcast. Marilyn Lovell is forced to go to the VIP room at Houston's Mission Control Center to watch her husband and his crewmates.

Television crews ask Marilyn Lovell for permission to set up transmitters on her front lawn. She tells them no and adds, "If they have a problem with that, they can take it up with my husband. He'll be home on Friday."

As scheduled, a television broadcast from Apollo 13 begins just fifty-five minutes after blastoff. Lovell, acting as emcee, shows the audience the interior of the craft. Again, the audience is limited by the fact that none of the major television networks are carrying the broadcast.

Approximately six and a half minutes after the TV broadcast, and during a routine cryogenic oxygen tank stir on Apollo 13, a fire starts inside an oxygen tank. The astronauts hear a loud bang and realize something is wrong. Liquid oxygen rapidly turns into a high-pressure gas, which bursts the tank, and a piece of shrapnel causes the leak of a second oxygen tank. In just over two hours, all on-board oxygen is lost, disabling the hydrogen fuel cells that provide electric power to the Command Service Module, Odyssey.

Swigert reports in to mission control twenty-six seconds later: "Okay, Houston, we've had a problem here," a message which is echoed soon after by Lovell.

The astronauts must immediately abort the moon-landing mission; the sole objective now is to safely return the crew to Earth.

Worldwide television coverage of Apollo 13 begins as soon as news of the endangered astronauts becomes public. President Nixon cancels appointments, phones the astronauts' families, and drives to NASA's Goddard Space Flight Center in Greenbelt, Maryland, where Apollo's tracking and communications are coordinated.

As the world learns of Apollo's serious situation, people surround their television sets to get the latest developments offered by the networks, which have interrupted their regular programming for bulletins.

Mattingly, having been replaced just prior to the launch, is currently at Houston's Mission Control Center, and because he is intimately familiar with the Apollo 13 spacecraft, he immediately takes on the responsibility of instructing the men how to get back to Earth.

Ten minutes after watching her husband inform Mission Control Center about a problem, Marilyn Lovell tries to find Ken Mattingly. She is desperate to speak with him. She picks up a phone, and one of NASA's operators answers. The operator places Marilyn on hold for two minutes, then informs her that Commander Mattingly is too busy to answer the phone. But Marilyn insists.

"Tell him it's Mrs. Lovell," she informs the operator. "Be sure to tell him it's Mrs. Lovell. I'm here in the VIP room. They won't let me into the control room. I know he's there. Please, tell Commander Mattingly I need to speak with him. Do you understand?"

"Yes ma'am, I do," the operator replies. "Would you mind holding once more?"

"Yes, yes, of course I'll hold."

After five minutes, Ken Mattingly picks up the line.

"Marilyn?"

"Ken, oh thank God. Do you think they'll make it? Ken, I'm so frightened," she says, her voice trembling.

"Of course, Marilyn, mark my words. I'm certain they'll make it home," he replies.

"You seem so confident," she says. "Why are you so sure?"

Mattingly pauses. "Because he has that goddamn lucky Boy Scout pocket watch with him, that's why."

"Of course, that pocket watch. I forgot about that." She laughs nervously, then begins to cry.

There are a few moments of silence.

"I'll help bring them back safely, Marilyn," he says.

"I know you will," she says, then hangs up the phone.

Using the lunar module as a 'life-boat' to provide battery power, oxygen, and propulsion, Lovell and his crew re-establish the free return trajectory that they had left and swing around the Moon to return home. Based on the flight controllers' calculations made on Earth, Lovell has to adjust the course twice by manually controlling the lunar module's thrusters and engine. Apollo 13 returns safely to Earth on April 17.

"CREW OF CRIPPLED APOLLO 13 STARTS BACK AFTER ROUNDING MOON AND FIRING ROCKET; MEN APPEAR CALM DESPITE LOW RESERVES"

– The *New York Times*

After the successful landing, Jim informs Marilyn he kept one hand on his brass pocket watch each time he adjusted Apollo's course. Lovell vows he will keep the watch close to him for the rest of his life.

CHAPTER 81

THE LUCKY POCKET WATCH

May 8, 1970

Jenny Genova is in her apartment in New York with her son, Jack, who is visiting from California. They watch as a newsman interviews astronaut Jim Lovell following the near fatal Apollo 13 mission. It is his first interview after being released from quarantine.

"Commander Lovell, I am David Brinkley from NBC News. We are live on television now. I know you must be eager to see your wife after being in quarantine for twenty-one days, but I must ask just one question—a question the public wants to know. Were there times on your most recent mission that you believed you and your crew were not going to make it back to Earth alive?"

Jim thinks for a moment, then smiles and says, "No. I never believed we were not going to make it." He takes a brass pocket watch out of his pocket. "See this watch here? Well, it's my lucky pocket watch, and I keep it with me all the time."

"You took this watch on your mission?"

"I sure did. I've taken it with me on all my missions— Gemini 7, Gemini 12, Apollo 8, and now Apollo 13. But really, honestly, we had great support from our team at mission control. I had the best crew up there, everyone remained calm, and most of all, we had Mattingly down here on Earth to give us excellent advice."

Jenny smiles, thinking to herself, *The brass watch longed for the brightest stars.*

"What's with the astronaut's watch, Mom?" Jack asks.

"Oh nothing, son. He just thinks his watch is lucky."

During Lovell's career as an astronaut, he received the Distinguished Eagle Scout Award and was also recognized by the Boy Scouts of America with their prestigious Silver Buffalo Award.

CHAPTER 82

MADAM GENOVA AND MONIQUE LECLAIRE

July, 2001

Jenny and Monique have spent the last two years at the 80th Street Residence Retirement Home, where maids set fresh flowers by their beds daily, chefs prepare the finest meals served on Paragon china dinnerware with Baccarat crystal stemware, and nurses change their beds daily with the finest linen sheets and pillowcases. Medical teams check in on them daily to ensure they are comfortable and in good health. Joshua stops by every day for a few minutes to make certain they are doing well.

Although the retirement home is largely devoted to Alzheimer's patients, Monique and Jenny show no signs of dementia even though they are the oldest occupants of the residence. Monique is one hundred and seven years old and has developed irregular rhythms of her heart and congestive heart failure. She has been largely bedridden for the past few months, using oxygen to help her feel comfortable. Recently, the doctors at the facility have informed Jenny that Monique has only days to live. Jenny, of course, already knows that. She sits by Monique's bed, holding her hand.

"Jenny," Monique says, "I don't know that we would have had such wonderful lives if you hadn't met Joshua."

"Well, Joshua definitely made our lives easier over the years, but so did Mr. Luciano, and that's all your doing," Jenny says and smiles.

"I am just grateful that I'm going to die before you," Monique says. "I don't think my heart could take it if you went first."

"Well, dear, you know I'll be following closely behind you."

They both smile.

"I know I'll meet you on the other side," says Monique. "And, like Houdini said to his wife before he died, if there is a way to contact you while you're still alive, you know I will find it."

"Yes, of course," Jenny says and smiles wider. "I know you will."

They sit for a few minutes.

"I hope Jeremy McMahon won't be waiting for me when I arrive," Monique says.

"Oh my God," Jenny says. "I haven't thought about him in years. He definitely deserved everything he got. I was thrilled to see that alligator chomp down on that asshole's body. Hey, and remember, the sheriff there really helped us out. Do you remember that?"

"Yes, yes. I remember," Monique says. "You know, Jenny, I used to have nightmares about that alligator. I had the exact same nightmare for years. In my dream, I would open the front door to my house and there would be that alligator on my porch, right in front of my door, blocking me from getting out, and always with a leg or an arm sticking out of his mouth... And he was always twice as large as the real one."

"Well, as I remember it, the actual alligator was pretty damn huge," Jenny laughs.

"Yeah, he was."

They sit in silence for a while.

"If you do happen to see Jeremy when you get to Heaven... or wherever one goes—actually, Jeremy would never be in Heaven...But if you happen to see him, punch him in the face for me, won't you?" Jenny asks.

"That's the first thing I'll do," Monique whispers and smiles. She pauses, then continues, "You know, Jenny, I love you very much, and the only reason I regret dying is that I won't see you every day. You really have been the love of my life."

"And you mine, my love."

Monique takes one last breath and is gone.

CHAPTER 83

JENNY GENOVA, 80TH STREET RESIDENCE RETIREMENT HOME

August 28, 2008

Jenny Genova now has the distinction of being the oldest living person in the retirement home at 109 years and is grateful to still see with her thick glasses and still hear well enough with her new-fangled hearing aids.

Joshua McMillan, M.D., the famous retired cardiothoracic surgeon and Chief of Cardiology at New York-Presbyterian Hospital, still looks after her after all these years and visits her often, living only one block from the retirement home in a fancy apartment. Jenny knew he would be her guardian angel since the first time she set eyes on him, almost a century ago now. Her son Jack would bring him to their apartment, and they would both observe her telling the future to her clients from the small grate in her closet.

Jack and his wife are both in their nineties and live in California. Two of his grandsons work for Google at their headquarters, the Googleplex, in Mountain View, California. Jack has long since retired and is now a great-grandfather of two young children.

So many wealthy people over the years wanted to know what to expect out of life, and Jenny was happy to tell them... for a price. And because of Joshua and Mr. Luciano, she now occupies one of the finest rooms in the most luxurious retirement home in New York—the 80th Street Residence.

She spends most of her days in her room, eating small meals and watching television. When she goes to sleep, the last thing she sees is a beautiful Gauguin painting, *Landscape near Arles*, hanging on her wall, given to her many years ago by Joshua. It remains her favorite work of art.

Jenny is thankful for everything and is not afraid to die, which she realizes could be any day now; however, she is afraid of pain. She doesn't want to be in any pain, and Joshua has assured her he will take care of everything and that she should never worry about it. He has promised her that all she needs to do is ask, whenever she is ready to go. He said he would help her and be by her side...and that her death would be painless.

After dinner most evenings, a nurse wheels Jenny out to the main living room for a few hours to watch television, mainly just to get her out of her room and to make sure she's still breathing. Today Jenny took a long afternoon nap to ensure she would stay awake for the Democratic National Convention. Baruck Obama has been formally selected as the Democratic Party nominee for President of the United States, the first Black man to do so.

"OBAMA'S CAMPAIGN SHIFTS TO A BIGGER STAGE FOR HIS BIG NIGHT"

– The *New York Times*

Last night, Jenny watched Senator Joe Biden accept the nomination for Vice President. This evening, her nurse and dear companion, Hattie, sits next to her waiting eagerly to listen to Obama's acceptance speech. In anticipation of the large crowd wanting to hear Obama's speech in person, the convention has moved to Invesco Field at Mile High in Denver, Colorado. The television reporter has just announced there are 84,000 people in attendance this evening. Jenny can feel the excitement in the air.

At 9:45, she watches as a television reporter approaches the presidential candidate and his family. He touches Obama's arm. "May I stop you for a moment, sir, and ask you a few questions? I'm Tom Brokaw from NBC television."

"Of course I recognize you, Tom." Obama smiles and nods his head. "Please excuse me just one second." Obama takes out a silver watch from his pocket, opens it up, glances at the time, and then puts it back in his pocket. "I have exactly two minutes before my family and I need to head toward the stage, so go ahead."

"First of all, congratulations, sir. We are all very excited about your nomination."

"Thank you. I am delighted, as you can imagine, with our party's decision," Obama says.

"I know everyone has asked you a million questions, but I see you frequently looking at your silver pocket watch. It looks quite old. Is it an heirloom? Has it been in your family long?"

"Well, Tom, I must admit you are the first person to ask me about my pocket watch." Obama takes the watch out of his pocket. "And yes, it is very dear to me. Nelson Mandela gave me this beautiful watch. He had received it as a gift, he told me, just prior to his release from prison, and he felt the watch brought him luck. He was kind enough to give me this watch, thinking that it just might bring me some luck, too. Of course I am not superstitious or anything like that, but perhaps the watch has brought me a little bit of luck…I am, after all, the official Democratic Party nominee. Let's hope the watch has enough luck left in it to see me all the way to the presidency," Obama says, smiling, as he places the watch back in his pocket.

"That's amazing, sir. I hope you're correct about your lucky watch. And what, Senator Obama, will be the official slogan of your campaign?"

The Senator pauses, then looks directly into the camera and says, "'Hope.' It will be 'Hope'…Hope for the American people and for the world."

I see the silver watch has finally found its home, Jenny thinks to herself and smiles. *It has found the man with the greatest hope.*

Obama walks onto the stage with his beautiful family. In the background, American flags blow in the wind. The family waves to the roaring crowd for a few minutes, then his wife and two young daughters leave the stage. Obama's formal acceptance speech begins a little after 10:00. He waits a few moments for the chanting of "Yes We Can" and the feet-stomping to die down before he speaks. As the television cameras pan the crowd, flashbulbs create thousands of flickering lights. Some in attendance are crying. Others are screaming for joy, waving their hands above their heads.

Obama scans the crowd and sees a small contingency of individuals to his right yelling and holding up signs stating, "Chicago loves you." The group has traveled from Chicago to Denver to listen to his acceptance speech.

"Hello, Chicago. If there is anyone out there who still doubts that America is a place where all things are possible, who still wonders if the dream of our founders is alive in our time, who still questions the power of our democracy, tonight is your answer." The crowd roars its approval.

After thanking his fellow candidates and his family for their support, Barack Obama proclaims it is time for Americans to come together as one family and to treat each other with dignity and respect. He concludes with statements emphasizing his campaign slogan of 'Hope.' "This is our time, to put our people back to work and open doors of opportunity for our kids; to restore prosperity and promote the cause of peace; to reclaim the American dream and reaffirm that fundamental truth, that, out of many, we are one; that while we breathe, we hope."

Jenny looks over at Hattie and sees she is crying. "Are you alright?"

"Yes ma'am. I'm just very happy. I never thought I would live to see this day."

"I didn't think I would either," Jenny says as she hands Hattie the box of tissues sitting on the table next to her.

A large fireworks display follows the acceptance speech, and when it is over, Hattie leans forward. "It's late, Miss Genova. Are you ready to go back to your room?"

She nods her head.

"Wasn't that the most thrilling speech you've ever heard?" Hattie asks as she wheels Jenny back to her room.

"Yes, I think it was."

While Hattie is helping her into bed, Jenny asks her to dial Dr. Joshua McMillan's phone number.

"It's pretty late, Miss Genova. Wouldn't you like to wait until morning?" she asks.

"No, I'm certain he's awake. Please dial his number for me." Hattie does so.

"Hello, Joshua, darling. I am ready."

"You are? You're certain?" he asks.

"Yes, I'm certain."

"I'll be right over," he says.

CHAPTER 84

DR. JOSHUA MCMILLAN AND MADAM GENOVA

August 28, 2008

"Well, I must tell you, you look pretty darn good for someone who's a hundred and nine," Joshua says as he enters Jenny's room, walking over to her bed. He kisses her on the cheek. "Good evening, Madam Genova."

"Good evening, Joshua. Thank you for coming so quickly."

Joshua takes off his light jacket, lays it neatly at the foot of her bed, and pulls a chair up close to her. He takes Jenny's hand in his. They are quiet for a few moments, and then he says, "You know, I've always dreaded this day." He looks away from her, takes a handkerchief from his pocket, and wipes his eyes.

"Oh, my, Joshua. Please don't be sad. I've had such an amazing life. It's just time for me to go. I've seen and done truly everything I've ever wanted to do."

Joshua nods his head.

"And besides, you know I can see the future. You and I will meet again, very soon. You'll see."

"Really?" he asks.

"Would I lie to you? Of course I will see you again. You've been like a son to me all these years...No, maybe even better than a son, looking out for me and always checking on me. I am so lucky to have had you in my life, and you know I love you very much."

Joshua looks down at his lap. "Remember when you used to let Jack and me hide in your closet and watch you work with your clients?"

"Yes, of course I do," Jenny replies.

"I remember when I was young, you saved me and my entire Boy Scout troop from being eaten by a bear."

"Yes. I remember that, too," Jenny says and smiles. "So many years ago."

"And then my father," Joshua says. "My father was beating my mother and me so severely. I had lost all hope."

"He would have killed you both. There was never any doubt," she says.

"I know you must have had something to do with his death...and with saving us from his abuse. I really believed there was no escape from our situation, but you...you somehow managed to save both my mother and me. You turned our lives around," Joshua whispers, and tears begin to drop onto his lap.

"I love you, Joshua."

"I love you, too, Jenny."

Joshua stands up, takes a drinking glass from the top of Jenny's dresser, and fills it halfway with water. He takes a bottle out of his pocket, unscrews the top, and with the attached eye-dropper, places six drops of fluid into the glass. He walks back over to his chair, sits down, and hands her the glass.

"You will feel no pain. You will just go to sleep. I'll call Jack. Are there any other arrangements you'd like me to make?" Joshua asks.

"No, everything has been taken care of, my love." Jenny picks up the glass and drinks it all. "Thank you, Joshua."

CHAPTER 85

THE POSTCARD

September 28, 2008

It's not unusual for Joshua to receive a note or card from one of his previous patients, so when he stops in the lobby for his mail, he's not surprised to find a colorful postcard among the stack of bills and advertisements. A large green alligator stretches across the front of the card. The reptile's mouth is wide open, showing off his pink tongue and numerous sharp, white teeth. The words 'Greetings from Louisiana' appear just underneath the alligator's powerful claws. Joshua turns the postcard over. It's blank, with the exception of a scribbled signature he fails to recognize. *Perhaps it's a sign from Jenny,* he thinks. He laughs out loud, then takes the elevator back up to his apartment.

REFERENCES

'Marilyn Monroe' (2020). *Wikipedia.* Available at https://
en.wikipedia.org/wiki/Marilyn_Monroe (Accessed: 03
November 2020)

'John F. Kennedy' (2020). *Wikipedia.* Available at https://
en.wikipedia.org/wiki/John_F._Kennedy (Accessed:
03 November 2020)

'Jim Lovell' (2020). *Wikipedia.* Available at https://en.wikipedia.
org/wiki/Jim_Lovell (Accessed: 03 November 2020)

'Fortune-telling' (2020) *Wikipedia.* Available at https://
en.wikipedia.org/wiki/Fortune-telling (Accessed: 03
November 2020)

'Tudor-City' (2020). *Wikipedia.* Available at https://en.wikipedia.
org/wiki/Tudor_City (Accessed: 03 November 2020)

'Marie Laveau' (2020). *Wikipedia.* Available at https://
en.wikipedia.org/wiki/Marie_Laveau (Accessed: 03
November 2020)

'Louisiana Voodoo' (2020). *Wikipedia.* Available at https://
en.wikipedia.org/wiki/Louisiana_Voodoo (Accessed:
03 November 2020)

'Pocket Watch' (2020). *Wikipedia.* Available at https://en.wikipedia.org/wiki/Pocket watch (Accessed: 03 November 2020)

'Joe DiMaggio' (2020). *Wikipedia.* Available at https://en.wikipedia.org/wiki/Joe_DiMaggio (Accessed: 03 November 2020)

'Ronald Reagan' (2020). *Wikipedia.* Available at https://en.wikipedia.org/wiki/Ronald_Reagan (Accessed: 03 November 2020)

'Nancy Reagan' (2020). *Wikipedia.* Available at https://en.wikipedia.org/wiki/Nancy_Reagan (Accessed: 03 November 2020)

'Betsy Bloomingdale' (2020). *Wikipedia.* Available at https://en.wikipedia.org/wiki/Betsy_Bloomingdale (Accessed: 03 November 2020)

'Alfred S. Bloomingdale' (2020), Wikipedia. Available at https://en.wikipedia.org/wiki/Alfred_S._Bloomingdale (Accessed: 04 December 2020)

'Mary Jane Wick' (2020) *Wikipedia.* Available at https://www.startribune.com/obituaries/detail/11986681/ (Accessed: 03 November 2020)

'Leonore Annenberg' (2020). *Wikipedia.* Available at https://en.wikipedia.org/wiki/Leonore_Annenberg (Accessed: 03 November 2020)

The Washington Post, "Not Swayed by Astrology, Reagan Says." By Lou Cannon and Donnie Radcliffe, May 4, 1988

'George H.W. Bush' (2020). *Wikipedia.* Available at https://en.wikipedia.org/wiki/George_H._W._Bush (Accessed: 03 November 2020)

'Barbara Bush' (2020). *Wikipedia.* Available at https://en.wikipedia.org/wiki/Barbara_Bush (Accessed: 03 November 2020)

'Marilyn Lovell' (2020). *Wikipedia.* Available at https://www.imdb.com/name/nm0522565/ (Accessed: 03 November 2020)

'Slinky' (2020). *Wikipedia.* Available at https://en.wikipedia.org/wiki/Slinky (Accessed: 03 November 2020)

'Richard T. James' (2020). *Wikipedia.* Available at https://en.wikipedia.org/wiki/Richard_T._James (Accessed: 03 November 2020)

'Betty James' (2020). *Wikipedia.* Available at https://en.wikipedia.org/wiki/Betty_James (Accessed: 03 November 2020)

'Ken Mattingly' (2020). *Wikipedia.* Available at https://en.wikipedia.org/wiki/Ken_Mattingly (Accessed: 03 November 2020

'Apollo 13' (2020). *Wikipedia.* Available at https://en.wikipedia.org/wiki/Apollo_13 (Accessed: 03 November 2020)

'Lucky Luciano' (2020). *Wikipedia.* Available at https://en.wikipedia.org/wiki/Lucky_Luciano (Accessed: 03 November 2020)

'Pierre C. Cartier' (2020). *Wikipedia.* Available at https://en.wikipedia.org/wiki/Pierre_C._Cartier (Accessed: 03 November 2020)

'Drakenstein Correctional Centre (formerly Victor Verster Prison)' (2020) *Wikipedia*. Available at https://
en.wikipedia.org/wiki/Drakenstein_Correctional_
Centre (Accessed: 03 November 2020)

'2004 National Democratic Convention' (2020). *Wikipedia*.
Available at https://en.wikipedia.org/wiki/2004_Dem-
ocratic_National_Convention (Accessed: 03 November 2020)

'Joan Quigley' (2020). *Wikipedia*. Available at https://
en.wikipedia.org/wiki/Joan_Quigley (Accessed: 03
November 2020)

'Nelson Mandela' (2020). *Wikipedia*. Available at https://
en.wikipedia.org/wiki/Nelson_Mandela (Accessed: 03
November 2020)

'Frank Sinatra' (2020). *Wikipedia*. Available at https://
en.wikipedia.org/wiki/Frank_Sinatra (Accessed: 03
November 2020)

'Charles Lindbergh' (2020). *Wikipedia*. Available at https://
en.wikipedia.org/wiki/Charles_Lindbergh (Accessed:
03 November 2020)

'Anne Morrow Lindbergh' (2020). *Wikipedia*. Available at
https://en.wikipedia.org/wiki/Anne_Morrow_Lind-
bergh (Accessed: 03 November 2020)

'Barack Obama' (2020). *Wikipedia*. Available at https://
en.wikipedia.org/wiki/Barack_Obama (Accessed: 03
November 2020)

'Marlin Fitzwater' (2020). *Wikipedia.* Available at https://en.wikipedia.org/wiki/Marlin_Fitzwater (Accessed: 03 November 2020)

'James Baker' (2020). *Wikipedia.* Available at https://en.wikipedia.org/wiki/James_Baker (Accessed: 03 November 2020)

'Iran Contra Affair' (2020). *Wikipedia.* Available at https://en.wikipedia.org/wiki/Iran%E2%80%93Contra_affair (Accessed: 03 November 2020)

'80th Street Residence' (2020). *Wikipedia.* Available at https://80thstreetresidence.com/ (Accessed: 03 November 2020)

'New Iberia Louisiana' (2020). *Wikipedia.* Available at https://en.wikipedia.org/wiki/New_Iberia,_Louisiana (Accessed: 04 November 2020)

'Western Astrology' (2020). *Wikipedia.* Available at https://en.wikipedia.org/wiki/Western_astrology (Accessed: 04 November 2020)

'Tarot' (2020). *Wikipedia.* Available at https://en.wikipedia.org/wiki/Tarot (Accessed: 04 November 2020)

'*Spirit of St. Louis*' (2020). *Wikipedia.* Available at https://en.wikipedia.org/wiki/Spirit_of_St._Louis (Accessed: 04 November 2020)

'Jacqueline Kennedy Onassis' (2020). *Wikipedia.* Available at https://en.wikipedia.org/wiki/Jacqueline_Kennedy_Onassis (Accessed: 04 November 2020)

'*Nancy Reagan: The Unauthorized Biography*,' Kitty Kelly, 1991, Simon and Schuster

'Mount Washington Hotel' (2020). *Wikipedia*. Available at https://en.wikipedia.org/wiki/Mount_Washington_ Hotel (Accessed: 04 November 2020)

'Gemini 7' (2020). *Wikipedia*. Available at https://en.wikipedia. org/wiki/Gemini 7 (Accessed: 04 November 2020)

'Gemini 12' (2020). *Wikipedia*. Available at https:// en.wikipedia.org/wiki/Gemini_12 (Accessed: 04 November 2020)

'Apollo 8' (2020). *Wikipedia*. Available at https://en.wikipedia. org/wiki/Apollo_8 (Accessed: 04 November 2020)

'Apollo 8 Genesis reading' (2020). *Wikipedia*. Available at https://en.wikipedia.org/wiki/Apollo_8_Genesis_ reading (Accessed: 04 November 2020)

'Madalyn Murry O'Hair' (2020). Wikipedia. Available at https:// en.wikipedia.org/wiki/Madalyn_Murray_O%27Hair (Accessed: 12 December 2020)

'Assassination of Robert F. Kennedy' (2020). *Wikipedia*, Available at https://en.wikipedia.org/wiki/Assassina- tion_of_Robert_F._Kennedy (Accessed: 07 November 2020)

'Miss America Protest' (2020). *Wikipedia*. Available at https://en.wikipedia.org/wiki/Miss_America_protest (Accessed: 07 November 2020)

'Lyndon B. Johnson' (2020). *Wikipedia*. Available at https://en.wikipedia.org/wiki/Lyndon_B._Johnson (Accessed: 07 November 2020)

'David Berkowitz' (2020). *Wikipedia*. Available at https://en.wikipedia.org/wiki/David_Berkowitz (Accessed: 12 November 2020)

'Jewish Women Archives. Irene Rothschild Guggenheim' https://jwa.org/encyclopedia/article/guggenheim-irene-rothschild

'Solomon R. Guggenheim' (2020). *Wikipedia*. Available at https://en.wikipedia.org/wiki/Solomon_R._Guggenheim (Accessed: 16 November 2020)

'Hilla von Rebay' (2020). *Wikipedia*. Available at https://en.wikipedia.org/wiki/Hilla_von_Rebay (Accessed: 16 November 2020)

'Solomon R. Guggenheim Museum' (2020). *Wikipedia*. Available at https://en.wikipedia.org/wiki/Solomon_R._Guggenheim_Museum Accessed: 16 November 2020)

'Vicki Morgan' (2020). Wikipedia. Available at https://en.wikipedia.org/wiki/Vicki_Morgan (Accessed: 9 December 2020)

Made in the USA
Columbia, SC
15 October 2021